CHARLOTTE: CASE SEVENTEEN

A LT. KATE GAZZARA NOVEL

THE LT. KATE GAZZARA MURDER FILES
BOOK 17

BLAIR HOWARD

1

Saturday, August 17, 5:55 a.m.

CINDY HALL WOKE UP WITH A START. SOMETHING WAS wrong. A sound echoed in her head, but everything was silent. Her nose wrinkled at an odor in the air, and she turned toward the bedroom window. Her husband, Darren, was still asleep.

They'd left the window open a crack to catch the cool breeze as they slept. She frowned; the acrid smell was smoke. She turned on her elbow and jostled Darren awake.

"Huh? What is it? Is it time to get up? Hey! It's barely..." Then the stench of fire reached his nose, and he jumped up. "Something's burning. Is it us?"

Cindy shook her head and pointed toward the window. Living at the end of a cul-de-sac, as they did, afforded a view of almost all of the houses on the entire block.

Darren stepped up to their second-story window and pushed it open wider, pressing his head to the bug screen. "It's coming from the Daniels house," he said, returning to the bed. "I can see it."

"Your phone's on the charger, over there on the table."

He nodded. "You call. I'm sure someone else has reported it already, but you go ahead."

Cindy jumped out of bed. "For heaven's sake, Darren. A house in our neighborhood is on fire," she said in a loud whisper as she picked up the phone, dialing 911.

"Emergency services," the dispatcher said. "Police, Fire, or Ambulance?"

"Maybe all of them," Cindy replied anxiously. "There's a housefire just down the street."

"What's the address?"

Cindy gave the street address of her own house. "That's my address, but it's a short street ending in a cul-de-sac. The fire trucks will see the smoke as soon as they turn onto the street."

"Any injuries that you know of?" the dispatcher asked.

"I have no idea. It's a family of five. I woke up, smelled smoke, opened the window, and saw flames."

"I'll put the call through to the fire department," the dispatcher said.

Cindy could hear the call to the fire station, then the dispatcher came back on the line. "They're on their way," she said. Then she asked for Cindy's details as the reporting party.

When the dispatcher disconnected the call, Cindy grabbed yesterday's shorts and tank top from the back of the chair, put them on and thrust her feet into a pair of yellow flip-flops. She turned around to find Darren still wearing nothing but his underwear.

"Aren't you coming with me?" she asked, surprised.

"Nope. I'll stay here in case the kids wake up."

"Darren! Our neighbor's house is on fire. Don't you want to see what's going on or if we can help?"

He returned a slow blink, then narrowed his eyes. "I wouldn't walk across the street to spit on Pete Daniels if he were on fire."

"Well, he probably is!" Cindy nearly yelled. "Don't you care about the kids?"

"I said I'd stay here in case they woke up."

"I'm not talking about our kids, Darren. Oh, never mind," she said, gesturing dismissively. "I'll be down the street if you need me."

LIEUTENANT TOMMY STEDKO, Station 7, had been the one to take the dispatch from the 911 call center. It was barely dawn. He knew the area well; it was a gated community in an upscale neighborhood where his cousin lived. *Maybe a gas leak*, he thought as he ran to the fire truck. *They don't have woodstoves in that community, and with good reason.*

Less than six minutes later, they arrived at the scene to see the west side of the house was already completely engulfed in flames. He looked at his watch. Nine minutes since he'd received the call from dispatch. *Not bad,* he thought as he jumped out of the truck. *Not bad at all. Looks like it's already too late, though.*

He directed Team One to start pulling hoses and watering down from either end of the house. He was glad he'd made the decision to bring two trucks because this fire would require that and more just to suppress it before it could jump to an adjacent house. His squad had been at the end of their shift, but the changeover hadn't happened yet. Luckily, it had been a quiet night, because this fire had taken hold and wasn't going to be easily extinguished. He gestured for Team Two to be ready to enter the house.

The air was still, so there were no shifting winds to spread the fire. But in these planned communities, the houses were built side-by-side with little room between them. Lt. Stedko immediately radioed for another truck which arrived in less than ten minutes.

Depending on how the fire had moved through the house, ceiling beams could start collapsing onto the lower floor at any moment. *How long had it been burning before anyone reported it? The explosion must have been what woke the person who called it in.*

By the time the third truck had arrived, the firefighters were shouting to one another for assistance. Quickly, he assessed the situation and then sent in Team Three to assist with outer suppression.

Neighbors were beginning to assemble. The first police car had arrived, and two uniformed officers were erecting a barrier to keep the crowd back.

Lt. Stedko ran the perimeter of the house, looking for a gas shutoff. He quickly found it and shut it down.

He headed back out to the street, where he caught a glimpse of a familiar face in the people behind the barrier. His cousin, Cindy Hall, was one of the first owners in the subdivision. He made eye contact with her and loped across the street toward her.

"Cindy! Do you know the family?"

She nodded. "Pete and Stacey Daniels."

"Dispatch said family of five?"

"Pete and Stacey, and three kids. Not little kids—the oldest is twenty-one but still lives at home. The two girls are in the upper grades."

"Good info, thanks."

He waved Team Two forward with instructions to enter the house, relaying the number of potential residents at risk with hand signals. Then he sent two police officers to tell the immediate neighbors that they should prepare to evacuate their homes.

He could see flames licking around the edges of a hole in the roof. It must have been created by an explosion and would have required a pressure buildup of some kind.

He directed the third team to connect the hundred-foot hose to quell the flames leaping out of the roof. His worst nightmare would be if the family had not gotten out. It chilled him to think that no one had come forward to claim ownership or occupancy of the house or to let him know whether everyone was safely out. Hopefully, the family was elsewhere.

But it wasn't to be. Firefighters Gray and Tamsin, both seasoned members of his team, brought out two victims which they had found under fallen ceiling beams in a downstairs bedroom. They laid them on the lawn and examined them for signs of life. Gray looked up and shook his head.

Lt. Stedko grimaced, sick to his stomach.

"I'll call the Medical Examiner," Tamsin said.

Lt. Stedko nodded. "Then call for a second ambulance. Check on the progress of the suppression and let me know when it's under control."

"Copy that, LT," she said.

Two EMTs ran to assist, bringing a gurney out of the ambulance.

Stedko and Gray went back in to continue looking for other family members.

Two other team members met them. "There's no one else in there, Lieutenant. We've searched the two main floors and the basement."

In another hour, the flames were out, and Stedko and Gray went back upstairs to check the damage. The fire had burned the west side of the house quickly, but the team had suppressed it before it spread too far into the east side.

"Lieutenant Stedko?" came a booming voice from the first floor. The Fire Marshal.

"Up here, Harris," Stedko responded.

Harris Wellington was a big guy—tall and broad-shouldered, weighing close to two hundred pounds. When he stepped onto the second stair, it groaned and creaked.

"We're going to have to do something about this staircase, and quickly," Harris shouted as he backed down. "It's not going to hold much longer. Better get somebody to shore it up."

Stedko acknowledged and dispatched Gray to find someone to work on the staircase. He cautiously descended to where Wellington was waiting for him.

"We found no evidence of anyone else in the house other than the two you've seen," Stedko volunteered.

Wellington looked around. "Has anyone called the Medical Examiner?"

Stedko nodded. "Yes, sir. He's already on his way."

"Any idea of the source yet?" Wellington asked.

"Nothing absolute yet, sir," Stedko replied. "I

thought maybe a gas leak or a kitchen fire at first, but there's no evidence of either. However, there is a serpentine burn pattern on the floor in the bedroom where the bodies were found, indicating some kind of... liquid accelerant."

Doc Sheddon, as he was affectionately called, arrived on the scene a few minutes later, signed in and, carrying his enormous black bag, went to the ambulance, had a quick word with Becky Tamsin, then dropped his bag, climbed into the ambulance, and began to examine the first of the two bodies. Becky Tamsin stood by at the rear of the ambulance.

After a couple of minutes, Sheddon looked sideways at her and said, "Tell me again, Becky. I want to know exactly how you found them."

"Both were in the same bed with fallen ceiling beams lying across them."

"In what position were they lying?" he asked.

"The woman was lying on her left side with her back to the window. This one," she said, indicating the second body, "was to her left, lying on its back."

"On its back? You're sure of that?"

"Absolutely."

"Interesting. Thank you."

Doc Sheddon got out of the ambulance and walked around the side of it for privacy, and he called the police chief, Wesley Johnston.

"Chief? Richard Sheddon here. I'm at a fire at nineteen Melrose Place. It's an upscale, gated community. It looks like we've got arson and two possible homicides. I can't tell you more until I do the autopsy. I wanted to give you a heads-up. I also recommend you send a detective and CSI right away... What? No, not yet anyway.

Yes, there are four uniformed officers on site. Yes, that's right, nineteen Melrose Place. Captain Gazzara? Yes. Good choice. Goodbye, Chief."

Doc Sheddon looked at his watch and made a mental note of the time. It was eleven minutes after seven.

2

August 17, 6:30 a.m.

I WOKE EARLY THAT SATURDAY MORNING IN AUGUST, clasped my hands together and stretched my arms over my head and glanced at my new smart alarm clock. So much better than any other alarm I'd ever had. For one, I could talk to it instead of having to grab it to shut it off. But since I didn't have to work that day, I'd turned the alarm off.

The sun was up, though low on the horizon, and bright coming through my open bedroom window. The beveled glass windows throughout the house were one of the features I found charming about the house. The French doors out to the backyard had them as well, as did the large window at the front.

The birds in the trees were twittering. I closed my eyes and smiled. It was something I hadn't heard in a long time, not during my long years in my apartment. Yes, I was still getting used to the quieter, more suburban life, and the birds, trees, and my big backyard were so inviting.

I glanced toward Samson's bed, where he was still lying, head up, alert, and panting expectantly. As soon as I looked his way, he gave a little whine.

The plan—as it always is when I have a day off which, I might add, is pretty rare these days—was to go for a short run and then come back, shower, and just enjoy a peaceful morning. I needed to do some grocery shopping, and maybe I would even hit the flower market on my way back. I'd been feeling changes in me since buying the house. I cared more now about things like having a colorful bouquet, or two, to brighten things up.

As soon as my feet hit the floor, Samson bounded out of his bed and led me to the kitchen to make sure I knew where his bowl was. I ducked back into the bedroom and slipped on a short, belted kimono. I keep forgetting that I have ground-floor windows now, unlike my former apartment, and that my neighbors have windows, too.

Samson usually waited patiently while I poured his kibble, but that day, as we entered the kitchen, movement outside the French doors to the backyard caught his eye.

He ran to the door whining excitedly, growling a little, and dancing back and forth, looking at me as if to say, "Something's breached the perimeter, and I must investigate!"

I backed up so I could see what he was looking at and saw a little brown bunny. It had caught Samson's dance moves and froze as it waited to see whether he was a threat.

I chuckled but then realized that it did indeed likely

mean there was a small breach somewhere in the fence where the rabbit could pass through, and I would have to find it and fix it.

Oh, well, I thought to myself. *If Mrs. Rabbit and friends start invading, they will have to deal with the terror that is Samson.* And I smiled at the thought. Fast as he was, Samson was no match for a rabbit on the run.

"You must be feeling lots better today," I said, stooping to scratch his head, putting my hands on either side of his neck, and checking his shoulder wound that was still healing. "You almost look chipper." *A day off will do him some good, too.*

He was healing well after taking a bullet in his shoulder a few months ago. He'd had surgery, but he was a big, sturdy dog, and fortunately, the bullet had not been a hollow point, so he'd pulled through okay.

I opened the door and let Samson out. The rabbit scampered quickly across the yard and disappeared. Samson did his business, then sniffed around a few minutes more while I sat on the back step. Finally, he gave up and came trotting back to me, and we went back into the house. He immediately went to his bowl and looked up.

"Now, where were we?" I said as I poured him a half scoop of kibble. I didn't like him to load his stomach before we went for our run.

I wasn't quite ready for breakfast yet, but coffee? Oh yes!

It's kind of funny how cops take coffee wherever they can get it, and for me, it used to be from McDonald's or the office coffee. But since I wasn't close to any fast food restaurants anymore, I'd invested in one of the pod-type coffee makers. Besides being better tasting, it was quick and easy. Mine made single cups and carafes. I made a carafe. A twelve-ounce cup in the morning wasn't enough. I needed a small bucket full.

I plopped onto the sofa in the new living room and reached for the remote, thinking maybe I could get some quick news before taking the run. Sammy climbed up, with some effort, to sit beside me, both of us pretending it wasn't against the rules. I just wanted him to be comfortable.

I tuned in to Chattanooga's local Channel 7 to be confronted with the spectacle of a raging house fire that had been filmed an hour earlier.

The reporter said no police or firefighters were available for comment, but two ambulances were on the scene, along with the county Medical Examiner, Doctor Richard Sheddon.

Sheddon? I thought. *That means there were bodies.*

I immediately took in the scenario, noticing three vehicles parked near the house—a sedan and a small pickup side by side in the driveway, and the back end of a camper van in the back yard.

Doc Sheddon's little bald head and corpulent body emerged from the house.

I had a sudden tingle run through me as though I knew what was next, and sure enough, my phone rang seconds later. It was my boss, Chief Johnston.

"Kate," he said. And I could tell by the tone of his voice he was in one of his no-nonsense moods. So much for my two consecutive days off.

"There's been a fire—"

"I know," I said, interrupting him; something I rarely did. "I'm watching the news."

He cleared his throat. "You know how much I hate

to call you when I've promised you the day off, but they're pretty sure it's arson."

Uh-oh. Suspected arson and dead bodies—a ready formula for a homicide investigation.

"I need you to get down there as soon as possible. Corbin's on his way, as well as others on your team."

I breathed a silent swear. "Okay, Chief. I'll be there."

"Quickly?"

"Quickly," I said and disconnected. He knew he didn't have to ask; I never dawdle when it comes to getting to a crime scene. Sometimes, I thought the chief was just trying to exert what little control he had over anything at the beginning of a case, which wasn't much. Being a controller myself, I didn't blame him.

So much for a morning run. If Corbin was there, he would see to it that the scene was secure. He was always Johnny-on-the-spot when we were called to a possible homicide.

I showered quickly, brushed my teeth and dressed in a pair of navy pants and a crisp, white, button-down shirt. I usually wore a leather jacket, too—I had several —but this summer had been unusually warm, with temps in the high nineties for the last several weeks. Add the humidity, and it was plain uncomfortable out there. So I grabbed a denim jacket instead, more to hide my Glock 17 than anything else.

By the time I stepped out of the bedroom, Samson was at the door, grinning, with his leash in his mouth. I sighed. I was such a tough gal at work, but where this dog was concerned, I was a pushover.

"Hold on a minute, Sammy. I need coffee to go."

3

Saturday 8:00 – 9:00 a.m.

I STRAPPED SAMSON INTO HIS SEAT HARNESS, RADIOED in and signed on, gave my destination, asked the status of Sergeant Corbin and was told he was already on location.

Knowing Corbin as I did, he was probably already being briefed by the ME, Doc Sheddon.

I wound quickly through my neighborhood. So nice to be in such a quiet, unhurried place. But one of my requirements in finding a house had been to be close enough to a prominent thoroughfare to get to a crime scene quickly.

I eased onto Highway 27 with no problem, but as I rounded onto I-24, I could see the freeway up ahead was packed with traffic. By now, on a normal day, I would already be in my office, readying myself for a team meeting.

The only way I was going to get where I was going

was to use lights and sirens to move vehicles out of the way.

I initiated the siren and the red and blue flashing lights and eased onto the hard shoulder. Once past the I-24/I-75 split, it was a straight shot to the East Brainerd Road exit and then a couple of miles more to the Melrose Acres gated community.

It was almost nine o'clock when I arrived at the scene. I parked as close as I could, which considering the size of the gathering of official vehicles, wasn't close at all.

I should leave Samson in the car, I thought. *But I can't; even with all the windows down, it's going to be too hot.* I couldn't imagine what it would be like as the day wore on. *It could be a real scorcher. Hah!* So I put him on a short leash, let him out of the car and, together, we walked almost half a block to the scene.

The area around the house was alive with onlookers. I figured most of the neighborhood was there, but the uniforms seemed to be doing a good job of holding them back. They'd extended the crime scene tape out across the street, which was good, because not only did it keep the onlookers at bay, but it would also keep traffic out.

As I approached, I could see Corbin talking to Doc Sheddon. The two of them were standing on a concrete step which, at one time, must have led up to a front porch, most of which was now a pile of blackened lumber.

A uniformed officer lifted the crime tape for me, and I approached. Corbin spotted me and beckoned while he continued to talk to Doc.

"What's the situation, guys?" I asked as I stepped up onto the bottom stair of the former stoop.

"Good morning, Kate," Doc Sheddon said, eyeing my sleek black and silver to-go mug distastefully. He knew this was coffee he couldn't "accidentally" steal. Coffee in a paper cup was always vulnerable when Doc was around.

"And good morning to you, too, Samson," he said, holding out his hand, which Samson nuzzled. It looked like instant affection, but I knew Samson was really sniffing Doc's hand to see if he had any tidbits to offer.

He moved toward Corbin, who held up his empty hands. "Sorry, Samson, the drive-thru line at Mickey D's was too long this morning."

"What?" I teased. "You're coffee-less, and Samson is completely surrounded by no chicken biscuits?"

"Yeah," Corbin said. "I need to remedy that situation soon. I'll send somebody. What do you want, Kate?"

Doc Sheddon cleared his throat.

"Later," I said to Corbin. "What've you found so far? The chief said arson is suspected and there are bodies. I see two ambulances, and they look like the same two ambulances I saw on TV more than an hour ago. And that means..."

"I haven't been inside the house yet to assess the scene, but Doc tells me there are two bodies in the ambulances," Corbin replied.

Doc Sheddon picked up from there. "I believe that we have two adults, male and female. From what I've seen so far, I'd say they were killed by smoke inhalation and then inundated by the fire, by falling beams. Of course, I won't know for sure until I've done the autopsies. Step this way," Sheddon said, gesturing toward one of the ambulances.

Corbin stood back and held Samson's leash. I climbed up into the ambulance with Doc.

"One of the firefighters that brought the victims out told me that this body was lying on its back. As I said, he or she must have already been dead by the time the two beams fell on them and turned them into crispies. But there's more, Kate. Come look at this. The firefighter said both of their heads were on what looked like melted foam, likely a foam pillow. Now then...."

Standing at the head of the gurney, Doc grasped the victim's head and turned it until I could see beneath it. On the backside of the head was a deep, bloody gash.

"I haven't talked to the fire marshal yet, but that's what makes me think this is arson and homicide. If he was on his back with his head on a pillow, how did he get the laceration? The size of it would have required stitches, there would have been a large amount of blood, and no one, well, no one sane anyway, would have just gone to bed with an open wound like that."

He paused, looked at me and said, "I can do the autopsy this afternoon or tomorrow morning, whichever would work better for your schedule."

"Can I get back to you on that?" I replied. "I need to see how this investigation goes. I need to see the scene for myself."

Doc nodded absently, and I jumped out of the ambulance and retrieved Samson from Corbin.

"What's the verdict?" he asked.

"Homicide," I replied. "No doubt about it. The guy... or woman, had a massive gash on the back of the head."

"He could have gotten that from the falling timbers," Corbin replied.

I shook my head. "Not if he was lying on his back," I said as we walked back toward the house, "and he was."

I needed to get a look at the crime scene, but I didn't know how long it would be before I could get inside because we hadn't yet gotten the all-clear from the fire marshal.

We stepped up to the house. I turned to Tonya Rivera, one of the CSI techs, with a bright smile—brighter than I felt.

She eyed me suspiciously but then put her hand out to grasp Samson's leash. "I don't mind," she said, smiling tentatively. "Really. There's nothing else I can do until we're summoned. Mike's chomping at the bit," she said, hitching her thumb toward Mike Willis, the CSI supervisor.

I glanced at him. He was pacing and frowning. Mike was... kind of obsessive about his crime scenes. He usually was king of all he surveyed once we were finished with our assessments, so it was hard for him to wait for yet another layer or two of whom he considered outsiders to do their thing.

I relinquished the leash, and Samson looked back at me as she turned away with his leash in hand. He was obviously concerned. I took two steps and bent down beside him, stroking his head. "It's okay, Sammy. No guns to worry about this time. You won't be getting injured again. I'll be all right. I promise. Now go with Tonya and be a good boy."

Tonya led him across the yard beneath a big shade tree, where he turned around and sat down, but he didn't take his eyes off me, not for a second.

"I'd be willing to bet that dog has separation anxiety," Corbin said.

"He does," I said, "but not the way you mean it. His job is to protect me, and he knows he can't do that when he's not at my side."

I found a box full of clean Tyvek suits, donning one myself and handing the other to Corbin.

"Let's go see how much they'll allow us to do," I said.

It was at that moment the fire marshal stepped out onto what was left of the front porch with a fire department lieutenant—whom I didn't know—by his side.

I flashed my badge. So did Corbin, and Mike Willis, who was right behind me.

The marshal looked me over skeptically.

"I'm Captain Kate Gazzara," I said. "Homicide. I need to take a look around inside."

Wellington shook his head. "Sorry, Captain. No can do. The fire hasn't cooled enough, nor is the structure stable enough for anybody but the fire department to be inside. Not even the police. Who called you in anyway? No one has declared this a homicide scene."

"We can talk about that when you walk me through," I said. "In the meantime, I'll take my chances. I need to see the scene as it is before your people start fooling with it. I need to see it, and I need photographs."

"It's not going to happen, Captain," he said. "I can't take a chance on something falling on you. I'll get you in ASAP. The bodies have already been removed. Our photographer took photos while everything was still in place, and of course we'll give you copies. We'll secure the scene behind us as we investigate. And we'll clear out as quickly as we can, but we've got some shoring up to do before we can investigate more thoroughly and prepare it for y'all. I'll call you just as soon as it's ready, but you shouldn't expect it before tomorrow morning."

I wanted to roll my eyes, but out of respect for his rank and position, I forced myself to just nod and hand him my card. "That's both my office phone and my mobile."

"Sure enough, Captain Gazzara. I'll call you just as soon as it's safe and when I know enough about what's happened here to walk you through the points of action in the fire."

I turned around. Willis had walked away and was standing under the tree with Tonya and Samson. He must have left as soon as he understood that we weren't getting in today. Guess he and Tonya must have been discussing what their next move would be.

The media was out in full force. Late-comers were snapping photos of whatever they could, and television crews were interviewing the neighbors and talking among themselves.

"Captain Gazzara?" came a voice from behind me. I turned to see a weary-looking fireman, the one I'd seen with the fire marshal. "I'm Lieutenant Stedko," he said, offering his hand. "My cousin, Cindy Hall, lives here on Melrose Place, five lots down that way." He nodded in the direction of my car. "It was me that took the dispatch, and we were first on the scene. I'll have a report I can send over to you later, but I thought perhaps I could answer some questions for you now."

"Thank you, Lieutenant," I said. "This is my partner, Sergeant Russell."

They shook hands, then Corbin looked at him, raised his eyebrows and said, "Occupants?" His notebook at the ready.

"The occupants are Peter and Stacey Daniels and their three children."

"Three children?" I asked. "Young children?"

"My cousin Cindy knows them. Some of their children are in school together. She went to get her husband. She said they'd be back shortly."

"They were here?"

"She was here earlier, one of the crowd."

"I'll need to talk to them," I said. "Any idea how long they'll be?"

He looked over my shoulder and nodded. "Here they are now. I'll introduce you."

4

Day 1, 10:05 a.m.

THE HALLS STEPPED UP TO THE TAPE, AND I WAVED TO the uniform to let them through.

"This is my cousin Cindy Hall and her husband Darren," Stedko said, turning toward them. "Darren, Cindy, this is Captain Gazzara and Sergeant Russell. They have questions for you. I'll leave you to it. I need to get back to my crew."

"Thank you, Lieutenant," I said. "Any chance I can have that report by the end of the day?"

"Yes, ma'am," he said. "I'll do my best."

I nodded and turned my attention back to the Halls. "Where exactly do you live?" I asked Cindy.

"We live down that way, at number ten, on the opposite side of the street," Darren answered for her. "We were the first to see it. Cindy called it in."

I eyed him. He looked away, seemingly a little embarrassed, and then looked back toward what was left of the Daniels house.

"What exactly did you see?" I asked.

"Nothing at first," Cindy replied. "I woke up and smelled the smoke. I had the bedroom window open, you see?"

"Yeah. I got out of bed and went to the window," Darren said. "I saw this billowing cloud of smoke coming out of the house." He looked past me and nodded at the hulk behind me. "We have a clear view of the street, so I knew right away it was the Daniels place."

Cindy nodded and said, "I told Darren to call 911, but he didn't, so I did, then I got dressed and came out," Cindy continued. "He stayed back with our kids. I had to get closer—they have kids. Two of them are the same age as ours. The firetrucks arrived just about the same time I did."

"What can you tell us about the family?" I asked.

"Wait," Cindy said. "I saw them bring out two bodies. Who were they?"

"We don't know yet," I said.

"Could have been anybody," Darren said.

I didn't miss the searing look she gave him right before she teared up.

"It was most likely Peter and Stacey," Cindy said. "But they could be any of them... Those poor kids. Are they all right?"

"Again, we don't know yet," I replied. "There were only two people in the house. We don't know who's missing. Can you give us some background on the family?"

"They moved into the neighborhood about... um... twenty years ago," Cindy said. "Yes, that would be right, because it was a couple of years before I got pregnant with our first, Marty. But they already had an infant when they moved in—that would have been Matthew, of course. He's twenty-one now but still lives at home. Then she—Stacey—and I were pregnant at the same time, their second go-round. I had our son, Jimmy, and they had Charlotte.

"Matthew's twenty-one now, and Charlotte's eighteen. She and my son are both seniors over at East Ridge High. The youngest, Emily, is eleven or twelve, a girl, the same as our daughter, Janene."

"Okay," I said. "Peter, Stacey, then the kids, Matthew, Charlotte, and Emily."

Cindy nodded. "The girls are a little odd, or so Janene tells me, and Matthew seems like he can be a bit of a troublemaker."

I pulled a wry face. "Odd how? Troublemaker, how?"

I glanced at Corbin. He was nodding even though his head was down and he was still taking notes.

"Well, as far as the girls being odd," she said, "you'd have to ask my kids."

"Can I talk to them?" I asked.

She looked at her husband, who shook his head almost imperceptibly.

"Uh—they're not up yet," she replied. "Maybe... another time?"

"Of course," I said and offered her my card, but she didn't take it. "It's important I talk to them, so please give me a call so we can set something up."

They looked at each other. They both looked tight-lipped, so I changed the subject.

"What about the three vehicles?" I asked, gesturing toward the house. "D'you know who they belong to?"

Cindy took a half-step to her left and looked around

me. "Hmm," she said. "It seems all the family vehicles are there. The pickup is Matthew's, the sedan is the family car, and the camper van..."

"Another family vehicle?" I asked.

"If you want to call it that," Darren said, giving Cindy an *if you know what I mean* look.

"Why the qualifier?"

"I think we've told you everything we can about the family right now," Cindy said hesitantly, searching for cues from her husband, "and I'm starving. Let's go somewhere for breakfast, Darren."

Now that seemed odd to me. Why would they not want to talk about the family vehicles? In fact, they seemed reluctant to talk about them at all, especially in the light of knowing that two were dead and three apparently missing. I decided not to question them any further at that point, but I would be back.

As the Halls turned to go, Cindy paused and looked back at me. Her mouth opened, but her husband shook his head just slightly, and she closed it again.

"You didn't take my card," I said.

I held it out to her, and she walked back the few short steps and took it from me.

"If you remember anything else, please give me a call."

I looked up into eyes that were obviously full of something she wanted to say, but she seemed to think better of it and turned to go.

I turned again to look at Samson. He'd been whining the entire time I'd been talking to the Halls. He was still sitting under the tree with Tonya but champing at the bit to get to me, having a hard time sitting as I had told him to.

Hmm, maybe Corbin's right about the separation anxiety thing, I thought. Then again, it was the first time I'd left him anywhere other than at home since his surgery. I took him everywhere with me.

I walked over to take him from Tonya. He put his ears back for a second, then they popped up again, and he tilted his head and started panting.

"I don't think he recognized you in that get-up," Tonya laughed. "I guess we're done here until we get the okay from you that we can go in. Mike says they'll have ladders for us, unless they're able to shore up the stairs so they're safe to use. Maybe we'll get the all-clear soon."

"I wouldn't hold my breath if I were you," I said. "The fire marshal said it would be tomorrow morning, so I'll have the uniforms secure the scene and we'll wait for a call."

"I guess," she said doubtfully. "Does Mike know?"

"He does," I replied.

"Well, all right, then," she said. "I'll see you tomorrow." And she nodded, turned and walked away.

"Let's go, Sammy-o," I said as I wound his leash around my hand, and we trotted side-by-side back toward the car.

Corbin caught up with us. "Do we need to issue an Amber Alert, Kate?"

"Hmm... At this point we have to assume that three of five family members escaped the fire," I replied, "but who, where did they go, and in what vehicle? I don't think we can assume anything right now."

"So what are you thinking?" Corbin asked.

I shrugged and said, "After looking at the scene, what little I could see of it without going inside, I'm thinking that the two victims must have been dead before they were inundated. They were lying in bed together, for Pete's sake. So they had to have died either from smoke inhalation or... someone killed them both. Either way, if it's arson, we have two homicides on our hands."

"Okay, I see that, and I agree," Corbin said. "But there are so many more possibilities and variables it's making my head hurt."

"That's because of what you've been breathing," I said.

"But what about what Doc showed you in the ambulance?" he asked.

"It's open to interpretation at this point. We won't really know anything for sure until the autopsy, and maybe not even then."

"That's going to make it rough to begin investigating," he said. "I checked on the registrations of the vehicles that we can see." He glanced at his notes. "The pickup belongs to the son, Matthew Daniels. The sedan is registered to an Anastasia Daniels—the mom, Stacey, I suppose—and the camper is in the father's name."

"It's hard to put out an Amber Alert," I said, "when we don't know who we're looking for... or what kind of vehicle. And if it's the older two, they're already of age, so it doesn't qualify, though the youngster, Emily, would. We'll see what the chief has to say."

"Hah, he's going to ask what you think, just like I did," Corbin said, grinning.

"Maybe," I said, "but once he's up-to-speed, he'll be able to make that decision."

Corbin tilted his head from side to side, saying, "Have you considered we could have a kidnapping on our hands? The kid's only twelve years old."

I sighed. "Anything's possible, Corbin. Our priority is

to identify the two victims. Then we'll know who's missing. A lot's going to depend on Doc Sheddon and the DNA results. We need to light a fire under him."

"No pun intended?" Corbin asked.

I narrowed my eyes at him but gave him a half-smile. "You stay here awhile and keep digging. Talk to the neighbors; see what you can find out. I'll meet you back at the station in... let's say at noon."

5

Day 1, 11:45 am

It was just after eleven-thirty when I pulled into my reserved parking spot at the police department. I gathered up my stuff, exited the car—my unmarked cruiser—put Samson on his leash, let him out and then headed for the elevator, the situation room and my office on the second floor.

I spent a few moments alone with Samson in my office trying to organize my thoughts, then I buzzed Detective Anne Robar and asked her to gather the rest of the team in my office forthwith, if not quicker.

I knew, deep in my gut, I had a double homicide on my hands, and God only knew what else. At that point all I had was two bodies, an address, some names, three vehicles and a whole lot of speculation. It was a weak beginning to a homicide investigation, but we'd had less to start with on other cases. Our task now was to follow the leads, do the interviews, and pull the threads. And above all, remember the motives for murder: love, hate, sex, jealousy, greed, revenge and, of course, money.

By noon, the rest of my team, Anne Robar, Detective Jack North, Sergeant Arthur "Hawk" Hawkins, Detective Tony Cooper, and Sergeant Tracy Ramirez, were all seated comfortably around the table; everyone except Corbin, who popped his head in five minutes later and said, "Have I missed anything?"

"What d'you think?" I replied. "Come on in and take a seat."

And he did, with a chicken biscuit in his hand.

I gave Corbin a look—he knew what it meant—but he just grinned and put the biscuit into Samson's bowl anyway. *I'm gonna have to have a talk with him about that,* I thought, frowning.

As hungry as I knew he must be, most dogs would have snapped at Corbin to get to the biscuit. Samson, however, was savvy enough to know not to bite the hand that fed him but only for people he trusted. So he sat politely, watching Corbin's every move. Then, when Corbin was out of the way, he grabbed the biscuit and swallowed it in three chomps.

Corbin grinned and turned around. "Have you ever seen this guy eat a cheeseburger?" he said, addressing the rest of the team. "He somehow eats it in three bites like he did the biscuit, but he leaves the lettuce in the bowl. I have no idea how he does that."

"Yup, he knows that iceberg lettuce is nutritionally worthless," I said sarcastically.

I was interrupted when the door opened and the chief stepped in. Samson immediately jumped into his basket under the window and sat at attention, his mouth shut and his ears pricked.

"Chief," I said. "We were just about to begin. You want to sit in?"

"Captain," he replied, using my rank to let me know he was going to say something important. Not that anything he said was ever unimportant. Chief Wesley Johnston was not one for idle chit-chat. He did seem a little rattled, though. Something we didn't see often.

"Kate," he began again, a little quieter. "The kids. They already have a six-hour head start. Do we have enough to issue an Amber Alert?"

I shook my head. "Not yet. We don't know exactly what or who we're dealing with. And, until we identify the two bodies, we won't know. My own thought is it's the parents and the three kids weren't there when the fire broke out, which means they could have been having sleepovers with friends. We don't want to make any assumptions. You and I both know how the press will be all over it. In fact, they already are."

He looked frustrated. "And if they're not, we'll really be for it. Kids gone? Geez, they must have left at... what? Before six in the morning? And if that's it, they—or one or more of them—could have set the fire... The fire marshal thinks it's arson, so I understand."

"Good point, Chief, but they could have been gone for a few days. I was just going to say we need to organize a door-to-door, which means I'll need some uniforms."

I looked at him expectantly.

"I'll have a word with patrol," he said. "Look, Kate, I'm getting pressure from the mayor's office. I need this thing solved and quickly. Geez, a neighborhood fire, two unidentified bodies, a possible arsonist, and maybe even a kidnapper. It's never good when there are children involved."

"Trust me, Chief," I said. "We'll have something for you ASAP."

He nodded curtly, grunted something unintelligible —something I didn't understand—and backed out the door.

It wasn't like the chief to jump to conclusions, like kidnapping. I figured he must have been brooding on it all morning.

"Okay," I said after the door closed. "We need to get a jump on this one. Corbin, what do we know?"

He flipped through his notebook.

"Just the facts, please. No speculation," I said, staring hard at him.

He nodded. "We don't have much," he began. "The facts at the moment are these: We have a house fire. Whether or not the cause was arson, we don't yet know..." He glanced at me and then added, "...for sure. We have two unidentified bodies. Both were discovered lying in natural postures." He looked at North, grinned and said, "That would be positions, Jack."

"Screw you, sergeant," Jack replied.

Me? I said nothing.

"The home is, was, occupied by five people: Peter and Stacey Daniels and their three children. Matthew, twenty-one, works in construction but still resides in the home. Charlotte, eighteen, a senior at East Ridge High School. And Emily, twelve, in Middle School, yet to be identified." Corbin flipped a page in his notebook.

He continued, "The two bodies were found in bed in a downstairs bedroom which, according to the fire marshal, also seems to be the source of the fire."

"Thanks, Corbin," I said. "What makes us suspect arson and homicide, you ask? One of the bodies has sharp-force trauma to the back of the head. That body was discovered lying on its back. We're waiting for info from Doc Sheddon, some of which we'll have following the autopsy."

"Jack," I said. "Give Doc Sheddon a quick call and ask him if he can schedule the autopsies for this afternoon."

"Right-o," Jack said and quickly left the room.

"So...where was I? Oh, yes. So Doc indicated we might be looking at a double homicide. I'll be attending the autopsy, so we should know something by the end of the day."

I paused and looked at my notes. "Hawk. I want you and Anne to go visit the Halls this afternoon. I spoke with them this morning, and they know something about the family they're not telling. 'Odd' was the word Cindy Hall used to describe them. She said we need to talk to her children about what that means. But the husband, Darren, warned her off. So, Anne, I want you to take the lead on the interview.

"Tracy, Cooper, I need you two to coordinate the door-to-door. We're looking for information—anything at all—about the Daniels family. I'll have Jack run full background checks on them, but I need the gossip. Know what I mean?"

They both nodded. They knew exactly what I meant, and Tracy was the ideal interrogator. If there was anything "odd," she'd find it.

Tony Cooper pulled up the street on his laptop and began to assemble a list of names and addresses of people they would interview during their door-to-door.

There were thirty-eight residences on the cul-de-sac, so it wasn't that long of a list, but I knew it would take them and at least two uniformed officers a full day to carry it out.

"It appears that Matthew Daniels already has a sheet," Ramirez said to no one in particular. "Nothing big. Once for soliciting a prostitute. Once for possession of marijuana. He had less than an ounce on him at the time. And a couple of petty thefts when he was a juvie: one was for a stack of porn mags, and the other was lifting a burner phone from Walmart. His last known address is the Daniels' address, and his place of employment is CDE Construction."

Prostitutes, porn mags, burner phones, and some weed. All petty stuff, and when Cooper handed me the sheet, I noted there was a span of months—in one case a year—between each of the offenses. *What kind of a path is this kid on?* I wondered.

"This is good," I said, "but it means little. Tracy, go ahead and call CDE Construction. Find out if he still works there."

She nodded, rose from her seat, walked to the door and stepped outside to return only a moment later.

"It's Saturday afternoon," she said, resuming her seat. "Call went to voicemail. We'll have to wait until Monday."

Hawk weighed in. "One more thing: the only relative we can find so far is a Rhonda Mackabee. She's Mrs. Daniels' sister. The address is in East Chattanooga."

"Okay," I said. "It seems we're stymied. The construction company is closed until Monday and so is the school. That leaves The Halls, Rhonda Mackabee, the door-to-door and the autopsy. So, first thing Monday, Hawk, Anne, I want to know if Matthew Daniels still works at CDE. See if you can interview his co-workers. And someone needs to visit the high school and see what we can find out about the kids and family and that would be... you, Tracy; take Cooper with you.

"In the meantime, Anne" I continued, "you and Hawk can go knock on the Halls' door and see what you can get out of them. Try to get the wife on her own. You talk to her, Anne. Hawk, you take the husband. And... somehow you have to persuade them to let you talk to their children. It was Janene, their youngest, who said the Daniels were, and I quote, 'odd.' So we want to know just what she means by 'odd,' right?"

Anne nodded. Hawk said, "You got it, boss."

I paused again and looked at my notes. "That leaves the walk-through, which I can't do until tomorrow morning, and door-to-door, which we've already covered." I looked at Tracy and said, "I suggest you two get yourselves out of here and go talk to the patrol commander. You know what to do."

They both nodded and began to gather together their papers and devices.

I paused, checked my notes again, then looked at Corbin and said, "You're with me. Give Jack a call and see if we're with Doc this afternoon."

"On it," Corbin replied and got up and went outside to return a moment later and said, "We're on for two-forty-five this afternoon."

I looked at my watch. It was almost one o'clock.

I reached for my cell phone and watched as they headed out to their various assignments.

Ramirez had a worried look on her face—probably why they had been quick about finding the family info. She had two teenage girls of her own and likely couldn't help thinking what if it was her two.

Tony Cooper was the youngest detective in the team: a big man—six-one, upward of two hundred pounds—with close-cropped brown hair and hazel eyes. He was kind, quiet, most of the time, and there was a time when that worried me, but no longer. He's an excellent observer and sharp as a tack, which was probably how he'd managed to work his way up to detective so quickly.

Hawk and Anne Robar made quite the pair of opposites. Hawk, still staving off retirement, complained he was always surrounded by females; even his dogs were female. Anne's family, however, was just the opposite—all male, even the dogs. They worked well together, and I knew I could count on Anne to keep an eye on him in the field. Not that he needed it, but he was "old-school" and tough, and didn't mind showing it.

And then there was Jack North, our cyber-forensic tech. He could be a whiner, but I knew how valuable he was when we needed access to a victim's phone, laptop or tablet, or whatever device. And he was a gifted hacker, though that was officially out of bounds. When he was in the office, he worked solo, immersing himself in a world all his own. He was a cyber wizard and was good with people, so occasionally, I sent him out on interviews with one or another of the other members of the team. What was it someone had said about him once? That he was great at social engineering. Solitary by choice, but he could turn on the charm if he wanted something from somebody.

According to the chief, Jack had an Internal Affairs

file six inches thick. Chief Johnston had told me that Jack was on his "last leg" with the force and that he didn't play well with others. But I found him to be something of a star at what he did in the tech field.

And, of course, some would say I didn't play well with others, either. I was constantly under the chief's scrutiny, but I'd proven myself enough times to gain his trust. Sometimes, though, I got the distinct impression he was just waiting for me to screw up somehow, but over the years, I'd become quite deft at skirting regulations, pushing the boundaries, if you will, in such a manner that nothing ever really came back on me.

I was just about ready to go get another cup of coffee when the chief poked his head in the door.

"Kate, do you have a minute?"

I sighed inaudibly and said, "Sure, Chief," with a measure of enthusiasm I didn't feel. And I stepped out into the situation room. I just knew he was going to ask for a progress report, and I was right. But there was precious little I could tell him other than Doc's conjectures and my own limited observations. I also told him it was too early and that we had the autopsy scheduled for two-forty-five, which seemed to make him a little happier. But I did wonder why he was riding me so much. It wasn't like him. It wasn't until later that I found out the press was already hounding him.

"Good," he said finally, wiping a hand over his shiny head. "Keep me informed, Kate." And then he turned and walked away toward the elevator.

Me? I looked at my watch. It was almost one-fifteen. Just a little more than four hours since I'd arrived at the scene of the fire; it seemed like a coon's age.

Corbin looked up at me as I stepped back into my

office. "Kate," he said, "you look roug... Nice." I glared at him. But before I could respond, he said, "How about I take you to lunch? All that coffee, and nothing in your sto... and nothing to eat."

I thought for a minute. *Where do I need to go next? Ah, yes.*

"Sounds good, but let's make it quick. I want to go see Stacey Daniels' sister, Rhonda Mackabee, before we head over to Doc's little house of horrors."

"Let's do the taco truck just down the road apiece. I've had all the fast food I can stand for today."

"And that's not fast food?" I asked.

"Home-made fast food," he replied with a grin. "It's a bit more nutritious."

At that, I had to laugh. "Seriously, Corbin," I said. "Have you ever seen what I put on my tacos?"

"Touché," he said.

"But I'll agree. It does sound better, in theory anyway."

I walked over to the corner where Samson was sitting on his bed.

"Okay, boy," I said. "Let's go get some tacos."

He leapt out of the bed, spun around, and shoved his head at me. I swear that dog knows exactly what I'm saying to him... well, sometimes.

I clipped on the leash, and he headed for the door, trailing it behind him.

It was at that moment my phone rang. It was Jack.

"Hey, boss," he said. "Doc called. He said for you to make it three o'clock. That okay?"

"It's perfect," I replied. "Thanks, Jack. That will give us a little extra time. I'll call you if I need to. Keep your phone turned on." I hung up, turned to Corbin and said, "The autopsy's at three. That will give us plenty of time to see Rhonda Mackabee and make it back in time." *I hope!*

6

Day 1, 1:15pm

THE ELEVATOR DOORS OPENED AND WE STEPPED OUT into the ground floor corridor, about to head toward the lobby and the front entrance when Chief Johnston stepped out of his office.

"Ah, Kate. Corbin," he said, walking swiftly toward us. "I see you're on your way out. A quick word before you go, if you don't mind. I need to talk to you about the press."

I turned back. The press was the bane of my existence.

"You saw the newscast earlier," he said. "It's all over the TV. Every channel in Chattanooga is carrying it. They saw Doc Sheddon and the ambulances there and the bodies being wheeled out, so they know there are two deaths. Of course, they're clamoring to know who they are."

"We can dodge that," I said. "*We* don't even know who they are yet. We can speculate that they are likely

47

Peter and Stacey Daniels, but not necessarily. We really won't know until Doc finishes the autopsy and we get the lab results. You can start there."

"I don't want it to sound like we know *nothing*," he said emphatically.

"You know what, Chief?" I said, thinking it out as I said it. "There's no reason the media should know we're involved at this point. We don't yet know for sure that it's homicide, although I highly suspect it is. Let's let the fire marshal handle the press until we know for sure. I'm attending the autopsy at three this afternoon. I should have some answers for you when I return."

He paused as if he was going to argue with me but finally said, "Fair enough," then turned, walked back down the corridor and ducked back into his office. And we were headed out to the taco truck.

I ordered two tacos al carbón with rice and beans. Corbin gave me a look of mock shock, but I waved him off. "Don't even say it."

I also ordered two for Sammy—sans the rice and beans. I'm sure he wasn't much of a connoisseur, but I'm also sure he appreciated the break from dog kibble.

We sat at a shady table outside on the block patio they had created for the truck. I took my two tacos out of the bag and started to unwrap one. Samson sat obediently, looking up at me. I ignored him. He snapped his jaws and licked his lips.

I narrowed my eyes and looked at him directly. He bowed his head off to the side and whined.

"Hush," I said, reaching into the bag again, this time for one of his tacos.

"This I gotta see," Corbin said as I extended my arm to hand the taco to Samson.

"Why? It's not like you haven't seen it before."

"Yeah, but how will he get all those little green shreds off? A cheeseburger is easier because it's usually all one piece, but this is..."

Before he had finished his sentence, Samson had already devoured the taco.

"What? Why did he eat the whole thing? I thought he didn't like—"

"Iceberg lettuce? You're right. He doesn't. But this is shredded cabbage. He eats that."

"A vegetable-eating dog?"

We finished our food, and I stood. "We've got to get over to see Mrs. Daniels' sister but I need to take Samson home first. Fortunately, she lives in East Chattanooga. So it's just a couple of minutes out of the way. Come on. Let's get to it."

WE HADN'T BEEN on the road for more than a couple of minutes when my phone rang. It was Mike Willis.

"Hey, Mike," I said as I pulled over and parked in front of Ace Hardware. "Whatcha got for me?"

"We're still at the Daniels' house—"

"Wait. What?" I said. "You're inside the building?"

"No!" he replied impatiently. "We're working the scene around the building. We're not going to get inside until tomorrow morning. What I wanted to tell you is that we found boot prints, size nine, under one of the rear windows. They look like cowboy boots. You know, the ones we used to call sh—"

"Kickers. I know, Mike."

"That may be how the arsonist got in," he continued.

"The prints are deep and recent. I can probably figure out how much the person weighed if that helps."

"Anything helps at this point," I said. "Good job. Gotta go, Mike. Let me know if you find anything else, okay?"

He said he would, and I hung up.

Ten minutes later, I was parked outside my house. I took Samson inside, made sure he was comfortable and then ran back out to my cruiser.

7

***

Day 1, 1:55 p.m.

LESS THAN TEN MINUTES LATER, I PULLED INTO
Rhonda Mackabee's driveway, parked, leaned back in my
seat and stared at the wide craftsman-style house,
thinking.

Waiting around for autopsy reports, lab reports,
DNA results and such was always torture. A four-day
turnaround was average for our lab; DNA could take up
to three weeks. I shouldn't complain, though. I knew a
lot of departments that were kept waiting four to six
weeks for their results. Luckily, Doc and I were friends,
and he was good friends with the head of the DNA lab
we used, so we usually got our results a little quicker.
Even so, when you don't even know who the potential
victims are, it can be frustrating. So, I was hoping
Rhonda Mackabee could enlighten us.

Rhonda's house was partially shaded by a huge oak
tree that also shaded my unmarked cruiser—I say
unmarked, but the driver's side spotlight and the

antennas were a dead giveaway—and the front porch, upon which, sitting in a porch swing drinking a cup of tea, we saw a middle-aged woman with dark blonde hair streaked with silver, and she was staring at us.

We exited the car and approached the porch.

She frowned, narrowed her eyes and said, "Who might you be? Not the press, I hope. I have nothing to say."

"No, not the press, Mrs. Mackabee. I'm Captain Gazzara, Chattanooga PD, and this is Sergeant Russell."

"Well, I have nothing to say to you either," she snapped. "The police have already been here to inform me about the fire at my sister's place and that there were victims."

"Mrs. Mackabee," Corbin began, "we'd just like to ask you a few questions... about your sister and her family."

She was mid-swallow and nearly choked. She looked from one to the other of us and finally sighed.

"All right," she said, setting her teacup down beside a teapot on a small side table. "You'd better come inside, then. The neighbors are already wondering what's up, and I don't need to air dirty laundry on my front porch."

I glanced at Corbin. *Dirty laundry?* I thought. *This might be just what we're looking for.*

She held the screen door for us, and we entered the living room. I stifled a gasp. It was not at all what I was expecting. All of the woodwork and exposed beams, the hardwood floors, and the kitchen off to the right had been renovated but still retained the original character of the craftsman home.

I was impressed. During my search for a new home, I'd looked at a number of these homes, most of them gutted and remodeled. The living room was tastefully furnished. I immediately spotted the antique table in the corner by the window upon which stood what appeared to be a Tiffany lamp with a grass green glass shade matching the color of the cathedral glass in the colonnades. The centerpiece of the room was, of course, the large stone hearth fronted by an antique wooden chest that obviously served as a coffee table, a leather couch and two gingerbread-colored chairs.

"Please. Sit down," she said, gesturing toward the couch and chairs.

I couldn't help but look around the living room, as much to see what I could glean from family photos as to satisfy my curiosity about the Arts and Crafts style décor.

I sat down and said, "Is it Miss or Mrs. Mackabee?"

"It's Missus. I was widowed six years ago. My husband was eighteen years my senior."

"I'm sorry for your loss. May I ask what business he was in?"

"Not that I see how the question's relevant to our subject, but..." She tilted her head to one side and chuckled sarcastically. "...you want to know how I could afford this house."

"No, I simply..." I had stepped in it now. It was not the way I usually handled an interview, but she was right. I did wonder how she could afford such a beautiful house and its furnishings. And, I have to admit, I was in love with her house. Especially now that I had one of my own.

"It's all right," she said, smiling. "We came here thirty-five years ago on a relocation assignment. My husband was a railroad executive. I have his pension, of course, but I also had my own money from when our parents died—Stacey was nine at the time—so I was able to put back a fair bit, and then we invested it, wisely, I might add. It's what helped me to keep Stacey with me instead of having to put her into foster care."

I'd been sitting on the edge of the seat, but seeing her relax, I decided I could too, at least a little, and sank back into pillowy couch cushions.

"Can I get you some coffee or something else, perhaps?"

"I'll have some coffee if it wouldn't be too much trouble," Corbin said.

That was unusual for him. Apparently, he thought we were going to be there for a while.

"Good!" she said. "What roast—dark, medium or light?"

"Dark," he replied. "Thank you."

"And for you, Captain?"

Now that I knew she was making pod coffee, I knew it would be quick, so I told her dark.

As Mrs. Mackabee walked toward the kitchen, Corbin shot me a quizzical look.

"This is quite a place," Corbin whispered when he was sure she was out of earshot.

I nodded, but said nothing.

When she returned less than five minutes later, Corbin raised his eyebrows. The coffees were in glass cups with beaded handles.

"I'm trying to be hospitable," she said after noting his expression. "Even as I deal with the possibility that Stacey died in the fire... and all that that means."

"We still don't know that she's one of the victims,

I'm afraid," I said. "It could take a couple of days or so. Do you know who her dentist is?"

"Yes," she replied. "It's James Tarbutt. He has a clinic on Chamberlain, close to the hospital."

"I know this is difficult for you, but I have to ask: what can you tell me about Stacey and her family?"

She sighed and shook her head, closed her eyes, then opened them again and said, "Well, you may be in for a surprise or two."

"Meaning?" I asked, frowning.

"It's not nearly enough to be much help to the police, I'm afraid. Just family gossip, really."

"You would be surprised how helpful that kind of thing can be," Corbin said.

"Very well, then. As I just told you, our parents were quite young when they died in an accident. I was just seventeen and Anastasia, Stacey, that is, was nine.

"We lived in a very small town where the entire school was housed in one building, so it wasn't too difficult, logistically, anyway, for me to remain in school and to keep Stacey, too."

"And where was this?" I asked. Corbin had opened a new, blank sheet in his notebook and was scribbling away.

"A little town in Kentucky called Rookery. It wasn't much then, so I'm sure it's little more than... Well, it was home."

"Anyway, I was able to graduate high school. I had wanted to go to college, but that was just not possible unless I relinquished Stacey."

"No other family members anywhere?"

Rhonda shook her head. "Our grandparents were

gone, Mom and Dad had passed, and neither of them had any siblings, so no cousins, either."

"I'm sorry," I said. "It must have been hard to be so young and responsible for your sister."

"I love my sister, Captain," she said, somewhat wistfully. "Which is why I insisted on keeping her with me. But you're right. By the time Stacey was a teenager, she was more than a handful.

"I met my husband when Stacey was sixteen. Everyone told me I was marrying my father, and in the back of my mind, I knew they were right, but it never caused any problems, even when he got older.

"We were married the following year, and Stacey moved in with us, of course. But that was hard on my marriage. My husband was handsome, kind, and generous—all the things Stacey was so desperate for. When he was firm with her about keeping her distance, she then became insanely jealous of my relationship with him."

I glanced at Corbin. He was making notes.

I nodded at Rhonda. "Please go on."

"And that's where my guilt kicks in. My husband and I were happy, but Stacey was unhappy and acting out. She was eighteen that year and often stayed out all night. I never knew where she was. I pleaded with her to get a job because I knew that my husband was ready to show her the door.

"She was always intelligent, so she went into a program where she picked up some secretarial and business assistant skills. Luckily, or perhaps unluckily, if I'm honest about it, she landed a receptionist job at a car dealership."

A car dealership. Interesting. I looked toward Corbin.

He glanced at me and wrote it down. *Didn't Cooper tell me that Daniels worked for a car dealership?*

"And that's where she met Pete Daniels," she said. "End of story."

"End of story?" Corbin asked, his eyebrows raised.

"For all intents and purposes, yes."

"What d'you mean by that?" I asked.

"Peter Daniels. They started dating. I had them here for dinner—once. Len and I did not like him at all."

"He was—odd?" I queried.

"No. Odd I could put up with. This was something else altogether. Back when we were growing up, we called it a bad vibe. But, since Len and I only saw him a couple of times, we never could put our finger on it."

"You lived here in Chattanooga, and you only saw him a few times?"

"A few times is being generous. They were living together right away. It relieved our problem, I guess you could say, but it was just sad. She invited us to their wedding, and we went. They got married at the courthouse by a Justice of the Peace, then Len and I—my husband's name was Leonard—held a small reception for them in that restaurant out by the river."

Obviously, Rhonda didn't get out much. There were all sorts of restaurants on the river now, but which one wasn't relevant.

"That was the last we saw of them until the kids came along. She brought Matthew to see us when he was just a few weeks old. I was delighted to have a nephew, of course, but it wasn't to be. The next time I saw Matthew, he was eight, I think. Charlotte had just started school, and Emily was a baby.

"Stacey brought them in under the pretense of

showing us the girls, especially the baby, but they hadn't been here fifteen minutes when she said she had to go grocery shopping and that it would be a lot easier if she didn't have to take the kids.

"I was reluctant, but I didn't want to make a scene or to take it out on the children. She didn't come back for them until almost midnight. I was fuming."

"Really?" I said, somewhat dumbfounded myself.

"Don't get me wrong. My husband and I enjoyed the children. We were fortunate to see them over the next couple of years. Stacey made no pretenses. She just sent the girls in with Matthew and the diaper bag.

"As I said, my husband and I enjoyed them, but the drop-ins became too frequent."

"What do you think she was doing when she stayed out those nights?"

"I have no earthly idea. I thought at first she must be seeing other men, but then I realized that Peter was always with her. So, what the two of them were doing, I have no idea. One time, my husband caught Matthew peeking at me in the bathroom while I was in the shower, and that was the straw that broke the camel's back.

"Usually, Stacey and Peter would drive up out front and honk, and I had to rouse the children and get them bundled up to go out. But that night, Len wouldn't let me. Finally, Stacey came in, and she and Len had words.

"That put a stop to the behavior, of course, but it had the consequence of not being able to see the children again at all. We sent birthday and Christmas presents every year, and the kids always called and thanked us, but that was the extent of our contact with them."

She plucked a tissue from a box on the side table, wiped away a tear and blew her nose.

"I went to Matthew's high school graduation," she said, "but I didn't see Stacey or Peter anywhere... I will be going to Charlotte's graduation, of course. Now, that's all I can tell you. I haven't seen either of them in years—Stacey and Peter, that is, nor the children, I'm afraid."

I nodded, placed my empty cup on the side table and stood up. I would have liked to have stayed longer, but tempus fugit, and we had to be at Doc's Forensic Center in less than thirty minutes.

"Thank you so much, Rhonda. You've been a great help." And she had. I now had something of an insight into the Daniels family. It was bordering on the bizarre. "Can I have a family liaison officer look in on you?"

She shook her head. "No. That won't be necessary. I'll be too busy with funeral arrangements if the adults... If they're Stacey and Peter. You will keep me informed as the investigation proceeds, won't you?"

"As much as I can," I replied.

"I understand," she said. "I'm just asking that you notify me when you've identified the victims. If they were in the house... well, they're family, aren't they?"

"Yes, of course," I said. "As soon as we know."

She followed us to the door. But, as I followed Corbin out onto the porch, I had a thought, and I turned to ask her about it.

"You mentioned that you always bought gifts for the kids. In the last couple of years, has anyone asked you for shoes?"

She looked taken aback for a moment, then her face lit up. "As a matter of fact, yes. Matthew asked me for a pair of cowboy boots last Christmas."

Cowboy boots. Bingo! "Do you, by any chance, remember what size they were?"

"No, I.... well, wait! I still have the receipt in my desk drawer in case he wanted to exchange them. Give me a minute." And she turned and hurried back into the house.

"Good catch, Kate," Corbin said. I smiled at him.

She returned with a yellow, hand-written sales slip and squinted at it. "Size nine," she said. "Yes, that's it. I should have remembered because I thought that was strangely small for a man almost six-foot-tall."

"Size nine. Thank you, Mrs. Mackabee," Corbin said, jotting it down.

"She's right, Kate," Corbin said as we walked to the car. "Size nine is small for a man Matthew's size. I'm only five-eight and I wear a size ten."

"Hmmm," I said. "Well, we'll see. Let's head over to Doc's little house of horrors and see what he's got for us."

8

Day 1, 2:50 p.m.

I WAS TEN MINUTES EARLY, BUT WHEN I WALKED INTO
the autopsy room Doc already had both bodies on the
tables and was waiting, impatiently, to begin.

"Coffee," he snapped. "Did you bring coffee?"

"Sorry, Doc, but I'll send Corbin across the road to
McDonald's for you when he gets here. You know how
squeamish he is."

"That would be top-notch of you, Kate," he said. "In
the meantime, please suit up. I don't have all day."

Corbin walked in some ten minutes later, and I intercepted him at the door and stepped out into the anti-
room. "Doc needs coffee," I said. "Can you see to that?"

Corbin nodded, looking relieved, even managing a
little smile.

"Take your time," I said.

He winked at me and backed out the door.

"Now then," Doc said, cracking his knuckles, when I

returned. "This is what I've been waiting for. Let's see if my theories pan out." He turned on the recorder, identified himself, me as an observer, and John Cluel as the photographer, and then stated the time and date and began.

"Victim number one," he began. "The body appears to be that of a well-developed, well-nourished adult Caucasian female aged between thirty-five and forty-five. One-hundred-thirty-five pounds and sixty-six inches. The body is extensively charred. Rigor mortis is present. Livor mortis is present on the left side of the body, purple in color, and blanches with pressure. There is scalp hair present also on the left side, blonde and... four to eight inches in length. The sclerae and conjunctivae are clear. The nose and ears are not unusual. The teeth are natural and in good repair. The tongue appears normal."

He paused and looked up at me. "She's not as badly burned as the other one, at least on the left side."

"I was told she was lying on her left side with her back to the window, facing into the center of the bedroom," I replied.

He nodded and continued his observations for several more minutes, then picked up a large scalpel and made the traditional Y-incision to expose the organs. It was usually his MO, during the many post-mortems I'd attended, to remove the heart first. This time, however, he removed the left lung, inspected it, then laid it in the scale pan to weigh it.

"Hmm..." he said. "Hmmm."

"What's up, Doc?" I asked, doing a fairly respectable impersonation of Bugs Bunny. He, in turn, gave me the stink-eye, and I laughed.

"Well," he began, drawing out the word as if giving himself time to think while the sound hummed in his throat.

"We do have some markers of asphyxiation by smoke, but not nearly as much as I would have expected. And fortunately, we have plenty of fluid to get a DNA sample.

"The thing is, though, I don't see a lot of dehydration. She inhaled some soot, but there's no indication of interior scorching. She does have edema in her lungs, but again, not as much as I would expect. The fact that she was lying on her side is probably why the body is better preserved. If you'll notice, the second victim is burned more extensively."

"Er, yeah," I said. The woman's skin and hair on the right side of her head were completely charred, making her virtually unrecognizable. But the second victim was charred black from head to toe, beyond recognition.

Doc turned again to the body on the table before him, tipped her head and stretched her jaw to look inside her mouth and down her throat.

"Hmmm. I do see a little scorching in her throat, but nowhere near what I would have expected. She either wasn't breathing very deeply, or she was breathing very slowly. I'm guessing it was the latter."

"Meaning?" I said.

"Meaning that she wasn't breathing deeply enough to... You know, I think she was drugged."

"Drugged?" I asked. "You mean like Valium or something?" I asked.

"Mexican Valium, more likely," he replied.

"Mexican Valium?" I repeated.

"Benzodiazepine. Rohypnol. Rufies. Perhaps even one of the muscle relaxants."

"Rufies? Is that a drug someone would give themselves?"

"Not in the quantity it would take to begin to paralyze the lungs unless, of course, the person was trying to commit suicide."

"Suicide, huh?" I said. "So maybe this isn't a homicide after all?"

"Let's not get ahead of ourselves," Doc replied. "Let's take a quick look at the other body. It's male and was, so I understand, found lying on its back next to the female."

"So I was told," I said.

"Victim number two," he said. "The body is extensively charred but appears to be that of a well-developed, well-nourished male Caucasian, age between twenty and fifty. Weight? One-hundred-ninety-five pounds and seventy-one inches.

"Is that the closest you can get?" I asked.

He looked at me as if I'd spit in his hand.

"Oops," I said. "Sorry, Doc. So, we can assume that what we have here are Mr. and Mrs. Daniels, then?"

"I wouldn't go that far," he replied, "not until I can formally identify them."

"Geez," I muttered.

"I heard that," he said as he lifted the lung out of the body.

"Uh, oh." I could see that the tissue was flat but grayish-pink. "Pink?" I said. "Does that mean what I think it does?"

"It does," Doc said. "This person's lungs are 'in-the-pink,' meaning..."

"Meaning he wasn't breathing when the fire started!" I said.

"Bingo!" Doc said. "Very good, Kate. This victim was dead before the fire started. Which brings us toooo..."

He gestured for me to help turn the body over.

Just then, Corbin opened the door with a cup holder full of coffees. I waved him away, and he set the coffees on the table closest to him, grabbed one for himself, and headed back out the door.

Once we turned the body, I could see that the back of the head had suffered little fire damage. True, it was coated in what looked to me like melted foam, but it wasn't completely charred. Doc scraped some ash away and exposed the wound; a deep, nasty-looking gash.

He looked at it for several moments as if considering his verdict, then excavated around the wound a little more. Then he paused to pick up shears and cut away the stiffened hair until finally, it was possible to see the gash was about three inches long and terminated at a right angle.

"Mm-hmm. The angle is too perfect to have been caused by his being struck by just anything; falling debris or timbers, for instance. This was something with a straight edge and a definite corner. And—"

It was at that moment my phone rang.

I took it from my pocket, glanced at the screen, looked up at Doc and said, "Sorry, Doc. I have to take this. It's Corbin."

He gave me a weird look as if he was about to argue, but instead, he said sarcastically, "Take your time, Kate. It seems I do have all day after all."

I smiled at him and walked quickly out of the room.

By the time I was out the door, he was already bent over the body again.

"Hey, Corbin, where are you?"

"Well, when you said that I could get my notes from the recording, I took the liberty of coming back to the office where I could make some calls. You still with Doc?"

"Yes, but not for much longer. I've seen just about all I need to see."

"Well, the rest of the gang is trickling in," he said, "so hopefully, they'll have plenty to report."

"See you shortly, then," I said and hung up and stepped back into the morgue where Sheddon was standing idle, his arms crossed.

"Sorry for holding you up, Doc," I said. "Now, where were we?"

"I was going to say," he said while pointing to the second burnt body, "that I think the wound to the back of the male's head could have been caused by the base of a lamp, or perhaps even a trophy or a small statue."

I curved my mouth downward and nodded thoughtfully. "Yes," I said. "I can see that. It makes sense, Doc. I'll let Mike Willis know. Maybe he'll find something.

"Look, my team is straggling in, and I need to hold a pow-wow before everyone disperses for the evening."

"I understand. You need to know, though, that it will take longer to get the DNA results on this guy because of the state of his body. I will, of course, request dental records for the entire Daniels family and send samples to the lab for tox screening."

"So," I said. "We have one male and one female. They were in bed together, so they are probably Peter and Stacey Daniels, but—"

"But not necessarily," Doc said. "The two bodies could have been placed that way."

"They could," I replied, "but why would someone go to the trouble?"

"To create confusion, my dear. To create confusion."

Day 1, Saturday 4:15 p.m.

IT WAS A LITTLE LATER WHEN I RETURNED TO MY
office that Saturday afternoon. Cooper and Ramirez
were at their desks in the Situation room. Jack arrived a
few minutes after I did, and Hawk and Anne a few
minutes after him. I texted Corbin and told him I was
back and that we were all to meet in my office in ten
minutes, then I dug out my single-serve coffee maker
and a bottle of water and made myself a mug of dark
roast and sat down at my desk to wait and to think.

I'd barely taken my first sip when Corbin stuck his
head in and asked if I was free.

I looked around, just to make sure, then said sarcastically, "Yes, I'm free. Come on in."

And he did. He came in and sat down at the table
and set his notebook, pen and phone down in a neat
little arrangement in front of him and looked at me
expectantly.

"Don't look at me like that," I said. "You already

know where I've been. Now sit still and shut up for a minute. I want a moment to think before the rest of the team comes charging in." But it wasn't to be.

Less than a couple of minutes later, Tracy and Cooper walked in, followed closely by Jack and then... The room seemed suddenly crowded and noisy, and my head was already beginning to ache.

"Okay, everybody," I raised my voice to be heard over the hubbub. "Settle down, please. Let's get through this and get out of here. Some of us have families waiting for us, including me."

"Oooooh," Jack said. "Her son, Sammy, is home alone waiting for her."

That brought some chuckles. Only Hawk kept his stolid composure.

"That's enough from you, Detective North," I said. "Any more of that, and you'll have another sheet in your already overflowing file."

He grinned at me, knowing I was joking and said, "You want me to write that for you, Boss?"

"I can manage, thank you," I replied. "Now, in light of your lack of respect, you can go first. How did the background checks go?"

"As yet," he replied, "not too well. There's nothing on the mom, Stacey, other than an arrest for DWI. Her credit is good. Score 715. Nothing outstanding. Her car's paid for. She has three credit cards, all of them fully paid up. Now Peter Daniels... That one's a bit of an enigma. As far as I can tell, he's clean. Good credit. No debts. No mortgage. No car payment. No rap sheet. He works as an accountant at a used car dealership, Roberts Auto Circus. Now how, I wonder, does he manage it? How does he manage to be completely debt free on fifty-K a year?"

I just shook my head, picked up the almost empty file and said, "Sounds like you need to keep digging, Jack." I turned my attention to Ramirez. "How did the door-to-door go, Tracy?"

Tracy inclined her head, thought for a moment, then said, "Okay, I guess. We finished at just after three-thirty and came straight here. Out of the thirty-eight residences on the street, Coop and I were able to talk to nine residents. We took two uniforms with us, and they were able to talk to eleven more, leaving eighteen that were either out or wouldn't come to the door. We left them there to make the rounds again. They're to report to either me or Coop when they get done." She paused, checked her notes, then continued.

"It was kind of weird," she said. "No one we talked to seemed to know much about the Daniels. The consensus was that they kept to themselves and didn't talk much to anyone. Now that could have been because that's the way neighbors are these days, but I got the distinct impression for two of my interviews that there was something strange going on there. You did, too, didn't you, Coop?"

"Yup," he said. "In fact, one of mine said she thought there was something unhealthy going on there. When I asked her to explain, she said it was just a feeling and that the kids always looked unhappy; even Matthew."

I bit my top lip and thought for a minute, trying to visualize the reception Ramirez and Cooper had received.

"What was the demeanor of the people you interviewed?" I asked. "Receptive or guarded?"

"A bit of both," Tracy replied. "The closer they lived to number nineteen, the more guarded they became. Farther down the street, much more receptive, wouldn't you say, Coop?"

Cooper nodded. "Yeah. We saw Hawk and Anne at the Halls but kept our distance."

I nodded and turned to Hawk and Anne Robar. "You and Hawk," I said, "were going to tackle the Halls. How did that go?"

"Not too well," Hawk said. "We were able to corral the Hall's son, Jimmy, but he couldn't tell me much. He did mention that Charlotte was often absent from school and that she was quiet and kept mostly to herself, though he had driven her home a couple times. She didn't have much to say even then, just answered questions he put to her either with a yes or a no. Odd was not a word he would have used, so he said, but he did say that his sister..." He paused, looked at his notes, then continued, "Janene did think she was a little off, mostly because she wouldn't talk to her." He looked at Anne.

"We also talked to Cindy Hall," Anne said. "She wasn't at all forthcoming. I got the distinct impression she was either hiding something or her husband had told her not to get involved. Anyway, all she said was that she didn't know the Daniels well, that they kept to themselves, and barely said hello when they bumped into them on the street.

"I also asked if we could talk to Janene, the twelve-year-old. She told me no, quite emphatically, stating she was just a child. We were going to talk to the husband, Darren, again but he'd gone out of town; at least that's what she said."

I nodded, leaned back in my chair and folded my

arms, staring at the whiteboard, trying to think, but my mind was as blank as the board.

"We need to identify the victims," I said. "Doc estimates the age of the female as between thirty-five and forty. That would be consistent with Mrs. Daniels. The other victim, the one with the wound to the back of the head, is male, age between twenty and fifty which means it could be either Peter Daniels or Matthew, which isn't very helpful." I paused, staring at the board. "Taking into account that they were in bed together, I have to assume it's Peter."

"I wouldn't be so sure," Hawk said. "There's something odd about the family, remember? It could just as easily be the kid."

"You mean Matthew was sleeping with his mother?" Jack said, shocked.

"Okay, that's enough," I said. "I think we can assume the female victim is the mother and male is... yet to be identified."

Everybody nodded slowly.

"If we only knew who it was that got clobbered," Corbin said. "And more important, who clobbered him? I can't believe it would have been Emily. I can't see a skinny twelve-year-old girl being strong enough to kill a full grown man, let's say she did; who helped her get him onto the bed? And who drugged momma? I can't see that being Emily either. So, what d'you say we eliminate her?"

"Ha!" Anne Robar said. "You should be glad you didn't meet me when I was twelve."

"And me," Ramirez echoed. "I grew up in a barrio where there were so many drive-bys the project slum lords knocked on people's doors saying, 'Please don't kill anybody.' I was pretty tough by the time I was twelve."

"Yeah," Anne said. "I was ninety pounds soaking wet, and I beat up my older brothers on a daily basis."

"Wow, that's quite a confession, Anne," Hawk said. "But we already knew that. You've told that story at least a half-dozen times to my knowledge."

She shrugged. "Yeah, but you don't know why I was beating them up."

"Somehow, though, I don't picture Emily 'tough' in that sense of the word," Ramirez said.

"Nor do I," Cooper said.

"Careful making assumptions, Coop," I said, teasing, "They have a habit of coming back to bite you in the ass."

He looked at Tracy, shrugged and pulled a face.

"Okay," I said, "There's not much more we can do today. I'll do the walk-through of the fire scene tomorrow. Corbin, you don't have to attend unless you want to. Monday, you and Coop go to East Ridge," I said to Tracy. "Hawk, you and Anne visit CDE and talk to Matthew's boss and co-workers. We'll all meet here at noon.

"All of you, thank you. Little by little, the pieces will come together," I said. "They always do. Oh, and one more thing; Matthew's aunt said she had purchased a pair of size nine cowboy boots for him last Christmas."

"Oh!" Hawk said. "Thanks for mentioning that. Anne and I stopped by the crime scene before we came back. There's nothing behind the Daniels' house. It's an empty lot, with the street just beyond. And we couldn't help wondering if that was how the killer made their escape. But, and here's the kicker—no pun intended— when we went to look for the footprints Willis found, we found they were facing only one way; toward the house and were directly under the upstairs window. What d'you make of that?"

All I could do was nod. I had no idea what it meant, nor was I going to speculate. I already had a headache and was wanting out of there.

There was a knock on the door. It opened and Chief Johnston walked in.

"How's it coming along, Captain?" he asked. "Are you making any progress?"

"I think so," I replied, though I didn't feel too confident.

"Good," he said. "Can you write up a short report of what you have so far so I can brief the mayor? I don't think the SOB ever takes a day off. Nothing extensive. Just a few paragraphs will do."

I looked toward Corbin.

"I can write that up for you, sir. I have notes on pretty much everything. I'll be sure it's on your desk before I leave tonight, Chief."

The chief gestured to me. "Fire Marshal Wellington handled the first press conference. But just as soon as you get the necessary information from Doc Sheddon, I'm going to ask you to take the next one."

"That's fine, Chief," I said.

Johnston looked around and said, "I want you all to go home. Take the rest of the weekend off. You've earned it. Start fresh on Monday morning."

"You heard the man," I said. "Go home. Have a good rest of the weekend. You have your assignments for Monday morning. As I said, we'll meet here in my office at noon. Lunch on me."

10

Day 1, 6:00 pm

IT WAS JUST AFTER SIX WHEN I PULLED INTO MY driveway that night. I didn't linger. I went straight inside to be met by an excited Samson. He rushed at me, stood on his hind legs and put his front paws on my shoulders and gave me a wet, slobbery licking.

"Ugh!" I said, pushing him away. He dropped down and turned and rushed to the back door and I let him out. He dashed across the deck, skittered down the steps and headed full speed across the lawn.

He's definitely getting better, I thought as I closed the door. Soon after, he was back inside, ready to reconnect after being alone.

I'd been home no more than fifteen minutes and was taking out the trash before having dinner when my neighbor in the second house to the west hailed me. He was also taking out the trash, but unlike me, he was dressed in a smart gray tracksuit and matching ASICS running shoes.

"Hey, good evening," he shouted. "You're our new neighbor," he said, stating the obvious as he walked toward me. "I'm Brad Little. I live one house over." Again, he stated the obvious. "I noticed you're refreshing your front yard... Oh, sorry. I'm not being nosey. It's just that I'm a professional landscaper and I notice things like that."

I perked up at that and told him I thought I had a mole problem and how pristine my yard had been when I'd moved in only a couple of weeks earlier. He offered to take a look, there and then.

"Oh, no," I said, shaking my head. "That's nice of you, but you said you were a landscaper, not an exterminator."

"No, no," he replied. "We deal with varmints all the time."

"Yeah? Me, too," I responded with a wry grin.

I had a sudden image of Bill Murray and his all-out war with a gopher in the movie *Caddyshack* and how the deviant little animal wreaked havoc on the golf course for fun.

I hesitated. It had been a long time since someone had offered to look at a problem for me. As a civil servant, it was always the other way around.

Finally, though, I nodded and showed him the way.

"By the way," he said as I led him through the side gate, "you never told me what you do."

He was right. I hadn't. Somehow, I always took it for granted people knew what I did just by looking at me. I mean, I can always tell a cop when I spot one, but apparently not everyone can.

"I'm with CPD," I told him.

"Really?" he asked. "How come I've never seen you in uniform?"

I just smiled. I'd given him enough information. When he saw that I wasn't going to say more about it, he smiled and said, "So, let's see what's going on back here."

He stood for a moment, surveyed the landscape, then bent down beside one of the holes, pulled back the grass in several places, then stood up, turned to me and said, "Well, the good news is you don't have moles."

"Great! And the bad news?" I asked.

"You have voles. Since it just started a few days ago, it may be just one or two right now, but unless you do something about it right away, there will be more. Maybe even an infestation."

"Voles," I repeated. "What's that, like a cross between a mole and a...?"

"Mouse," he filled in the blank, grinning. "Yep, they're built more like a mouse than a mole, and they make tunnels, but differently from a mole. Their tunnels run along the surface, tearing up the grass and digging down just a couple of inches to eat the roots of the plants instead of digging deep and tunneling under like a mole does. Voles will make a track across your yard that will look like tiny armies are dividing up your land for battle."

"Oh, that's just great," I said.

It was at that moment we heard the French doors rattling. We both turned to look and could see Samson jumping up and down.

"Ah," Brad said. "That's your first line of defense right there."

"What, Samson?" I asked, and immediately regretted

it, wanting to kick myself for mentioning his name.

"If that's Samson," Brad said, pointing toward the house, "yes."

"Are you okay with dogs?" I asked.

"Sure, I have a couple of my own. Let him out."

I stepped up onto the deck and opened the doors, and Samson bounded out. He didn't go far, though. He came to me and sat down beside me, on the alert, sniffing the air.

"It's okay, Sammy," I said. "This is our neighbor, Brad."

Sammy stood, then moved cautiously forward, studying Brad. After a second, he seemed to sense that Brad wasn't a threat, so he diverted to the vole tracks.

"So, you must be a K9 officer?"

"K9 Detective," I replied.

"Wow," he said. "The only K9s I've met were rescue dogs."

"Yeah," I said. "Sammy's a breed unto himself. What were you saying about him being my first line of defense?"

"This vole activity looks very recent," he replied. "Apparently, it hasn't encountered Samson yet."

"Well, he's with me most of the time," I said without thinking. I'd just told a stranger that my house was empty all day. I should have known better, but the guy was so disarming that it was difficult to think of him as a stranger at all.

But that's exactly how they worm the information out of you, isn't it? I thought.

And then I began to look at him in a different light. Did *he* release the vole into my yard in order to gain entrance and my confidence? *Oh, for Pete's sake, Kate. You need to stop thinking like a detective every waking minute*. But I knew I couldn't. I also knew I shouldn't.

"I'm having to adjust to being home more," I said. "I used to live in an apartment, so this is all new to me." I waved my hand at my extensive backyard. "How I'm going to keep up with all this, I don't know."

Brad laughed. "Maybe I can help you with that... By the way, Miss K9 Detective, you haven't told me your name."

Again, I was tempted to ignore the question, but I knew Samson had a brain of his own and didn't take all his cues from me. So, I figured if he could trust him, I probably could, too.

"It's Kate," I said. "Captain Kate Gazzara, Homicide." I wanted Brad to know I was somebody to be reckoned with. There, now; how controlling is that?

Brad's eyebrows went up, and he gave a low whistle. I saw Samson's ears prick up and look our way, but he quickly resumed nosing the ground.

"Whoops," he said. "I completely missed that one. Well, I'd better let you get back to what you were doing..."

"Before taking out my trash?"

"Yeah, that," he said, grinning. "I need to go for my run before it gets too dark. I'll check in on you in a few days to see if Samson's having any success. If it seems like it's getting worse, please..." Brad said, handing me his card.

I wasn't sure I knew anyone who kept business cards in the pocket of their tracksuit. Other than me, that is. But then, I never knew what I might find on a running trail.

"Thanks," I said. "I appreciate it."

11

Day 1, 8 p.m.

AFTER GOING BACK INSIDE FOLLOWING MY DISCUSSION with neighbor Brad, I took a long hot shower to wash away the grime after a long day. And my cases often started on a weekend. Most regular offices were shut down, but not us—crime has no regard for time or place —and that can be very frustrating. I dressed in sweats and wandered downstairs to the kitchen, heading to the fridge where I knew I had half a pan pizza—supreme, of course—and almost a full bottle of Chablis. Yay me!

I removed the pizza and the wine from the fridge and set them on the table. Taking care of my canine partner next, I filled Sammy's bowl with five cups of his favorite salmon kibble. Then I left him to it and took my pizza and wine into the living room, where I poured myself a large glass of wine, sat on the couch and reached for the TV remote.

I paused. "No," I told myself, laying the remote back onto the side table. "Kate, you need some quiet time to think and wind down, not numb your brain." And I needed to free up my mind and analyze what little we had so far or I'd never get to sleep that night.

Yeah, I know. Work, work, work. It seems I can never let go, but it's what I do and it's how I get things done, so please bear with me.

I picked up a large slice of pizza and ate it, almost without stopping, then I grabbed another, ate it and washed it down with two big gulps of wine.

Only then did I relax my shoulders and settle back into the cushions. They seemed to mold themselves around me. *Ah, yes. That's why I purchased this model.* I closed my eyes and willed my mind to clear itself, then turned it loose to do its thing.

If the subtle inferences regarding the parents'—the Daniels, that is—strange behavior had any weight to them, I needed to know. I put my hand to my face and pinched the bridge of my nose to alleviate what felt like an approaching sinus headache.

I need to interview Darren Hall formally, I thought. *Should I bring him in? And what about the boot prints under the window? Were they made by the boots Rhonda bought Matthew for Christmas? Sheesh! We're not likely to find them in the house, now are we? And all the family vehicles were at the property. Okay, so if we assume the female victim is Stacy Daniels and, by default, we assume the male victim is Peter Daniels, where the hell are the three kids? Are they taking shelter somewhere nearby? Did someone pick them up? That would make sense... But what if the male victim is not Peter? Geez. That would open up a whole new set of unknowns. In that case, who the hell is the male victim? Matthew? Doubtful! He wouldn't be in bed with his mother... would he? Nah! So, if it isn't Peter, and it's not Matthew, who is it?*

You're just complicating it, Kate. The simplest theory is almost always the answer. And the most logical conclusion is that it was Peter Daniels in bed with his wife. But who clobbered him, and why? And by the same token, who started the fire? Yikes. Who knows what was going on there?

Just as I was about to launch into another round of fruitless calculation, my phone rang, causing me to almost jump out of my skin.

I looked at my watch. It was ten after ten. *Who the...* "Gazzara," I said.

"Hey, it's me," Jack said. "I just found a bit of information that I wanted you to know about right away."

"Are you still at the office, Jack?" I said. "You know you're disobeying the chief's order?"

"Yeah, well. The rest of you have families. What do I have to go home to?" he replied despondently.

Jack had recently broken up with his long-time girlfriend, Maria.

"You need to get a dog, Jack."

"Why?" he asked. "So I can worry all day about having to go home and let it out to pee? It's all right for you. You get to bring Sammy to work with you."

"Point taken," I said. "So, what's up?"

He hesitated for a second, then said, "Peter Daniels is a registered sex offender."

That blew my mind, just a little, and yet not so much when I remembered Darren Hall's unspoken implication.

"For what, specifically?" I asked.

"Public indecent exposure to a minor, and solicitation of a prostitute."

I remembered the bit from Matthew's record that he, too, had been picked up for solicitation. "Wow," I said. "Like father, like son. Let's hope Dad is the second victim."

"Kate! That's cold. You surprise me," Jack said.

I knew he was mocking me, but I let it go saying, "I have no tolerance for old men taking advantage of underage girls—or boys. Does it say the gender of the victim or victims? Do you have a name?"

"Not in the database. Tomorrow, I'll request the full file."

"Why don't you put in that request right now and then get the heck out of there and go home and take tomorrow off. Captain Kate's orders. Do it now, Jack."

"Okay, okay. Fear not. It shall be done."

I disconnected, sighed, stood up, grabbed the pizza box and walked into the kitchen to set the box back in the fridge, figuring I'd eat cold pizza for breakfast. Then I walked to the French doors, opened them, and took a deep breath of air, good clean air—no car fumes or fast-food smells. Sammy got out of his day bed and came and stood beside me, looking up at me.

"Go on, Samson. Do your thing and sniff around a bit, then we're going to hit the sack."

I sat on the back porch for a couple of minutes, nursing the dregs of my second glass of wine and looking at the stars. Having moved to the suburbs, I was actually able to see what was in the night sky. The constellation of Orion was a little to the south and I wondered, *Are we really alone in the universe?*

All was quiet except for the sound of the breeze ruffling the leaves of my two Chinese Elms. The cicadas had tuned up for a while but quit shortly after I sat down. No crickets either, which I thought was odd.

It reminded me of a poem I read when I was a kid. It

was something about "when the crickets quit," and every verse ended in: "And the goblins will get ya if ya don't watch out!"

I laughed to myself. With Samson on guard, there would be no goblins... Except... there was this tiny, persistent sound as if something was munching on the roots of my grass. But maybe that was just my imagination, or perhaps the wine.

12

Day 2, Sunday, August 23, 7:00 a.m.

I WOKE EARLY THE FOLLOWING MORNING, SUNDAY, feeling better than I had in days. It had been a full 24 hours since the Daniels' fire and the discovery of the two bodies.

Corbin had been right; a good night's sleep had given me a new perspective on the case, but I still had to keep reminding myself what the real focus was. We were investigating a potential homicide stemming from arson. The missing kids, the unknown victim, so many balls to keep in the air. But I was invigorated and ready to tackle it anew.

I climbed out of bed and headed downstairs with Samson at my heels. He took a long drink of water from his bowl, then headed straight to the French doors, so I let him out and left the doors open to catch a little breeze blowing in through my kitchen.

I made coffee and grabbed a bagel and slipped it into the toaster, waited the two minutes it took to turn it golden brown, then smothered it in cream cheese. Finally, I sat down at my small kitchen table, wanting to take a little time to sip and contemplate.

Barely had I sat down when there was a series of short, sharp yips and barks that got me up again. I arrived at the door just in time to see Sammy dig out what I assumed was one of the voles. He dropped it, then looked over his shoulder at me, picked it up again and trotted back to the deck, up the steps, sat down in front of me and dropped it. Fortunately, it was dead.

I looked at Samson. He had his ears pricked, his mouth open and his tongue lolling out, obviously proud of his conquest.

"What are you? A cat?" I asked him, laughing. "I didn't know that dogs did that."

I was going to pick it up by the tail and toss it in the trash, but thought better of it and decided to bury it at the bottom of the garden. So, still in my robe, I grabbed a shovel from the shed and less than two minutes later, the little critter had been given a decent burial.

"C'mon, Sammy," I said. "You gotta eat, and I need to take a shower. Then, we're on our way."

IT WAS a little before nine-thirty when I arrived at the police department. I know the chief said to take the rest of the weekend off, but I'm pretty sure he knew when he said it that I wouldn't. I took the elevator to the second floor and walked across the situation room to my office and the sound of my phone ringing.

I quickly unclipped Samson's leash, thinking he would follow me inside, but Corbin whistled and he turned and ran to see his friend. I smiled. Corbin had always had a fond relationship with Samson, and I was pretty sure he had a treat for him.

I ran to my desk and grabbed my phone.

"Gazzara," I said.

"Kate! I was just about to hang up and try your cell phone."

"Whatcha got, Doc?"

"The good news is, Kate, that I'm fast-tracking the DNA samples and other lab work on the two victims. Of course, I'll keep working on it, but don't expect results on them anytime soon. I'm sorry."

I sighed. "Okay, Doc. Not your fault. I appreciate everything you're doing." I disconnected.

So, I thought. *We're supposed to do the walk-through today.* I looked at my watch. It was still only nine-forty-three.

I sat down at my desk, picked up the file, and opened it. It was pitifully thin. I didn't even have Doc's autopsy reports.

And then, reluctantly, I began to write up my own report for the chief. True, Corbin had already done that for me, but, me being me, and in the hope it might bring some inspiration, I began to type.

13

***

Day 2, 11:30 a.m.

AT NOON, MY PHONE RANG. I CHECKED THE SCREEN.
It was a local number but not one I recognized.

"Captain Gazzara," I said.

"Good morning, Captain. Fire Marshal Wellington
here. The Daniels house is ready for your walk-through."

"Thank you, Marshal Wellington," I said. "When
would you like to do this?"

"At your convenience," Wellington replied.

"How about right now?" I asked.

"Suits me. I am at the site now."

"I need to give Mike Willis in CSI a heads up, and
then, at the very least, my Sergeant and I will meet you
there in say... forty-five minutes, at twelve-forty-five."

"Perfect," he said and disconnected.

I tapped in Corbin's three-digit number and waited
three rings before he picked up. "Yes, Cap?" he said.

"The Fire Marshal just called," I said. "We're to meet
him at the site at twelve-forty-five. You coming?"

"Sure," he said. "Let's go!"

"Give me a minute," I replied. "I have a couple of calls to make first."

I disconnected and punched in Mike Willis' number.

"Mike," I said when he answered, "the CFD Marshal just called and says we can do a walk-through now. We're supposed to meet Wellington at twelve-forty-five. Does that work for you? Good. Yes. Okay, see you then."

I looked over at Sammy, and he sat up in anticipation of wherever we were about to go, and I was about to disappoint him.

"Sammy, you need to stay here. It's the safest place and the coolest."

We were at peak heat for the day, and I was already dreading it myself. I was pretty sure the ruin would still be warm, and with that, the sun, the dust and the ashes, it was not, I was sure, going to be a fun hour or so.

So I refreshed his water, told him to be good, and walked to the door, where I looked back at him and received a baleful look in return. I shook my head, smiling, and then locked him in.

I knew it wouldn't take long. Not more than a couple of hours anyway.

"AH, THERE YOU ARE, CAPTAIN GAZZARA," Wellington said as I stepped onto the Daniels' front lawn. "You and your partner can come in now, but booties and suits on first, please. Believe me, you don't want to take this stuff home with you," he said, pointing to the wet soot and what must have been mounds of ash before it was soaked by fire hoses.

I turned around, and a member of the fire investigation team shoved a white Tyvek full-body suit and booties into my hands. I donned it and the booties as quickly as possible, hoping I wouldn't be wearing it for more than ten or fifteen minutes, but I understood the necessity of it. I also strapped an N95 surgical mask over my nose and mouth, hoping it would keep the crap out of my lungs.

As we ventured inside, Wellington leading, it quickly became apparent the fire damage was more severe than I first thought. I hadn't been to that many fire scenes, but the ones I had seen were much less drastic. Here, everything was blackened, and boards hung down where the fire had penetrated the ceiling. Every piece of furniture was burned black, and there wasn't a scrap of fabric to be seen on any of the chairs or what once had been sofas and couches.

Wellington led us first to the master bedroom on the ground floor where the victims were found. "The evidence suggests the source of the fire is here," he said as Corbin and I followed him into the bedroom. "See this serpentine pattern on the floor? That's where an accelerant was poured. It started here and quickly penetrated the walls and the electrical wiring."

I nodded as I surveyed the rest of the room. Other than accelerant, there was nothing I could see that would help my investigation. I was ready to move on.

By then, Doc had also joined, and he and Corbin were whispering and gesturing toward the room, their heads close. When I returned to the hallway, they both straightened up. I was curious, of course, but I just wanted to see what we came here to see and get out of there. Corbin and I could come back later.

Wellington pointed up the stairs. "Go on up if you want to look around."

We all trooped up the stairs, one at a time since they still weren't sure how much weight they would bear. Wellington brought up the rear.

I stepped up to the fire-chewed frame, which had been a bedroom door and looked inside. Nothing. Everything had been burned to a crisp.

I looked around in all three bedrooms. It was strange. The one room on the west side of the house—Matthew's room, so I learned later—was completely burned, while the two bedrooms on the east side of the house not so much.

Wellington told us that the dark alligator pattern in the blackened walls of the rooms on the left—west—side of the hallway was an indication of a hot and rapid burn. I didn't know that, but I did know that heat rises and the higher it gets, the hotter it gets; hot enough to melt steel beams in an industrial building.

The two rooms on the east side of the short hall were badly damaged but not nearly as extensive as the two on the west side. Strangely, though, both of the upstairs bathrooms were virtually intact, as were the contents: towels, mats, cabinets, etcetera. I made a mental note to have someone come back and check them out.

Then, as we all trooped back down the stairs, I heard a crack as loud as a gunshot as Mike stepped down onto the fourth step from the top.

"Whoa!" he yelped.

"Go on, go on," Wellington said from behind him. "You're okay now," Wellington told him. "I'm going to get down another way, but we'll have to make sure the stairs are properly reinforced. I assume, CSI Willis, that you'll be using these stairs extensively."

"Terrific," Willis replied. "I suppose that means it will be even longer before me and my team can get to work. How long before they'll be shored up?"

Wellington nodded. "I suppose you're as nimble as a fireman, so if you're really anxious to proceed, I can have a ladder brought in."

Mike calmed a bit and said, "That will work. In the meantime, if it's all right with you, we can start downstairs and in the garage."

Wellington nodded. "That works for me. I'll make sure we have something for you when you're ready for the second floor."

It was at that moment I had a sudden impulse to walk through the whole house again, by myself.

"Marshal," I said, "if you don't mind, I'd like to do my own walk-through now. I'll be as quick as I can, but I need to fill in some blanks in my head. It won't take long, I promise."

"But the stairs..." he started to protest.

"I weigh a whole lot less than Willis. My feet will barely touch them." I smiled at him.

"Why by yourself?" he asked.

"I need to be able to think clearly," I replied, "and I can't do that with other people talking to me and getting in my way. And my senses just work better that way."

He looked at me as if deciding, then said, "Okay. Be quick, but please be careful."

"That I will do," I said.

Time was of the essence. I'd tried to make speculations, but it was ridiculous to speculate on anything until we had at least a few bare facts. We were going to have to dig—deep and fast. And besides, I still had my Tyvek "getup" on.

As I worked my way through the house, I packed my impressions away in the corners of my mind, hopefully to bring them forth again when the conditions were more conducive. I glanced in the downstairs bedroom, but Mike had already moved his forensic team in there, so I didn't dawdle.

I stepped gingerly up the staircase and ventured a little deeper into the two west side rooms this time. One was a bedroom—Matthew's, as I'd previously assumed—but the other, much smaller, was set up as an office. There was nothing much of interest to see in either room; they were pretty well destroyed, so I figured I'd let Willis and company do their thing in there.

I stuck my head into both girls' rooms again, just glancing quickly, trying to take it all in.

By the time I got back downstairs, Wellington was in the doorway of the master bedroom, observing the forensic team *and likely making them nervous as hell,* I thought.

Next, I took a quick tour around the kitchen, walked around the island, saw nothing that grabbed my interest and then on into the living room. Again, as I glanced around the room, there was little to see except scorched furniture—obviously expensive—but it wasn't until my last look around from the doorway when I saw something that struck me as odd. Behind the once beautiful couch, I spotted a melted plastic box screwed to the wall. I could see the screws had been loosened by the heat of the fire, and the box was now virtually hanging off the wall. Upon closer inspection, I could see it was a wi-fi modem. I stood and stared at it, wondering why I found it so odd, until it struck me. I had not seen a single computer in the house. And then I remembered seeing a melted monitor in one of the burned-out bedrooms. Back up the stairs, with Wellington watching me, shaking his head, I walked into the bedroom at the far end of the hall, and, sure enough, there it was. On the charred remains of a desk under the window—now sans glass—was the monitor, but nowhere could I see the CPU.

I took out my cell phone and called the office.

"Jack North," I heard.

"Hey, Jack," I said. "Everything okay? Good. Look, I need you to find out who the Daniels' internet provider is and, if possible, I'd like to know how many internet-connected devices there are in the home, and when they were last used. And I need cell phone records for all five family members."

"Can do, Cap," he replied. "I should be able to have that for you sometime tomorrow. Anything else?"

"No, not right now," I replied. "But thanks. See you tomorrow bright and early." And with that, I disconnected.

I looked at my watch. It was almost one o'clock.

It was time to get back to the office, write up my notes and finish that report.

14

Noon, Day 3

I SPENT MOST OF MONDAY MORNING CATCHING UP ON my paperwork, not just for the case in hand, but also for several other cases that had been temporarily shelved for one reason or another.

I knew Tracy, Cooper, Hawk and Anne were out working their morning assignments. Jack was running down internet providers and phone records, and Corbin was off doing something on his own, as he often did, though I suspected he was doing some digging on the arson case. Somehow, he always managed to gather additional information on the human-interest aspect of each case. He was a deacon at his church, after all, so maybe he was watching out for the soul of each person involved.

Surprisingly, the morning flew by quickly, and when I glanced up at the clock, I saw it was already eleven-thirty and that my team would be arriving soon.

I'd promised to buy lunch. I knew the department

would reimburse me anyway, so I bought a round of pizzas. It was going to be another long day.

I called my order in and was told it would be about forty-five minutes, which gave me time to get somewhat organized. I stacked the shelved files neatly and put them on the credenza behind my desk. Then I made myself some coffee, glanced up at the two whiteboards and shook my head. It needed some work, in the worst way.

Corbin arrived first, followed by Hawk and Anne, then the pizza, followed by Ramirez and Cooper. Jack walked in with a sheepish grin on his face some ten minutes later. So, by twenty after twelve, they were all seated around the table, while I was at my desk, eating giant slices of pie and mumbling incoherently to one another. Sammy was, as usual, lying in his bed waiting patiently for someone to hand him a sliver of pepperoni which, of course, Corbin was only too happy to do, along with the bigger half of a slice of pie. *I'm going to have to talk to him about that when I get a minute,* I thought for the umpteenth time.

"Okay," I said after wiping my mouth and taking a stiff gulp of lukewarm coffee. "Let's get on with it, shall we? Tracy. You went to East Ridge this morning. How did that go?"

"Yes," Tracy replied. "We went to both the high school and the middle school, and we talked to several of the teachers in both schools." She paused to glance at her notes, then continued. "In all cases, the teachers said that the girls were good students, that both were smart and had been accepted into the advanced programs."

"Had been," Cooper said, correcting her. "It's true they were both accepted into the advanced programs, and Emily is still there but hanging on by a thread. Charlotte was in athletics—basketball, I think. They also chose her for a program for kids gifted in math. Apparently, she signed up but then dropped out of the program before school started the following year."

"Agreed," Tracy said. "Charlotte's homeroom teacher —a Miss Smidt—said that Charlotte was showing signs of depression in her sophomore year, and by the middle of her junior year, last year—she's a senior now—she was missing a lot of school with no explanation. Apparently, they called the parents and sent them letters and emails, but they never heard back. She said it was clearly a departure from Charlotte's earlier behavior and her middle school performance level. She also said Charlotte was clearly a troubled young lady and had been in counseling, but she refused to talk about it, especially her home life. I asked why they hadn't gotten CPS involved, and the answer to that was, and I quote, 'she's eighteen and an adult,' which, I suppose is true, but only just. School started back two weeks ago, on August six. She's supposed to graduate next May. I asked how the first two weeks of school went and all I got in return was a shrug and a vacant look."

"So," I said, "Charlotte has problems. Hmmm. Problems at home?" I asked.

Tracy shook her head and said, "I don't know, and neither do her teachers. We did talk to two of her friends—with teachers present, of course—but they both looked kind of guilty and said they thought she was okay, and they didn't think anything was wrong with her."

"Well, they would, wouldn't they?" Cooper said. "No kid that age is going to rat on a friend. If we're going to find out what's wrong with her, we need to talk to Emily or Matthew. And we can't do that until we find them."

I nodded. "What about Emily?"

"Now that was also revealing," Tracy said, taking up the narrative again. "Emily was in sixth grade last year—she was eleven then—and was doing well. But, when school started back—and this is according to her home-room teacher, Miss Truitt—there had been a significant change in her demeanor and her school work was suffering. She was of the opinion that something must have happened during the summer recess. What it was, she didn't know; the kid refused to talk. She just said nothing was wrong. That's all."

"So," I said thoughtfully, "There was obviously something seriously wrong going on at nineteen Melrose Place. Jack, you told me that Daniels is a registered sex offender—"

"What?" Tracy snapped, obviously shaken.

"Yeah," I said. "Five years ago. He was cited for indecent exposure to a minor in a public restroom and solicitation of a prostitute. The guy has... had problems."

I blew air out through my lips and shook my head.

"That it, then, Tracy?" I asked.

"Yep. That's it," she replied.

I nodded and said, "Then let's move on. Anne and Hawk, were you able to track down any of Matthew's co-workers?"

"We were," Anne replied. "We arrived early at CDE Construction, at around seven-thirty, before they dispersed to their various jobsites. And we were able to talk to several of the workers, all of whom knew surprisingly little about Matthew, considering he had worked there for about a year. As far as we could tell, they didn't seem like they were hiding anything. They just... didn't know him, right, Hawk?"

Hawk nodded, and Anne continued, "He doesn't attend social functions, doesn't go out with any of the crew, and keeps to himself. He's well-liked and apparently very skilled at what he does, but he keeps most everyone at a distance."

"That's been the theme throughout this investigation," I said. "I take it Matthew didn't turn up for work this morning."

Anne shook her head and said, "No. Not while we were there, and I did leave mine and Hawk's cards with the office supervisor with instructions to call us if he turned up."

She took a breath, looked at Hawk and nodded.

"There was this one guy that we talked to, a Vincent Miller," Hawk said, "who worked with Matthew from time to time. He said he didn't know much about him, but he referred us to a Parker Morris. Morris is supposedly Matthew's closest friend or acquaintance, and Miller seemed to think if anyone could tell us something about the boy and, by extension, his family, it would be Morris. He also said that Morris used to talk about Matthew and his family. I asked him what kinds of things Morris had said about them, but he just shrugged and replied, 'Better ask Parker.'"

"Then we'll do just that," I said. "Did you get an address?"

"We did," Anne replied. "We spoke to the office supervisor who gave us Morris's address and told us that he had last seen Matthew at close of business last Friday."

"Good work," I said, reaching out to take the slip of

paper with Morris's address. "Anything else?"

"Nope," Hawk said. "Other than no one seemed to have a bad word to say about the kid. The consensus was that he's a hard worker but a bit of a loner."

I nodded, turned to Jack and said, "How about you, Jack? Were you able to come up with anything new?"

Jack heaved a big breath and said, "Not that much, not yet. I managed to find out that the Daniels have an Xfinity account and that there were four computers and an iPad connected to WiFi. I also found out they have a Verizon account, but that's all. It's going to take a search warrant to get the phone records. By the way, during your walk-through, did you see a landline, by any chance?"

I had to think about that. I hadn't noticed one, but that didn't mean there wasn't one. "I can't say that I did," I replied. "Get hold of Mike Willis. If there is one, he'll know. In the meantime, keep digging. About the search warrant; you'll need to see the chief. How about the background checks?"

"Still working on them, boss," he replied.

I nodded. "Tracy, Coop, you need to go back to Melrose place and see if you can interview any more of the neighbors. Maybe someone we haven't already interviewed will know something."

I paused for a moment, thinking, then said, "Anne, Hawk. There's someone we've kind of ignored. See what you can find out about Stacey Daniels. If you think you need to, make contact with her sister. You good?"

They both nodded.

"Corbin, you and I will see if we can't track down this Parker Morris guy. All right, everyone. Let's get to it."

15

IT WAS ALMOST ONE-FORTY-FIVE THAT MONDAY afternoon when Corbin, Samson, and I took off to find Parker Morris.

It wasn't difficult. The address in North Chattanooga Hawk had been given was good, and we arrived there right at two o'clock.

Parker Morris lived in an upscale home in a gated community. That being so, I figured he, like Matthew, must still be living with his parents.

Having no gate code, however, all we could do was sit and wait for someone to either go in or out. Not a big deal, especially as we had to wait no more than a couple of minutes before the gate opened and a woman in a Range Rover drove out. We slipped in before the gate could close.

We rang the doorbell, but there was no immediate answer. We rang again with a similar result and were just about to leave when the door opened, and a disheveled, sleepy-eyed young man peered out at us.

"Police," I said, flashing my badge. "Open up!"

The door closed, then opened again, and Sleepy stepped out onto the stoop wearing only boxers and socks.

"Can I help you, officers?" he asked, bleary-eyed.

"I'm Captain Gazzara and this is Sergeant Russell. We're looking for Parker Morris. Is that you?"

"Um, yeah... What d'you wanna see me for?"

"Can we come in?" I asked. "And you need to put some clothes on."

"Oh." He looked down at himself. "Yeah, right. Yeah, come on in. Wait! You can't bring the mutt in," he said.

Samson laid his ears back and kept his eyes on Morris.

"Oh, but I can," I replied. "It's too hot to leave him in the car. And he's not a mutt. He's a K-9 officer, as you can see from his harness and badge, and he's as much my partner as Sergeant Russell here."

He shrugged and said, "Have it your way." And then he turned away, walked back into the house, and led us through to the kitchen.

"Take a seat," he said, nodding toward the kitchen table. "I won't be a minute. Make yourselves some coffee, if you want to. There are pods and cups in the cupboard next to the sink and creamer in the fridge."

"That won't be necessary," I said as I gifted Corbin with a pointed look.

Parker nodded and left to return a few moments later wearing a pair of yellow and white shorts that came down below his knees, a white T-shirt and flip-flops.

Had we been in California, I'd have pegged him for a surfer dude.

"So," he said, taking a seat at the table opposite us. "What can I do for you?"

"You're a friend of Matthew Daniels, right?" Corbin asked, taking the lead, as we'd arranged during the drive over.

He nodded. "Yeah, I guess you could say that. So what?"

"Are you aware of the fire at the Daniels' home early Sunday morning?" Corbin asked.

I hadn't mentioned that we were from Homicide, something we'd also arranged in the car.

He looked off to the side, apparently thinking. "Yeah, I guess my mom said something about it before she left for work."

"You don't seem too concerned," I said.

"Why would I be? What's it got to do with me?" he asked testily.

"We talked to Vincent Miller earlier today. He told us you and Matthew are best friends."

He shrugged. "Used to be."

"A minute ago you said you were friends," I snapped. "Which is it? Either you're friends, or you're not. Did you have a falling out?"

"Yes, and no. We just don't get together anymore."

"Why not?" Corbin asked.

No response. He was tapping the heel of his right foot up and down as if he was uncomfortable speaking with us.

I narrowed my eyes and said, "What can you tell us about Matthew Daniels?"

He didn't reply. His jaw was set and his eyes were narrowed.

"Look," Corbin said, "we can do this here or we can take you downtown and do it there. Your choice, buddy."

"So, is Matthew dead?" he asked.

I thought for a moment about how I wanted to answer the question. Usually, I would say something to the effect that it was an ongoing investigation and that I couldn't talk about it, but in that particular case, I had nothing to talk about. So I looked him in the eye and said, "We don't know. That's why we're here. We need to know who and what he is and where he and his two sisters might be."

He looked at us for a long moment, then said, "Okay. I'll tell you what I know. Ask your questions."

I turned on the record app on my phone and set it down on the table in front of him, then asked his permission to record the interview. He agreed, and I looked at Corbin and nodded.

"How do you know Matthew?" Corbin asked.

"We were at middle school together," he replied. "We didn't really start hanging out until high school, though."

"And you were best friends?" Corbin asked.

Again, he looked irritated and began tapping his foot again. "We spent a lot of time together, yes."

"And you spent a lot of time in his house?" Corbin said.

Morris cracked a smile. "Er yuh! He has sisters. Of course I spent a lot of time there."

"How did that go?" Corbin asked.

He shrugged again. "Not well. I was really interested in dating Charlotte a couple of years ago, but Matthew warned me off. I pursued it for a while, but when she told me in no uncertain terms, that she wasn't interested, I kind of lost interest."

"How about his parents? Did you see much of them?" I asked, changing the direction.

"The first couple of times I was there, they invited me to stay for dinner." He paused. "The whole family together is just, you know, strange."

"Strange how?" Corbin asked, looking up.

"No small talk. The girls were completely silent, and the only thing I heard from the adults was, 'Pass the potatoes,' 'More green beans?' Stuff like that. Even Matthew. If he wanted to get something across to me, he just gestured."

That was interesting. "So, were they strict?" I asked.

"I honestly don't know. I don't think any of them said more than a couple of dozen words either time I saw them. It was like... Aw, hell. I don't know what it was like. It was weird, is what it was. After those first two times, I didn't see much of them. We just hung out in Matthew's room."

That struck a note. "Can you tell us which rooms were upstairs?"

"Uh, yeah. Matthew's was at the top of the stairs on the left. Emily's was across from his, and Charlotte's room was down the hall on the right."

"Charlotte's bedroom," I repeated. "So, what happened between you and Matthew? I'm sure it wasn't just because of Charlotte."

"He was obsessed with his sisters."

"What do you mean by obsessed? Unhealthily obsessed?"

Morris shrugged. "Isn't any obsession unhealthy?" He

looked away to his left, toward the dining room. He was either about to start lying or he was pondering how much or how little to say.

"He was protective of them. Took them everywhere. Brought them everywhere. He dropped them off at school in the morning and picked them up in the afternoon. When we went out at night, he always brought Charlotte. It made it hard to do any guy stuff, you know?"

"Did he bring Emily, too?" I asked.

"Sometimes, but less often than Charlotte."

"Had he changed his mind about you and Charlotte?"

"Hell, no. If anything, he was more adamant that I keep away from her. That was hard. I just got tired of it, that's all."

"So, that was your falling out?"

"Like I said before, yes and no," Parker replied.

"Meaning?" I asked.

"Meaning it was part of it, but it was more than just that."

We waited for him to say something else, but he didn't.

"Come on, Parker," I said. "Don't make us drag it out of you. If you know something that might help us with our inquiries, spill it. What was more?" I continued.

"Aw, jeez. I don't like ratting on someone, even if he's no longer my friend."

"Ratting? As in ratting him out?" Corbin asked.

"Yes, as in ratting him out," he said with a mocking smile on his lips.

Now I was getting irritable. Parker Morris was getting on my last nerve.

"Since 'ratting' was your choice of words, I'm going

to suggest you explain what you mean by it," I said sharply.

He jutted out his bottom lip and shook his head. "I just said I don't like doing that."

I took a deep breath, letting it out with some exasperation in my voice. Morris grinned.

"Okay, buddy," I said, now out of patience, "if you know something about illegal activities Matthew Daniels was engaged in, you'd better tell us now. Otherwise, I'll arrest you for obstruction of a police investigation and withholding evidence."

Parker's eyes opened wide. "Hey! I didn't say anything about illegal!" He paused for a moment, the color gone from his face, then said, "It mostly started when he got in with some bad people doing bad things. One guy cozied up to Matt, and our relationship—Matt's and mine—quickly became subordinate to theirs.

"See? Matt and I had always been open with each other about everything, but suddenly, he didn't want to talk to me about anything. Nothing personal anyway. He tried to stay friendly, you know? But even that seemed like too much of a burden after a while. He was always gone, staying out late with Charlotte in tow. I guess, in the end, we just stopped trying and drifted apart."

I thought about what Rhonda Mackabee had said about Peter and Stacey, always out late, doing what she never knew.

"Okay, that's good," I said. "Very helpful, but you still haven't told us what he was into."

Morris put up his hands as if in protest.

"I don't really know how deep Matthew's involvement goes or anything about it. But I will tell you, under duress, that the guy he started hanging out with was linked somehow to some kind of sex... I dunno, ring? Sex ring? Prostitution?"

"What d'you mean, a sex ring?" Corbin asked.

"Wait a minute," I said. "Let's make sure we're on the same page here. Are you talking about sex trafficking?"

He shook his head. "No. I know the difference. This is about underage girls, you know?"

Now that caught me by surprise. I was no stranger to the concept; and I knew that—as it was in any and every other large city—happening in Chattanooga. But not being on the vice squad, it didn't often cross my radar.

"Okay," I said. "I need more. What was going on with Matthew and the girls? Was he pimping them out?"

"No! I don't know. I didn't read that into it, but this guy... he seemed to have a lot of influence over Matthew."

"Has he got a name?" Corbin asked.

"Uh, Terry something... no, Terrance. That's it. Terrance."

"Terrance who?" I asked. "And I need an address."

"I don't know... Knowles, maybe? I dunno. But that's it," he snapped. "I'm done. I've told you everything I know. And I don't know the exact address. Hey! You're cops. Surely you know about the operation on Green Lane."

I didn't. But I sure as hell was going to find out. And what was Matthew Daniels doing tied up in it?

"Where on Green Lane?" I asked.

"Toward the north end," he replied. "Fourth house from the end on the right. That's all I know. I told you; I'm done talking. Now please go."

I stared at him for a long moment, then looked at Corbin. He nodded.

So I shortened Samson's leash—he was lying under the table—and thanked Morris for his cooperation, told him we might want to talk to him again.

He gave me a quick, expressionless nod. We got up, and he escorted us back to the front door and, without saying another word, quickly shut it behind us.

"Soooo..." I said as we walked to the car. "I guess you learn something new every day. Terrance Knowles, huh?"

"You know," Corbin replied, "that boy told us a whole lot more than he thinks. A sex ring on Green Lane! Who would have thunk it?"

"Now you're confusing sex trafficking for commercial purposes," I said. "Sex rings usually, but not always, involve children and cater mostly to pedophiles."

He shrugged. "Whatever. It's still men exploiting young women and girls."

"Right. I believe the charge in this case would be sexual exploitation of a minor. Unfortunately, Vice doesn't share everything with us. I'm sure they keep something like that on the down low. That tells me one good thing, though."

Corbin looked at me, his eyebrows raised in question.

"Apparently, no one's murdering these girls, or we would have seen it by now," I said, half joking.

"Maybe, until now." Corbin was not laughing. "Green Lane, though?"

"Yes," I replied thoughtfully. "That's a bit of an enigma."

Corbin grimaced. "I always picture something like that only happening in large mansions patronized by rich white men."

"I try not to picture it at all," I said dryly. "Let's get back to the office."

———

WE ARRIVED BACK in the situation room some fifteen minutes later where I found most of my team at their desks; they occupied a small section on the east side of the room just a few feet from my office at the north end.

Jack, of course, was nowhere to be seen, but it didn't bother me. I knew he was probably in the cyber forensics lab digging into... what, I had no idea.

The other four members of my team were at their desks. So, I parked myself on the corner of Hawk's desk and said, "How did it go with the elusive Mr. Hall?"

"Still elusive," Hawk replied. "We did manage to have a word with his wife, Cindy. She said he was out of town. Anne tried to question her, but she would have none of it. In fact, she was still kinda pissed that we talked to her son and threatened to make a formal complaint if we so much as went near her daughter. I think we've gotten as much from that family as we're going to."

I nodded and turned to Tracy. "Any good news?" I asked.

Tracey shook her head. "Nope. Most of the close neighbors were at work," she replied. "We were able to talk to three more people, but it was the same story: No one seems to know anything about the Daniels." She shrugged. "How did you do? Were you able to find this Morris guy?"

I turned to look at Corbin, who was leaning nonchalantly against one of the support pillars, his arms folded across his chest and his legs crossed at the ankles.

"It seems Matthew Daniels is involved in, or at least has dealings with, some kind of a sex ring at a home on Green Lane."

"Green Lane?" Anne said. "No way! For real?"

"That's what Morris said," Corbin replied. "Hard to believe, right?"

"Hard to believe," I agreed. "I haven't had a chance to check with anybody in Vice yet, but Morris seemed to think we know all about it. We, being the police."

Cooper sat forward in his chair and cleared his throat to get our attention.

"What is it, Coop?" I asked.

"A while back, when I was still in Vice, me and my partner arrested a couple of guys on theft and drug charges. They were just small fry, street-level pushers, you know? So, during the initial interview, we offered to go easy on them in return for information about where and how they were getting their product. Failing that, the idea was to turn them; make them CIs. We offered to turn them loose in exchange for any drug or crime-related info.

"One of them asked if that included prostitution. That piqued my curiosity, so I told him it did. And he said he'd heard that there were girls available for pretty much anything down on Green Lane. I asked for an address. He said he didn't have one, that it was just something he'd heard, so we put 'em in holding, and Jerry and me went to check it out.

"Well, we didn't find anything. Green Lane is in a quiet, upper-class neighborhood in East Brainerd—not exactly the kind of place you'd expect. We saw nothing that indicated criminal activity of any kind. We figured they were just trying to make brownie points." He shrugged. "We turned 'em loose anyway. Wasn't worth the time and effort to charge them."

"If it's the kind of prostitution we think it is," Corbin said, still leaning against the pillar, "there wouldn't be anything to see. They wouldn't advertise it, and there wouldn't be any street activity. Maybe your guy didn't know that."

"Hmmm," Tracy said. "I wonder if it isn't connected to what Parker Morris told you, though. Maybe it's worth another look, and not in broad daylight," she said, looking askance at Cooper.

"Uh, yeah," he said. "What she said."

"Stakeout tonight?" Tracy asked, looking at me.

"Sure," I said. "If you're up for it."

I heard the elevator door open and turned to see Chief Johnston step out. Corbin immediately straightened himself up and tried not to look self-conscious.

"Good afternoon, Kate," he said and nodded at the rest of the team. "What's the latest?"

I quickly brought him up to date. He seemed happy enough when he left, so I went to my office, closed the door—wishing I had a Do Not Disturb sign to hang on the handle—turned on the coffee maker, then sat down at my desk and closed my eyes.

16

Day 3, 3:45 p.m.

IT COULDN'T HAVE BEEN MORE THAN FIVE MINUTES later when there was a knock at my door, and a young, uniformed officer poked his head inside and told me I had a visitor.

"I do? Who is it?" I asked.

"A Miss Ella Sanchez, ma'am," he said. "She said she wants to talk to you about Matthew Daniels."

"Did she now?" I said. "Bring her up, please."

Okay, for some reason I can't explain—maybe it was just a gut feeling—I was pretty sure Matthew Daniels was not the unidentified body in Doc's little house of horrors. And I was hoping this Ella Sanchez person could shed some light on where he and the two girls might be.

I picked up the phone and buzzed Ramirez. "Tracy, my office, please," I said when she picked up.

She arrived almost immediately, notepad in hand, and two minutes later the young officer arrived with a tall, Hispanic woman whom he introduced and then stepped aside for her to enter.

"You want me to wait, Captain?" he asked.

"Yes, grab a seat outside," I replied. "I'll call you when we're done. Thank you...?"

"Dennison," he said. "Officer Dennison."

I nodded and he closed the door.

"Miss Sanchez," I said. "I'm Captain Gazzara. This is Sergeant Ramirez. Thank you for coming. Please take a seat." I gestured toward the table.

Samson caught her eye, even though he hadn't moved.

"Are you afraid of dogs, Miss Sanchez?"

"No! I love dogs," she said, "but police dogs always seem a bit, I dunno, scary."

"Would you rather I remove him?"

"Nah. He's fine. He seems pretty chill," she said.

"He is," I said, smiling.

"So, tell me about Matthew Daniels," I said. "What is your relationship to him?"

She nodded. "Sure," she said. "I'm Matthew's ex-girlfriend."

"Okay," I said. "So why don't you tell me why you're here? You do know this is the Homicide Division, right?"

She nodded, then took a deep breath. "I went through high school with Matthew. We went out for about three years until we broke up just a few weeks ago. I still... Is he...?" She paused. Looked at me, then continued, "When I heard the news about the fire, I knew I had to talk to somebody. I called Matthew's aunt, who wasn't sayin' much, but she did give me your name and number. She told me you were the person I needed to speak to."

"You knew Matthew's aunt?" I asked, frowning. I was curious because Rhoda Mackabee had told us she'd had little contact with any of the Daniels family, except at Christmas, so I was pretty sure Matthew hadn't introduced Ella to her.

"No. I don't know her at all," she replied. "But just before we broke up, Matt called her and told her about me, and he told me she was his emergency contact if... something should happen to him. I just wanted to see if she had heard from him since the fire."

"And?"

"She said she hadn't seen him since Christmas, then she told me about you and gave me your information."

"That's fine," I said. "So, what did you want to talk to me about?"

"We were friends first, then started dating. He's the best guy I've ever dated, but..."

"But?" I asked.

She sighed. "Matthew was always very sweet to his sisters. The last year that we were together, he brought them almost everywhere we went, which I didn't mind at first, but it's like they were just tolerating me. Neither of them liked to talk, so it was hard to get more than two words out of either of them.

"But soon, Matt's insistence in keeping them so close became really old. I mean, it was weird, and then he began to shut me out."

"How did you feel about that?" Tracy asked. "It must have hurt, right?"

"Well, it didn't feel good, that's for sure. I mean, we'd been together a long time. It was the strangest thing. He shut everybody out, even Parker—him and Parker

Morris were best friends for years. But then even he stopped coming around. And then I found out that Matthew was hanging around a new guy and... some other people. They seemed..." She shrugged. "I dunno. They made my frickin' skin crawl."

"Why was that?" Tracy asked. "Were they on drugs?"

"No," Ella replied. "They're just sleazy. Frickin' nasty."

I sat back in my chair, watching her face and began to sense that she was about to go into withdrawal, just as Parker did. I got the feeling she was frightened that perhaps she was saying too much. So I tapped my left forefinger three times on the table, a long-time prearranged signal to Tracy—and to the rest of my team —to keep quiet and see what she'd do next.

There followed a long moment of silence until she sighed and said, "It just doesn't add up," she said. "Matt, being so overprotective of his sisters, and yet he was hanging around these guys. I don't know for sure, but I think they're involved in prostitution... and who knows what else."

She sat back for a minute, steadily popping her gum, then continued. "Suddenly, he had more money than he ever had, and I knew he hadn't gotten a promotion at work. I mean, he only makes sixteen dollars an hour. He bought that blue crew cab pickup and gave his sisters money. I could tell 'cause they started dressing up more and wearing makeup."

"Charlotte never wore makeup before?" Tracy asked.

"She did, but it was like a kid using her mama's lipstick. Once Matthew gave them money, well, I think she must have gone somewhere to learn how to do it properly. I mean, she looked really good."

"Could he have been pimping his sister, d'you think?" I asked.

"I don't know. Maybe. But Matt... I can't believe he would do something like that. He's a loving guy, which is why I said nothing to him about his sisters coming with us all the time."

"Did he ever talk to you about prostitution?" Tracy asked. "Did he ever suggest—"

"What? No! Hell no!" she snapped, interrupting Tracy. "He sure didn't try to involve me if that's what you mean. No way I would put up with that kind of shit," she said, looking down at her perfect red and black gel nails. The nail on each ring finger was decorated with a sugar skull.

"You said he might be involved in prostitution. Do you know where?"

"Not exactly. It's a house somewhere in the East Brainerd area, but I've never been there. That's really about all I know about the situation." She paused for a moment, then said defiantly, "And I think there's some real trouble going on at home."

"What makes you say that?" I asked.

"Because of the way he keeps those two girls with him. I mean, they're either at school or they're with him; never at home. It makes no sense, does it? Anyway. That's all I know. Now, it's my turn. D'you know where Matthew is? Did he die in the fire? Please. I need to know."

Inwardly, I sighed, then said, "Ella, the answer to both questions is, we don't know. The investigation is still ongoing. I know that doesn't help, but right now, it's all we have. We were hoping you'd be able to provide answers to some of our questions, and you have. You've been very helpful." She really did look devastated. "I'm sorry, Ella."

I looked at Tracy. She nodded imperceptibly and said, "Thanks, Ella, for coming forward. We're almost done, I think. Just a couple more questions."

"Just so you know," she said, "I'm not trying to get anybody in trouble. I was really worried when I heard about the fire."

"I know," I said. "When was the last time you saw Matthew or his sisters?"

"It was a couple of weeks ago."

"Did he share any of his plans with you?" I asked.

"Ha! No," she said. "He barely spoke to me."

"Okay, then," I said. "One more and we're done. You mentioned this new friend of his. What's his name?"

"Terrance Knowles, with a K. And before you ask, I know nothing about him other than he's not a nice guy. In fact, he's a frickin' total sleaze."

"Thanks," I said and watched as Tracy made a note of the name.

"Terrance Knowles," I said. "D'you have his address?"

"No!" she snapped. "I really don't know anything else... Will you please let me know when you know something?"

"We will," I said. "Thanks again, Ella. You've been most helpful." We all stood, and I shook her hand. "We may need to speak to you again, so if you'll give Sergeant Ramirez your contact information, we'll know how and where to get hold of you."

I went to the door and called Officer Dennison while Tracy wrote down her information.

"Please show Miss Sanchez out," I said, then thanked

Ella one last time and watched her walk with Dennison across the situation room to the elevator.

Then I turned to Tracy and said, "Does the name Terrance Knowles ring any bells for you?"

She shook her head. "Not me. I'll ask the others."

"Good," I replied, "and ask Jack to run a full background check on him? I'm thinking from what Ella said, he's probably got a record." I paused and thought for a moment, then continued, "I'm going to send Hawk and Robar to Peter Daniels' car dealership. Robert's Auto Circus. It's on Rossville Boulevard, I believe. And, if Jack can provide us with an address for Terrance Knowles, Corbin and I will head out there," I said. "Thanks, Tracy."

"No problem, Kate." And she nodded and then turned away and left my office, presumably to talk to Jack.

17

Day 3, Monday 4:15 p.m.

IT DIDN'T TAKE LONG FOR JACK TO COME UP WITH AN address, and by four-fifteen we were on our way.

The upscale development where Knowles lived was impressive. The row of townhouses was a new development—not more than a couple of years old. The houses were in pairs with narrow gaps between each pair. Built-in garages flanked the front doors, which were side-by-side.

I looked up as we approached the house. "Three frickin' floors? What's that about?" I asked out loud.

"Well, two and a half, by the look of it," he said, "but it sure is big."

I parked my unmarked cruiser at the curb in front of a recessed front door; a small porch, I guess you'd call it.

We rang the bell and knocked using the ornate brass knocker but without response. I stood on tiptoe and peered through the window in the door, but all I could see was a wide-carpeted stairway leading up from a small foyer.

Corbin knocked, harder this time. Still no response.

"I'll go around back," Corbin said. "He could have slipped out. If he has a rap sheet, cops wouldn't exactly be welcome. And that cruiser of yours is a dead giveaway. We should have used my car."

"All right, smart ass," I replied. "Go on, see what you can see round the back."

I hammered on the door again, but still there was no response.

Corbin had been gone for perhaps a couple of minutes when I heard a voice behind me.

"Looking for the occupants, officer...?"

I turned and looked at him. Despite his silver hair, I figured he was probably in his mid-to-late forties. He wore running gear and had, by the look of his glistening skin and reddened cheeks, just come from a run.

I stepped forward, badge in hand; it was on a chain around my neck.

"Gazzara. And it's Captain."

He stepped closer, leaned forward and looked at it. "Oh!" he said. "Yes. I see that now. Sorry."

"That's okay," I said, releasing my badge to flop back onto my chest. "Yes, I am looking for the occupants," I said. "That's not you, I suppose?"

"No. I live two doors down. That way." He pointed to his left. "We kind of watch out for one another around here. There's only one occupant now, I guess. There used to be a young woman named Sandy living here, but I haven't seen her for some time. The only occupant I know of is Terrance."

"Terrance Knowles?"

"That would be him," he said.

"What about Sandy?" I asked. "Do you know her last name?"

"No, I never actually met her. I just saw her coming and going. I only know her first name because I saw him chase her into the street one time, yelling her name."

"Do you know a Matthew Daniels or ever remember seeing him here?"

"No. That name doesn't ring a bell."

"Are you home a lot, Mr...?"

"Burnett. Paul Burnett. Yes, I'm a data analyst, and I work from home. My office window gives me a good view of the street, day and night."

"Nighttime, too?"

"Yes, I have several security cameras with broad views of the street," Burnett said.

"Why is that?" I asked.

"Why is what?"

"Why do you have cameras that monitor the street day and night?"

He grinned. "I'm a great believer in CCTV. The Brits use it extensively and to great advantage, and being in tech, I have a thing for gadgets. I'm single and have lots of time on my hands."

"The neighborhood voyeur, then?"

He knit his brows together. "You can call it whatever you like," he snapped. "We don't see a lot of your people, so why not?"

"Sorry. Just kidding," I said. "But seriously, you need to be careful. People can be funny about their privacy."

"There's no such thing as real 'privacy' anymore, what with satellites and drones and those idiotic devices people have in their homes that listen to and record every word they say. Don't talk to me about privacy, Captain. It doesn't exist. I'm much more interested in security. It's a jungle out there." He paused and raised his shirt to reveal what looked like a Sig P938 on his hip.

"D'you have a permit for that?" I asked.

"Of course I do, but as a police officer, you should know I don't need one anymore."

I nodded, staring hard at him.

He blanched, then said, "I really do keep a lookout on the comings and goings around here."

"Is that why you're telling me about Terrance Knowles?"

"Er... Yes. I suppose it is," he replied.

"Tell me more," I said. But before he could, Corbin reappeared.

He shook his head and said, "There's a gate back there that opens into an alley. I was able to get into the backyard and look in the windows. It looked kind of deserted to me. I don't think there's been any activity for at least several days."

"You're right, I think," Burnett said. "I haven't seen his car come or go since last Friday."

I introduced Corbin and then said, "What sort of vehicle does he drive?"

"One of those big, black SUVs," he replied.

"Like the cartels use?" Corbin asked, grinning.

"Yes, I suppose so," Burnett replied. "I hadn't thought of it like that, but it has tinted windows. One of those big Chevys."

My interest was piqued, but before I could ask further, Burnett said, "Look, you're welcome to look at my security footage."

It was an offer I couldn't refuse.

"It runs twenty-four-seven," he said, "so we should be able to determine the last time that Terrance was in residence."

"How long have you been doing this video surveillance, Mr. Burnett?" I asked.

"A couple of years now, I suppose," he said.

"What do you do with the recordings?" Corbin asked him.

"I review them every morning. I have an archive on my laptop of everything more than a week old, unless I find something interesting and isolate it."

"And have you?" I asked.

"I have a few, but they're more of an interest to me than they would be to you."

"Really," I said. "You might be surprised what would be of interest to me."

"How about first we go take a look at the files for the last week and see if we can figure out when Terrance was last here."

"That would be great," I said and glanced at Corbin. "But it's hot out here, Mr. Burnett. I have my K9 in my car. I'd like to bring him with me if that's okay."

"Why yes, of course. That's okay," he replied. "I like dogs."

I thanked him, walked to my car, put Sammy on his leash and let him out.

"Heel to me, Sammy," I said, not wanting him to walk ahead as he usually does.

"Wow! He's beautiful," Paul said and reached down to scratch Sammy's head, not something you'd want to do with a regular K9 officer. You'd be likely to lose a finger, if not your hand.

Paul laughed. "Wherever did you get him?" he asked. "He's too... friendly to be..."

"Samson's kind of special," I said, not wanting to get into a long-winded explanation.

"Wow, you even have a badge," he said, looking at Sammy.

I smiled and said, "We're kind of short on time, Mr. Burnett, so, if you wouldn't mind...."

"Oh, sure. Sorry. Just come on up. It's upstairs."

And together, the four of us walked the short distance to his house, a twin of the Knowles home. We stepped inside and made our way up two flights of stairs to a wide, open landing on the second floor, with a large window, his desk, several computers, and monitors.

"See? Just like CCTV," he said, grinning, as he brought up the live view showing five different angles of the street below.

"Let's see, this is Monday, so let's take it back to last Friday morning at... let's say—"

"One in the morning," Corbin said.

Burnett glanced round at him and nodded.

"There! How's that?" he asked.

The monitors now showed five different views of the darkened street, all time and date stamped.

"That's good," I said. "Now please fast-forward." And he did, slowing only when a car or person came into view.

Finally, at nine-seventeen that Friday evening, a vehicle appeared. Burnett paused the video. "That's it," he said. "That's his black SUV."

I glanced at Corbin. He shook his head. It was too dark to see the driver.

"Please continue," I said to Burnett.

The car slowed and then made a slow turn to the right, presumably into Knowles' garage. Again, we had a good view of the driver's side window, but it was too dark to see the driver.

"Okay, so we know he was here on Friday night. Let's go through the weekend."

He nodded and fast-forwarded quickly through the rest of the night until ten after six on Saturday morning when the car backed out onto the street and parked at the curb. The driver's side door opened and the driver stepped out and walked back toward the house, presumably into the garage.

"Stop!" I snapped. "Back up a little. Is that him?"

He paused the video. It wasn't that good of an angle. The man had his face turned away from the camera.

"Yes, that's Terrance," Burnett said. "Let's run it through the rest of Saturday, Sunday, and Monday," he said.

"No!" I said. "Back it up a little, there. That's better. Can you magnify the image? I'd like to get a good look at him."

He managed to bring up the blurry figure. It wasn't great, and his face was still turned away from the camera, but it was enough for me to get a rough idea of his build.

Knowles wasn't a tall man, probably around five-nine, but he had a broad, stocky build, well-muscled, and I wondered if he might have been a wrestler or played football when he was in high school. It was an idle thought that meant nothing, but there you are. It's strange, the thoughts that go through your mind, especially in times of stress, which this obviously wasn't. But the thought took me back to the trophy.

"Can you enhance that for me?" I asked.

Burnett looked at me as if I was an idiot.

"Er... No," he said. "I'm not running a forensic lab here. I can make a copy of the footage for you, though."

I sighed and gave him what I considered a withering look, which didn't faze him one bit, so I thanked him and told him to continue. Which he did.

We watched Knowles come out of the garage and drive away down the street.

"You get that plate number?" I asked Corbin.

Now it was my turn to receive a withering look. I grinned at him, then turned back to the video monitors. Burnett was finishing up his search.

"Nope," he said. "He doesn't appear again after Saturday morning. I brought it all up to the moment. See?" he said, pointing to my car on the street below.

"You realize we've just provided Knowles with an alibi?" Corbin said. "If he was here in the house until just after ten on Saturday—"

"He couldn't have been at..." I stopped, not wanting Burnett to know what we were thinking.

"Are there back entrances to the houses?" I asked Burnett. "Could he have gotten out that way?"

"He could," Burnett said. "These houses back onto Mitton Lane. It runs between this street and the next."

"And could he have had access to another vehicle back there?" I asked.

"He could have used the SUV. The garages to these houses are through and through."

I looked at Corbin, sighed and shook my head. Then I turned again to Burnett and said, "D'you have cameras out back?"

"Unfortunately not," he replied.

It was on the tip of my tongue to ask why not, but I thought better of it. He had, after all, provided us with a lot of information we didn't have.

"You've been a big help, Mr. Burnett," I said. "Thank you."

"What, exactly, are you investigating," he asked, frowning, his eyes narrowed, "and how does Terrance fit into it?"

"I'm sorry," I said. "It's an ongoing investigation and I'm not at liberty to divulge that kind of information."

"Well, all right, then," he said. "Just like on TV, huh? Glad I could help."

"Out of curiosity, why *were* you so eager to help. I mean, you approached me with a lot of info from the get-go."

He shrugged. "Well, I fancy myself as a bit of an amateur sleuth," he said. "Data analysis is what I do for a living, but I do research and write true-crime as well."

"Ah," I said.

"To tell you the truth, Terrance has always been a bit of an enigma to me; shady, if you know what I mean. Unlikeable. But I'll admit that I haven't had many dealings with him. I suppose it's my curiosity combined with my imagination, my constant what-ifs."

I smiled and said, "In that case, we might be back to pick your brain." *Geez, this is all I need: an amateur detective.*

"I would like that, very much," he said. "And be sure to bring Samson with you," Burnett said, crouching down and giving him one last ruffle.

"Will do," I said, smiling. "We can show ourselves out," I said, handing him my card. "If you see *anything*..."

"Only too happy to oblige," Burnett said as we retreated down the stairs.

As soon as we closed the door behind us, Corbin asked, "What was that? A mutual admiration society?"

"Just humoring him. You never know when someone like that can be useful. And, if you think that was mutual admiration, just wait until you meet my new landscaping neighbor."

Corbin glanced at me with raised eyebrows. "You forget I know you too well, Kate."

"Meaning?"

"I'll just let you chew on it for a bit," Corbin said.

18

Day 3, 4:30 p.m.

AS WE WALKED BACK PAST THE KNOWLES HOUSE, I stopped for a moment in front of it.

"What're you thinking?" Corbin asked. "This is a big house. Five, six bedrooms. You have to wonder why he doesn't run his operation from here?"

I chuckled. "Maybe he moved it. I'm sure he was on to Mr. Burnett's surveillance."

Corbin nodded, looked up at the facade, and said, "It would be nice to get a hold of something that could be used to test for DNA."

"It would," I agreed. "But we have no probable cause."

"Health and Welfare check?" he asked. "Nobody's seen the guy since Saturday."

I smiled. "Two days?" I said. "That's hardly enough to justify our breaking in, and if he was inside, dead or incapacitated, where's the Tahoe?"

"Maybe somebody else drove it away?"

"Yeah, right?" I said. "You're grasping at straws, Corbin. You made a note of the license number, right?"

He gave me another withering look, then said, "Yeah! Got it right here." He tapped his jacket pocket.

"Call Jack and have him run it—"

"What if..." Corbin started to say, interrupting me. "What if the Daniels kids are hiding out here?"

"Well, that would certainly be probable cause if we truly thought they were here, but..." I turned my head and looked at him.

"But we're grasping at straws. I know."

"Go on," I said. "Call Jack."

He called Jack while I put Samson in the back seat of my cruiser.

Corbin laid his notebook on the hood to have both hands free to write. "Yeah... Mmm-hm... What? Yeah, give me that address." He picked the phone up, disconnected and laid it down again while he finished his note.

He looked up at me and said, "Okay, the Tahoe's not registered to Knowles. It belongs to a Tina Stafford. I have an address."

"Good," I said. "But first, I'm starved."

"Me, too," Corbin agreed. "What do you want? Burgers? Tacos? Subs?"

"You know what? For once, we're not in a hurry. How about we go to the Public House over in Southside? They serve the best trout."

Corbin narrowed his eyes at me. "What? Now that you live in a fancy neighborhood, you want fancy food?"

I rolled my eyes. "Public House trout is not fancy food, nor is my neighborhood fancy—well, not too fancy," I said with a grin. "The food's good, and fish is brain food. I'll even spring for a beer if you like."

He reached out and put the back of his hand to my forehead. "Nope, no fever. Not sick. Let's go then."

Ten minutes later I leashed Samson, straightened his K9 harness and let him out, and we walked to the outdoor dining area, the last table at the end.

"Samson!" Mandy, our server said. "You're back! Be with you in a minute, folks."

"They know you here?" Corbin asked.

"We've been here three or four times," I said.

He looked around. "They allow dogs here?"

"They allow 'service dogs,'" I said.

"That's kind of stretching the definition of service dog."

I shrugged. "It works."

The server returned to take our order.

I ordered the Carolina Trout, and Corbin had fried chicken and fries—hold the kale salad, he told them.

I checked the menu again for a second and turned to the server. "You know the four-ounce, cold, grilled chicken breast that you have for salads?"

Mandy nodded.

"Can I get one?"

"Which salad?" she asked.

"No salad," I answered. "Just the chicken."

She smiled. "Oh. Right. It's for Sammy."

"Why are you eating like a bachelor," I said to Corbin when she left.

"My wife makes fabulous, healthy, wholesome food meals at home. Having an occasional decadent meal when I'm out on the job won't hurt. Besides, I'm regulation weight," he said, drumming on his stomach muscles. "I believe, if I recall, that you ate only fast-food right up until a couple weeks ago."

"Touché," I said. "But it'll catch up with you sooner or later."

He rolled his eyes, then laughed. "Actually, my wife's out of town."

I laughed too. He usually wasn't one to joke around like that about his personal life.

The server brought our non-alcoholic IPAs and left again after promising our order would be just a few more minutes.

"So," I said. "To recap, we have two victims from a deliberately set fire—one of whom we can assume is Stacy Daniels—thus making it a homicide."

"Or manslaughter," Corbin said, "depending on the intent and whether the arsonist knew they were in the house."

"Oh, he knew all right. He smacked the male victim over the head with a five-pound trophy."

Corbin shook his head. "You think it could have been this Terrance Knowles guy?"

"I'm not thinking anything yet," I replied. "We still have little to go on. If the male victim is Peter Daniels— and I think it must be—then the prime suspect has to be the son, Matthew."

Again, Corbin shook his head. "It could have been any one of the three kids, or all of them... if he, Daniels, was abusing them."

"And see," I said, "we still don't know the half of it. We don't yet know what Daniels or Matthew were into. No, there's a lot we still don't know, and until we do, we can't make *any* assumptions."

"And who is this Tina person?" Corbin said.

"We need to find out," I replied. "She could be

involved or, more likely, she's Knowles' girlfriend and she lets him drive her SUV."

"What was the woman's name that Burnett mentioned... Sandy?" Corbin asked.

"Uh-huh."

"Do you suppose Tina and Sandy could be two of Knowles' sex workers?"

"And driving a Chevy Tahoe? I doubt it." But then I had another thought. Suppose it wasn't street prostitution he was running. Suppose it was high-class escorts. That would explain how they were able to keep it on the down-low in a suburban neighborhood. It might even explain why the Daniels girls were able to wear expensive clothes, as Ella Sanchez had mentioned. I shuddered.

I could see Charlotte as an escort, perhaps, but Emily? A twelve-year-old girl? Judas Priest. How twisted was all this? She was obviously not high-class escort material. She was underage... And then it clicked! "Pedophiles," I muttered.

"What?" Corbin asked.

"Nothing," I said. "I was just thinking out loud."

Mandy brought our food; Samson's chicken was brought to us in a doggie bag. It even had a picture of a cute Scottie wearing a bib on it.

I thanked her and turned again to Corbin.

"I think we're looking either at a high-end escort service or some kind of pedophile ring," I said, "and I think it's being run out of Green Lane."

Sammy growled. I looked at him. "What?" He pawed my leg, and I realized he was growling because I hadn't given him his chicken. I quickly put that right, and he lay down and scarfed it down in three bites.

"Wait," Corbin said. "Are you psychic or something?"

I looked at him. "What are you talking about, Corbin?"

"You said Green Lane?" he replied. "Are you connecting Green Lane with Knowles?"

"It's a bit of a leap, I know. But you weren't in on the Ella Sanchez interview."

"I wasn't invited," he said.

"Don't take it to heart," I said.

I took a moment to think, then said, "As much as I hate the idea, I think I need to talk to Henry Finkle. Pick his brain." Captain Henry "Tiny" Finkle, my one-time nemesis, was head of the vice squad.

"Or you could pick Harry Starke's brain," Corbin said, smiling.

It wasn't a bad idea. I could talk to them both, but since Finkle was supposed to be the one who had his finger on the pulse of the seamy side of the city, I'd talk to him first. Then I'd get a more balanced picture of what might be going on from Harry.

"Finkle? Are you serious?" Corbin asked. "After what he put you through?"

I frowned, narrowed my eyes and turned to look at him. "How d'you know about what I went through?" I asked.

"Come on, Kate. You don't think the whole department doesn't know, do you, especially as he was busted for it."

I gave him the "look" and let it go.

"I'm hoping he can provide me with some information about what's going on at Green Lane."

"But?" Corbin asked.

I shrugged. "I think he'll probably try to blow me off."

"Then why bother?"

I gave him a cagey smile, and Corbin looked askance.

"Good Lord," he said. "Why would you put yourself through that?"

"Because now we're of equal rank, so if he gives me any shit, I can handle it in ways I couldn't before."

Corbin smirked and shook his head.

The server returned to the table. "Anything else I can get for you? Dessert?"

"No dessert for me, thanks," I said. I didn't dare look at what they were offering.

She looked at Corbin, and he shook his head and thanked her.

"Let's go back to the office," I said. "We'll have Jack run a background check on Tina Stafford before we go see her. I'll collect any new intel that's come in—if any— then we'll call it a day. I need to go home and freshen up. Then tonight, you and I will take a trip down Green Lane to see what we can see."

"Sounds like a plan to me," Corbin said.

19

Day 3, 5:25 p.m.

"GATHER THE TROOPS. MY OFFICE. FIVE MINUTES," I said to Corbin as we rode the elevator up to the situation room.

I went straight to my office, where I found an envelope lying on my desk. It contained a thumb drive and a note.

"I thought I should bring this to you in case you need it for evidence. Sorry I missed you. Hope we can catch up sometime." It was signed Paul Burnett.

And then Jack stepped into my office and laid a piece of paper before me. I read it and mouthed "thank you" to him and told him to sit down.

While I waited for the rest of my team to arrive, I popped Burnett's drive into my laptop and brought up the file. It contained the footage of the black Tahoe and Knowles entering and leaving his garage.

I ejected the drive and handed it to Jack. "I need you

to enhance the images on this video file. In particular, those of the guy, Terrance Knowles."

"I'll see what I can do, Cap," he said.

"Oh, and do a background check on Tina Stafford. Here's the address."

By then, we were all present, so I said, "I'm not going to keep you long. I have just a couple of things to go over and get your feedback on where you've been this afternoon."

I waved the sheet of paper Jack had given me. "Jack just handed me this. Apparently, there are eleven devices in use at the Daniels residence. One of them was online at three-thirty-eight Saturday morning; after that, nothing. Unfortunately, none of the devices were found in the house."

"If they're all mobile devices—" Cooper began.

"Uh-uh," I said, interrupting him. "At least one of them was a computer. A desktop. The monitor was there but not the CPU."

"Geez. Who takes a desktop with them?" Corbin wanted to know.

"Nobody," Anne Robar said. "Mobile devices can sync with the CPU, so any info on the CPU is also likely on at least one other device. All three kids would have laptops and probably tablets as well."

"Unless someone took it, stole it," Cooper said.

"That would mean someone else was there before or when the fire started," I said.

"Or," Corbin said, "someone's trying to cover their tracks."

"Okay," I said. "That's it for the conjecture. Hawk, Anne. How did your visit to Peter Daniels' place of work go? Robert's Auto Circus, right?"

Hawk looked at Anne. She nodded and said, "We were directed to the owner, John Roberts. Now there's a weird one. He acts like the friendliest and most helpful guy you could ever want to meet, but there's something about him that's just too over-the-top to be real."

"Daniels is the dealership's accountant," Hawk said, "and apparently, he and Roberts are good buds. Roberts painted a rosy picture of the Daniels family, especially of Peter and how he loved his kids so much, and it was truly a shame he died in the fire."

"Now, we didn't tell him we hadn't identified the victims yet, but he seemed sure that his accountant was one of them," Anne added. "I had the impression the guy is a walking cliché—the quintessential used car sales-man. We asked him if Daniels had ever talked to him about trouble at home. His only comment was that Daniels had told him that Matthew could be a rabble-rouser when he wanted to be."

"Huh," I said, "that's a strange choice of words, 'rab-ble-rouser.' You sure he didn't say troublemaker?"

Hawk nodded. "No. He used that very word."

"Really?" I said, thinking out loud.

"There's a difference?" Cooper asked.

"Yes, there's a difference," I said. "A troublemaker is someone who goes around making and getting into trou-ble, while a rabble-rouser is someone who's always trying to stir things up. Why would Daniels use that word, I wonder?"

"Maybe he was covering his own ass," Hawk said. "After all, the man's a pedophile with daughters."

"The way both Parker Morris and Ella Sanchez tell it," I said, "Matthew is extremely protective of his sisters. That could cause some emotional and physical wrangling at home."

"Protective?" Tracy said. "Then what's he doing hanging out in a brothel?"

"Yeah," Cooper said. "And where's the mom in all this, anyway?"

I had to shrug at that one. "I don't know. We've talked to her sister and gotten some good background information, but nothing about the Daniels family dynamics."

"Then maybe that should be our next avenue of inquiry. Find out more about Momma Daniels," Corbin said.

"I'm not sure that will be easy," I said. "If she's dead, she can't talk, and apparently, she has no friends or relatives to speak for her other than her sister, who doesn't seem to really know her. We've got to find those kids and talk to them."

"I just hope we don't find out that Matthew is the second victim," Corbin said.

"In bed with his mother?" Anne said. "I should hope not.

"Do we know for sure that it *is* Mom?"

"No. We can only guess," I said. "And mine would be the two bodies are those of Peter and Stacy Daniels, and that the three kids are in the wind."

"Any word on the DNA results yet?" Tracy asked.

"Nope," I said. "It's only been three days. I'd say it'll be at least another week."

"All right, then," I said, wrapping up the meeting. "We've gone as far as we can until the lab catches up with us. So, it's back to old-fashioned police work.

Corbin and I will be out on Green Lane tonight, and we'll see what we can shake loose. That being so, I'm going home for a couple hours. So's Corbin. Y'all know what to do."

20

Day 3, 7:15 p.m.

WHEN I GOT HOME LATE THAT EVENING, I LET
Samson out into the backyard, filled his bowl with Fresh
Pet, and then microwaved a chicken fried rice dinner
from the freezer and sat on the couch with a glass of
seltzer water and lime. I could have used a glass of red,
but I was going out again and didn't want to have
alcohol on my breath during a stakeout.

I'd barely scooped my first forkful when there was a
knock on my front door. I rose and went to answer it,
taking my dinner with me. Even though Samson was
outside, I'd developed the habit of always carrying my
food with me because otherwise it would not be there
when I got back.

Looking through the peephole, I saw it was Brad. I
opened it and stood on the threshold. *Oh crap!*

"Hey, Brad," I said after I opened the door. "What's
up? Oh, and by the way, thanks for bringing my garbage

bin up to the gate. It's still a new routine for me, so it's easy to forget."

"Hey, yourself. It's no problem." He glanced at my plastic bowl and grinned. "So you're single, then?"

"Just in a hurry. I'm going back to work tonight."

"Oh, sorry," he said. "Don't let me hold you up. I was just checking on your varmint problem."

"I'm pretty sure I heard critters with tiny teeth chomping on my grass last night." And then I told him about Samson catching a vole and ceremoniously laying it at my feet.

He laughed. "I told you he was going to be your first line of defense."

"Yup, looks like it," I said. My phone rang.

"Thanks again, Brad. I have to take this call."

"Sure enough," he said. "Talk at ya later."

I waved goodbye and closed the door, walking quickly across the room to grab my phone. It was Corbin.

"Are you ready?" he asked. "How 'bout I pick you up at the station at seven-thirty?"

"Seven-thirty?" I said. "It's August. It won't be dark until after nine."

"Okay. Eight-thirty, then."

"That works," I said. "See you then." And I disconnected.

I set the phone down on the kitchen table, alongside my half-empty bowl, thinking about Brad. He was beginning to get on my nerves, commenting about my eating habits and his line, "I *told* you he would be your first line of defense." *Does he think a homicide captain is somehow clueless about life outside her job?*

I hope I won't be forced to read the riot act to his snarky, sexist, landscaping ass. Who the hell does he think he is?

Wow. Where did THAT come from? I wondered. *Doc Chandry was right: I need to do some serious self-care.*

I forced myself to sit down and finish eating.

I'd gone to my doctor a while back because no matter the food or what time I ate, I always woke up with heartburn in the middle of the night. I knew she would lecture me, and she did not disappoint.

In addition, she gave me a prescription for Omeprazole and handed me a brochure with a lot of stuff in it about self-care, especially when I felt anxious or stressed. "If you don't take this seriously, Catherine, you'll end up with reflux damage to your esophagus." And then she went on to describe said damage in great detail, and I decided I should probably give it a try.

When I read the brochure, though, I'd rolled my eyes and scoffed, knowing I'd never have time to do even half of it: yoga, meditation, mindfulness classes. The only thing I *was* doing was getting plenty of exercise and taking the O pill every day.

I finished my meal and went out to sit on the back deck with Sammy for a while. He raced around the fence and then came and sat down beside me. I felt relaxed, focused. Stakeouts weren't that bad. With minimal physical effort, I could potentially open a couple of new doors.

Thirty minutes later, I was back inside and dressed in black jeans, boots, and a T-shirt. I told Sammy to be good, slipped into my shoulder holster, grabbed my black leather jacket and headed out the door.

GREEN LANE WAS in an older district of Chattanooga. The entire street was comprised mostly of beautifully restored turn-of-the-century homes.

The lawns were just as tidy and pristine as the houses. Not at all the kind of neighborhood where one would expect to find a house of ill repute.

"North end. Fourth house on the right," I said.

"That one," Corbin said. "That's it, if Morris was telling the truth. Doesn't look much like a brothel to me."

"Do they ever?" I asked sarcastically.

Like those on the rest of the street, it was an older, two-story house, by no means shabby, but it was easy to see it hadn't been updated as recently as the others.

I set a reminder in my phone to have Jack check out the property's history and to find out who the present owner was.

"Are we sure this is the right place?" Corbin asked.

"That's what he said," I replied. "Drive on a bit."

"I'm going to drive around the block," he said, leaning forward to stare out through the windshield.

As we drove slowly past the house, I could see a garage in the back.

"Drive on, Corbin," I said. "You're going too slow. You'll attract attention."

"Okay, okay," he said and sped up a little and circled the block. I had him stop along the way so I could get in the back seat, and then he drove on. Eventually, we parked half a block from the house on the left side of the road, and we watched.

For almost an hour nothing happened. Then a car pulled up at the end of the driveway to the left side of the house. A figure walked quickly along the driveway to the car, opened the door and got inside, and the car drove away. Some fifteen minutes later, it happened again.

Corbin turned to look at me and said, "What's that about?"

"Discreet is what it's about," I replied. "These girls are not streetwalkers. Look, there we go again." And, sure enough, another car had pulled up at the end of the driveway and a young woman ran to it and got inside.

"You want to give it a try?" I asked.

"Sure. Why not?" he replied.

He pulled up to the house and stopped at the end of the driveway. By then, I'd slid as far down in the back seat as I could, but not so low I couldn't see the garage.

The garage side door opened and a young woman stepped out. She was wearing a tight, butter-colored V-cut sweater with a black mini-skirt, boots, and patterned hose.

She walked quickly to the car, jerked the door open and slid inside.

"You lookin' for something, mister?" she asked.

Corbin looked at her, then said, "Maybe. How much for a hummer?"

She rolled her eyes. "Dunno, you'd have to ask your Humvee dealer," she said. "But if you're looking for a blow, it's a hundred bucks."

I smiled to myself.

"A hundred?" Corbin said. "Are you kidding?"

"Okay, okay," the girl said. "Drive on, for God's sake. We don't sit out here and negotiate. This is your first time, right?"

Corbin pulled away from the curb.

"There's a park a few blocks down that way," she said. "You can park there."

He drove on, and then she said, "Drive around the block so the car is pointing east, and the driver's side is up against the curb. I'll walk back after we're done."

He parked, and she turned sideways in her seat to look at him and said, "So you look like a guy on a pretty tight budget. Seventy-five, then."

Again, I had to smile.

"Fifty?" Corbin countered.

"Fifty?" she echoed incredulously. "Are you out of your mind? Maybe you should go home and ask your *sister* if she'll do it for fifty!"

I could see her face in the rearview mirror. She rolled her eyes again as if lamenting her under-appreciated lot in life. She looked truly offended. She was a pretty girl with bleached blonde hair with black roots.

"Seventy-five," she said, "or I get out. What's it to be?"

Corbin nodded.

"Payment is up front," she said, "and this is a one-off. You come back again, you pay what we ask. And never flash your lights; we don't want to alert the neighborhood. Just pull up and wait. We have a sensor, so we'll know you're there."

"Got it," he said.

"Good. When we're done, I'll give you my card, so you can make an appointment next time."

She was poised and professional. She operated like she was taking our food order at a drive-through. She was not my idea of a call girl.

"I'm Sandy, by the way," she said. "You can pay me now."

That was my cue. I sat up into her field of vision. "Nice to meet you, Sandy."

She shrieked and whirled toward me. "What the hell is this?" she cried, looking daggers at Corbin. "What kind of kinky... You know, kinky is extra."

When she turned back to me, I was holding up my badge.

"Oh shit!" she said and scrambled to open her door, to no avail. Corbin had the safety switch on and the door wouldn't unlock.

"Take it easy, Sandy," Corbin said. "We're not here for you. We just want to talk."

"I should have known you were too good to be true. You're just a little bit too clean and good-looking for the average John."

"Why thank you," he said with a grin. "Or do you say that to all the boys?"

"Sandy," I said. "We're not here to arrest you. Not if you're willing to answer some questions."

She heaved a deep sigh, laid her head back against the headrest and closed her eyes. Then she opened them again, twisted around in her seat so she could look at me and said, "You promise?"

"If you cooperate," I replied, "yes, I promise."

"Okay. Go ahead. Ask your questions."

I nodded and said, "Tell me about Terrance Knowles."

"How do you know Terry? Is he in jail?"

"I don't know him," I said. "I know of him, and I know you were once his girlfriend." That was a bit of a stretch. I didn't know if she was his girlfriend or not, but I figured it was worth a try. "Oh, and that he has a black Chevy Tahoe," I added.

"It's not his," she said. "It's Tiana's."

"Who's Tiana?"

"His new bi—, his new girlfriend," she snapped.

"How long ago did you and Terrance split up?" I queried.

"About four months ago, I guess," she said, shrugging.

"Do you still see him?" I asked.

"Do I still see him?" she repeated. "Only every damn day."

Inwardly, I smiled. "Why's that?" I asked.

And… she clammed up. Her lips might not have been moving, but her body language was telling me there was something about her relationship with the guy that went beyond emotional attachment. Was it business? We let her sit in silence for a minute, then she said, "Can I go now?"

"No," I said. "I haven't finished with the questions yet."

"What if I don't have any more answers?"

"Oh, you have answers," I said.

"I know you can't hold me, not without charging me."

"Wrong again," I said. "I can hold you for up to forty-eight hours, and then I can charge you with solicitation. You want to go that route, we can."

Corbin gave me a "back off" look. "Sandy," he said softly. "We need you to talk to us. We can either talk here and be comfortable and quick, or we go downtown and put you in a holding cell for the night."

"Been there, done that, not going back," she said.

"Good, then we're in agreement. Now, let's talk," I prompted.

She turned and stared out the window, then looked back, her eyes darting between mine and Corbin's as if assessing whether, or how much, we believed her.

"I see him every day because this is his operation," she answered.

"His operation?" I repeated. "He's your pimp?"

"No. He just comes to take his share of our money. He's afraid if he doesn't pick it up every day, we'll steal some of it."

"So, who is your..."

"My pimp? Well, it should be Matthew."

My ears pricked up at that. "Matthew Daniels?" I asked. "And you said 'should be.' What did you mean by that?"

"Yeah, him. That's his job. He helps us keep things organized, and he does the books, but he's more like our angel." She smiled with genuine affection.

"How's that?" Corbin asked her.

"Matt is way too kind to be a pimp. He just keeps watch over us and protects us. Terry has a temper, and Matthew keeps him from hurting us."

"And Matt's sisters; are they involved in this operation too?" I asked.

She turned toward me with a look of fear. "You want to know about Matt's sisters," she said, more as a statement than a question.

"They're always here with us from right after school until he goes home, and that can be late, really late. But they're not being pimped out or anything. Matthew would die before he'd let that happen."

"Why does he keep them with him, then?" Corbin asked.

She shrugged. "I can't say for sure, but one of the

other girls mentioned a while back that she thinks it's not safe for them at home."

"Not safe in what way?" I asked.

"I'm not sure. I can only guess, and I'd rather not." As if to signal her discomfort, she glanced back over her shoulder. Both shoulders, actually, as if she had a feeling that someone might be watching her.

"All right, Sandy," I said. "I get it." I didn't, but I knew I would sooner or later, so I moved on. "Tell us about Tina."

"Tina? We call her Tiana. That's her working name. She's one of Terry's escorts. Her real name is Tina Stafford."

"There's an escort service, too?" Corbin said.

She nodded. "That's why he only has time to collect our money. Once he started managing the escorts, he had less time for us. The escort service is where he makes his real money."

"Is the escort service run from here, too, from the Green Lane address?" I asked.

"No," she replied. "They were when it started out, but it got too busy too fast, and the powers-that-be were afraid there would be too much activity to keep a low profile in the neighborhood. So, they were moved."

"To Terry's house?" Corbin asked.

"For a little while, but apparently this creepy guy down the street was watching them with cameras, so he had to move them again."

I suppressed a smile. *So they know about Paul Burnett, crime writer; that's just too funny.* And then I realized he must have known what was going on at Knowles' house, but he hadn't mentioned it. Why not?

"So where are they working out of now?" Corbin asked.

"I don't know," she replied. "They're keeping that pretty much on the down-low. That's all I know, honest. Can I go now?"

Corbin looked at me, his eyebrows raised in question,

I nodded, and he said, "I'll gladly take you back to the house and drop you off."

She shook her head. "I'll be fine," she said, reaching for the door handle.

"Hold on," Corbin said as he reached inside his jacket and took out his wallet. "Here, take this," he said, handing her seventy-five dollars. "We wouldn't want Terry thinking you're skimming, now would we?"

She smiled at him. He released the safety, and she opened the door and was about to step out when she turned and said, "There is one strange thing. We haven't seen Terry since Friday. I mean, he takes off once in a great while, and Matthew stays over with us, but that's the weird part. We haven't seen either him, Matthew, or the girls."

"Wait!" I said as she hopped out of the car. "When, exactly, was the last time you saw them, any of them?"

"I saw Terry late Friday afternoon, and Matthew and the girls Saturday evening."

"Thanks, Sandy," I said, handing her my card. "What's your full name, by the way?"

"Seriously?" she asked.

"Yes, seriously," I replied.

She thought for a moment, then said, "It's Sandra, Sandra Tatum."

"Thank you, Sandra." I smiled at her. "If you think of anything..."

"Yeah, yeah. I know," she said, glancing at the card. "Call you. I know the drill."

"I'd appreciate it," I said.

And she quickly disappeared into the night.

21

Day 3, 10:35 p.m.

CORBIN AND I SAT IN SILENCE FOR A MOMENT, digesting the information Sandy had provided. Her words hung in the air like the scent of her perfume. Finally, Corbin sighed, cleared his throat and, staring out into the park, said, "Well, that was enlightening."

"Was it?" I said skeptically. "Maybe... if we were Vice, but I'm not sure how much it helped our case. She talked, and now we have even more questions than answers."

"C'mon, Kate," he countered. "We now know that Terrance, Matthew, Charlotte, and Emily are all in the wind."

"Together, d'you think?" I asked.

"Most likely. I mean, it's doubtful they scattered in different directions, wouldn't you say?"

I shrugged and let him continue.

"It could just be the three siblings on their own," he said thoughtfully. "Or maybe he picked them up and took them someplace he thought might be safe for them."

"You're reaching, Corbin," I said. "Or, maybe he kidnapped them, killed their parents, stole the computers, and set the place on fire."

"Why would he do that?" he asked.

"Why would Matthew?" I countered.

"None of it makes sense," Corbin said. "Unless there's more to Pete and Stacey than we know."

"True," I said. "But here's the question we need to ask ourselves: what's the Daniels—Pete and Stacey, I'm talking about—what's their relationship to Terrance Knowles?"

"Maybe he's just playing chauffeur."

"Bullshit!" I snapped. "The guy's a pimp."

"There's that," he agreed.

"Oh, this is all so hollow," I said. "Shit. We might even be barking up the wrong tree. What if it's just a crime of opportunity, an intruder looking to steal some drug money. It happens all the time. You know that. Hell, it might even be a dissatisfied customer from the dealership or some random arsonist." I was joking, of course, but I knew from past experience that the simplest explanation is often the right one.

"But knowing about the sex biz and that Matthew and Knowles are both part of it..." Corbin ran out of things to say.

I shook my head. "I don't know. In truth, we have nothing, just a whole lot of wild suppositions. We don't know if they're all together. Sandy said Knowles is religious about collecting his money on a daily basis and hasn't done so for the last two days, so you have to ask yourself if he's even alive. As for Matthew being their guardian angel, that's really odd, and I doubt it's a coincidence that no one has seen any of them since just before the fire."

"Absolutely, Kate," Corbin said. "What I want to know is, when do you think we're going to hear from Doc? We have to know who the victims are. That's pivotal to solving this thing."

"Think sometime early next week," I said, fumbling with a pack of chewing gum. I offered Corbin a stick, which he declined. "Until the lab offers up some clues, we'll just have to rely on good, old-fashioned policework: knocking on doors and asking questions.

"We should talk with Tina Stafford tomorrow. Maybe she knows where her Tahoe is. I also want to reinterview Darren Hall about the nasty implications he made about Pete Daniels; this out-of-town shit's not getting it. I think he's avoiding us.

"And, after what Sandy said about the creepy guy down the street from Terrance, I think we need to bring Paul Burnett in. I think he knows more than he's telling."

"You said you were going to check in with Vice," Corbin said.

"It would certainly be nice to pick Finkle's brain about the Green Lane operation," I said.

"Ooh," he said, "that one's on you."

"Yeah, right," I said, "and thank you for the kind words. Let's go home."

22

Day 4, Tuesday, August 20 7:30 a.m.

I ROSE EARLY THAT FOLLOWING MORNING, BEFORE five, took Samson for a long—well, longish—walk and was in my office by seven-thirty.

I sat down at my desk, and Sammy went to his bed under my window, where he laid his head down and stared at me.

Me? I figured it was going to be a busy day so I began to organize myself, my notes and the growing stack of information; not that it meant much, not at that point, anyway. And I knew Corbin had more, and so I hoped did Jack, and it would all have to go up on the boards when they arrived.

I hadn't been at it long when, much to my annoyance, my phone rang. It was Mike Willis.

"Are you ready for an evidence walk-through? I've got it all set up in the conference room," he said.

"Sure, I'll be right there."

The door opened, and I looked up, waved Corbin in,

hung up the phone and took a few minutes to chat with him. Then together we went to see what Mike had put together for us.

He met us at the conference room door, giving us a look of "this is too good to be true."

"We made some good finds yesterday, especially the one at the end of the table," he said. "Come on. I'll show you."

We followed him to the far end of the conference table. "This is the trophy we found," he said. "If you recall, the headboard was against the east wall of the room. We found this underneath the bed. How it got there, I have no idea, but there's blood spatter around the rim of the cup; nothing on the base, though. I've taken a sample and sent it away to the DNA lab."

"Blood? And it survived the fire?" I asked, turning it over in my mind.

"Yes," Mike said. "The bed protected it, so I was able to get a viable sample."

"It couldn't have been the weapon," Corbin said. "The shape of the wound suggests it would have been made by the base, but you say there's no blood present, so the blood must be spatter caused when—"

"It could have been made by any number of things," I said. "And here we are waiting for DNA again."

"Aren't we always?" Corbin said.

"You said you found it in an upstairs bedroom?" I asked.

"The last one on the right," he replied.

Charlotte's room, I thought. *But the victim was found in the ground floor bedroom.* I pursed my lips, blew air out through them, then shook my head and said, "Hmm... so we've got what looks like blood spatter in an upstairs bedroom, and the victim in or on the bed in the master bedroom on the ground floor. That makes no sense. It has to be a coincidence—old blood. I don't usually believe in coincidence, but in this case... it has to be."

I paused, stared at the trophy, then said, "Thanks, Mike. I wonder who it belongs to." I bent down to look at it closer. "The plaque's broken. Nothing on it but the year; 2018."

"Well, that narrows it down a bit," Corbin said. "How about prints?"

"Nope. Sorry."

"Thanks again," I said sarcastically. "Wiped?"

"Probably," he replied. "They do clean these things, you know?"

I looked through the various items he had tagged as potential evidence, and I took photos of some of the items with my phone. I knew Mike would provide me with an itemized list I could compare with my photos.

"How long will you keep the display here?" I asked.

"At least until Friday," he said, "and beyond if need be."

"Thanks, Mike," I said. "Please let me have the list as soon as you can. Come on, Corbin. My office."

By then it was almost eight-thirty. Everyone was at their desks and busy organizing their own tasks, I assumed, so I buzzed Hawk and asked him to notify everyone that we'd meet in my office in ten minutes.

Once everyone was seated, I had Corbin give them a quick rundown of last night's stakeout, but I was more interested in what they'd been working on. After all, prostitution was Vice's domain. My only interest in it was how it might affect my investigation and how it might help us track down the Daniels family.

Corbin explained that we'd confirmed prostitution activities at Green Lane and the specifics of how it worked: how the women are approached and dispatched, and that we'd made contact with one of the sex workers and how cooperative she'd been.

"But more about that in a minute," he said. "Captain?"

I nodded and said, "Corbin, I want you to work on the boards and bring them up to date." All we had at that point were some questions and a few photographs I'd put up on Saturday. "I want every scrap of info we have up on the boards."

"That's not going to take long," Corbin said, smiling ruefully.

"True," I said. "What we do have is a lot of unanswered questions and some bits and pieces. We just don't know how the pieces fit together. Also, if any of you have what you believe to be pertinent questions, put them up. Jack, take my phone and print the photo of the trophy. That needs to be up there, too. And, Jack, I want you to pull the records of... I want photos of the victims and everyone connected to them, however loosely. Got it?"

"Got it, boss," Jack replied.

"Got it, Corbin?" I asked, frowning at him.

"Yes, ma'am," Corbin replied. "I'm on it."

"Good," I said. "And, of course, we'll expand from the Daniels family nucleus and add persons of interest and other peripheral parties as they introduce themselves."

"What photos do we already have?" Corbin wanted to know.

I opened the file and said, "Here's one of Stacey Daniels. I got it from her sister—not sure how old it is."

Jack spoke up. "I have yearbook photos of each of the kids. Of course, Matthew's was taken three years ago, but the girls' photos are recent."

"I'm sure he won't have changed much in three years," I said.

"I remember seeing several photos of Pete Daniels at the dealership," Hawk said. "One of them was for employee of the month. I have more questions for John Roberts and we'd planned to go by there today, so I'll grab one."

"Sounds good," I said. "Jack, print out driver's license shots from the DMV database. Those always turn out swell, right?" That elicited a few chuckles and groans from the team. I saw Jack handing over the pictures to Corbin. "A mug shot of Daniels wouldn't hurt, either."

"Do we have anything of Terrance Knowles?" Anne asked.

"No," Jack said. "His juvenile offenses are still sealed. Other than that, he has a clean record. He was arrested a couple of times for soliciting prostitution but somehow avoided processing. So, no photo nor prints."

"What?" I said, stunned. "How can that be?"

"The charges were dropped without a hearing," Jack said. "He obviously has friends in high places. Family connections, I'd say. His father is a diplomat serving in Serbia."

"That might explain why he's never been processed," I said thoughtfully. "One phone call to Dad and..."

"And phones light up from Czechia to Chattanooga," Hawk said dryly.

"Yes, but still..." I said. "I wonder if Vice has

anything to do with it? It sounds like something Finkle would pull."

"It also explains why he's got that big empty house all to himself," Corbin said. "The old man keeps the roof over his head while Junior maintains a life of leisure."

"And Daddy's connections might have benefited the escort service as well as the house on Green Lane," Ramirez conjectured. "Somebody's been turning a blind eye while this enterprise has prospered and grown."

"I still think Henry Finkle might have a finger in the pie," I said. "Okay, Corbin. Put out an APB for Knowles and the Chevy Tahoe. I want them found, soon."

He nodded and made a note of it.

"Have we checked phone records on any of the Daniels yet?" I asked.

"Contacted," Jack said. "They should be coming soon unless they're going to ask for a subpoena."

"Good," I said. "Let's see if we can't get phone records for Terrance Knowles as well."

"That would be a forlorn hope," Hawk said. "I guarantee he's using burners."

"Probably, but give it a try anyway," I said, then turned my attention to Cooper and Ramirez. "Tracy, Coop, I want you two to focus on Stacey Daniels. Track down anything you can find on her."

"Anything specific in mind, Cap?" Tracy asked.

"I don't know. Use your imagination," I said with a grin. "Employment history. Education. Prior marriages, domestic disturbance, anything. Talk to her friends. Did she have a life before she married Peter? Was she cheating on him? Hobbies, social media, affiliations, the works. Come on, you two; you know this stuff. It's basic. Detection 101. Who knows? Maybe she's our way into this maze. We barely know anything about her, and we need to know more."

I turned again to Jack and said, "Backgrounds on Peter, Stacey, Matthew, and Charlotte Daniels and on Terrance Knowles, Sandy, and Tina Stafford, especially financials, right?"

He nodded.

"I also want you to check on the property records for the Green Lane house."

Finally, I gave Corbin the nod, and he took the floor, summarizing once again the highlights of last night's stakeout, particularly our tête-a-tête with Sandy.

"That's a lot to spill," Tracy said. "Why was she so loose-lipped?"

It was a good question, the kind we all ask whenever someone appears to be overly helpful. What's in it for them? Is it a rehearsed response designed to get them out of a jam?

"I have a feeling that she's worried about Matthew," I said, "especially the Daniels kids."

"Enough to reveal so much about the operation?" Cooper asked.

"I got the impression that she was, perhaps, in charge of the working girls since they've essentially been abandoned," Corbin said.

"If so," Anne said, "You'd think she'd be even more tight-lipped. Me? I'd take it all with a grain of salt. What did you say her name was?"

"I didn't, but she told us it's Sandra Tatum," I replied.

"Maybe she's just holding down the fort," Corbin said. "I think she was concerned with being arrested, though, and the house being raided. In other words, she talked to us because she knew she had to."

Hawk spoke up. "That's the strangest prostitution operation I've ever heard of. Curb service, for Pete's sake! And helpful hookers. Oh yeah, somebody's on the take. And somebody pretty high up, if you ask me."

"And I'm willing to bet Vice is all over it," Hawk said sarcastically.

"It's different," I said, "but you have to give them some credit for their business model, I suppose. They're not walking the streets, attracting trouble and upsetting the neighbors. It's quiet, it's confined, and they must be doing something right because this is the first we've heard of them, right? Okay. Time's a-wasting. You've got your tasks. Let's make some progress."

After the meeting had dispersed and the door had closed behind them, I stretched out my legs, pushed back in my chair, linked my fingers together at the back of my neck and stared up at the ceiling.

I thought about the trophy. Mike Willis had said that the blood was on the cup itself, not the base. *Has to be blood spatter, and probably old, too,* I thought.

I picked up the phone and called Doc. "Doc? Do you have a minute to show me the male burn victim again?"

"Of course," he said. "But I don't have any more information for you."

"I know, but I wanted to run something by you."

"Come on over," Doc said.

"See you in five," I said.

"Not if I see you first." He chuckled and disconnected.

"Geez! The oldest joke in the world." I sighed.

I walked the three blocks to Doc's Forensic Center

and arrived to find him pulling the victim out of the cooler.

He pulled back the sheet, and the smell of burned flesh hit me like a hammer blow.

"Ew!" I said. "I thought that the cold was supposed to suppress the smell."

"It does a little," Doc said. "Dead flesh is one thing, but burned flesh is something else altogether."

"I want to look at the gash again if I can."

I told Doc about the trophy, and he nodded his head side-to-side, considering it.

"I don't think this is from being struck by the base of a trophy, or a lamp, or anything remotely similar," he said. "Look how long the gash is. A trophy with a base that size would have required someone the size of a linebacker to swing it."

"Matthew's a construction worker," I said.

"Still not the weapon of choice," Doc replied. "Of desperation, maybe. But if you say there's no blood on the base..."

I nodded, shook my head and stared down at the body. "You're probably right—"

"Probably?" he said, sounding thoroughly outraged. "Not probably, Catherine. Definitely."

"All right, Doc," I said dryly. "Have it your way."

I paused for a moment, still staring at the body, then said, "We know nothing yet about Peter Daniels' body size, and the only thing we know, and not even for sure, is that the son, Matthew, is six feet tall. So this could be either one."

Doc tipped his head to the side in acknowledgment. "True. But there's little we can do until we get the DNA results. One thing is certain, though." He smiled at me and then continued, "It can't be both of them. Maybe you'll get lucky and find one of them."

"Maybe," I said. "We've learned a lot, but we still don't know where Matthew or the girls are."

He looked at me, sighed and said, "I know, Kate. It seems the more you uncover, the harder your job becomes."

"You got that right," I said. "Too many damn variables."

"Well, I can state quite categorically that this wound was not made by the rim of a trophy. The base? No! Not possible, in my opinion. My guess is that it's the result of a fall against a table or some similar piece of furniture."

"Could be, I suppose," I replied. "Tables, desks, you name it. There are plenty there. Most of them ashes, but still... Oh well, that's CSI's job. If there's anything to it, Mike will find it. I'll let him know what we're looking for."

I held up my phone for Doc to see, pointing at it as I walked toward the door.

"Thanks, Doc," I said. "See ya!"

I dialed Mike Willis's number.

"Hi, Kate," he answered.

"Mike, d'you have that evidence list for me yet?" I asked him.

"Ask and ye shall receive," he said. "Carol just handed it to me."

"Good. Just one bit of direction," I said. "The gash on the male victim's head. Doc thinks it could have been made by a fall; that he hit his head on the edge of a table, or something similar. Any thoughts?"

"You may be in luck. Marsha found dried blood on the corner of what once was a desk in one of the upstairs bedrooms. We cut the corner off, took a sample of the blood and sent it to the lab for DNA analysis. Piece of wood, we bagged and tagged."

"That's the best news I've heard all day," I said, feeling somewhat relieved. "In one of the bedrooms, you say?"

"Correct," he replied.

"Which one?" I asked

"The last one on the right."

"Great work, Mike. Thanks," I said. "Give Marsha a pat on the back for me."

I returned to the refrigeration room in time to see Doc slide the body back into the cooler.

"Willis says they've found something that might just be what we're looking for. Again, we have to wait for DNA results. I'll give you a buzz when I know something."

"Excellent! I look forward to it."

23

Day 4 10:00 a.m.

TIANA

BY TEN-THIRTY I was back in my office. Corbin stuck his head in the door and said, "Everything okay, boss?"

"More evidence piling up," I said. "I just got back from seeing Doc. We pretty much discounted the trophy theory in favor of the corner of a piece of furniture of some sort. And Mike confirmed they had indeed found blood on the desk in the bedroom. So, it proceeds, though be it at an extremely slow pace. I guess the blood on the desk throws a whole different light on things. If it was an accident... well... Any thoughts?"

"Well, yes," he said, taking a seat at the table. "It makes more sense than the trophy. What else did Doc have to say?"

I sighed. "He's still prodding the lab to get the DNA analysis done, and we just keep adding to the pile."

"We do know the male victim was already dead before the fire started, and that the female was... I dunno; close to it?"

My desk phone buzzed. I picked up. "Gazzara."

"There's a young woman," the operator said, "a Tina Stafford, asking to speak with you."

"By phone?" I asked.

"No, ma'am. She's in the lobby."

"Even better," I said. "Please have someone bring her up to my office."

"Tina Stafford," I said to Corbin.

"Boss, I'm sorry," Corbin said. "I should have mentioned it earlier, but I've got a dental appointment in about twenty minutes."

"Go, go!" I said. "I'll have Ramirez sit in and bring you up to date later."

I WOULD NEVER HAVE GUESSED that Tina Stafford was an escort; she looked more like a sophisticated, high-class model. Her chestnut hair was pulled back into a chignon, and she wore loose, linen, light gray pants with a white blouse and bohemian pearl sandals. She removed her gold-trimmed dark-lens sunglasses as she entered my office. I stood and shook her hand as we introduced ourselves.

"My real name is Tina," she said, "but everyone calls me Tiana. It's... a bit more exotic," she said, wrinkling her nose and smiling.

"What would you like me to call you?" I asked.

"Probably Tiana. I'm so used to it, you know?"

"Tiana, then." I nodded and gestured for her to sit

down. "That's Samson," I said, gesturing toward him. "I hope you don't mind. He sits in on all my meetings."

"Of course not," Tiana said. "Beautiful dog."

Samson raised his head and sniffed the air, then laid back down, seemingly unconcerned.

I smiled at her and said, "And this is Sergeant Ramirez."

"Nice to meet you, too," she said, offering Tracy her hand.

Tiana leaned forward and spoke softly as if confiding in me. "I spoke with Sandy, and she suggested I come talk to you. She said you were very nice to her and that you seemed genuinely concerned about the Daniels kids. That it wasn't just another case to you."

I nodded, then said, "Thank you for coming in, Tiana. You've saved me a trip. I was going to come looking for you this morning. Would you like some coffee? It's not very good, I'm afraid, but it's strong and does the job."

"No. Thank you. I've already had two cups this morning," she replied. "So, how can I help you?"

"How long have you been working for Terrance Knowles?" I asked.

"Terry, you mean? Hmm, it would be... two years come September," she replied.

"And he treats you well?" Ramirez asked.

Tiana looked at her, then nodded and said, "As well as can be expected, I guess."

"The black Chevy Tahoe he's driving," I said. "It's registered to you."

"That's right," she said with a smile.

"Are you living with him?" I asked.

She shook her head. "No! I was when he ran our

escort service from his house, but when he told us we had to get out, I moved to an apartment of my own. He wasn't happy about it. He doesn't like us to be independent, but he couldn't do anything about it. It was after the move that our relationship started to go downhill. He began treating me more like a commodity than a girlfriend, which I suppose I am."

"Tell me about yourself, Tiana," I said. "How can an escort afford to own a Chevy Tahoe, for instance?"

"Why would that surprise you, Captain?" she said with a sly smile. "The escort biz is more lucrative than you might think. Even with all the hands in the till, I make enough to live on my own in a luxury apartment— not quite a penthouse, but you get the idea. I also drive a new vehicle, as you know, and I'm paying my own tuition at UT."

"UT?" I said, beginning to think I was in the wrong line of work. "What's your major?"

"Public policy," she replied. "You'd be surprised how much of my life as an escort prepares me for policy and financial negotiations. Of course, I'll need a master's eventually, so... no rest for the wicked!"

"Really?" I said dryly, then paused for a moment, looking at her. She maintained eye contact, a slight smile on her lips as if she knew I was assessing her, which I was.

"So, Tiana," I said, "People in your line of business usually steer clear of the police, so why are you here?"

"As I said," she replied, "Sandy called me last night. She confirmed you cared and she talked about some of the things I was worried about. I saw the Daniels family fire on the news. Can you tell me who the victims are, Captain?"

"I'm sorry, I can't," I replied. "Not because I don't want to, but because we don't know. We're still waiting for the DNA reports. Why are you so concerned?"

She shrugged, tilted her head back and looked up at the ceiling. "I've been running it through my mind over and over. Sandy told me Matthew and Charlotte are missing, and I haven't seen Terry since last Friday afternoon, so I don't know what to think. But what Sandy doesn't know, though, is that my best friend, Amelia, seems to have disappeared, too. She lives in the apartment next to mine, and I haven't seen her since Saturday."

Oh boy, I thought. *Another one? What the hell's going on?*

"Is it possible that she would have gone out of town with a client?" I asked.

She shook her head. "Something like that is carefully planned by Terry. Besides, Amelia would have told me if she was planning anything like that."

"Any chance that, with Terry out of the picture, she could have agreed to something like that herself?" Ramirez asked.

She looked at her and shook her head. "That's completely against the rules," Tiana said. "She'd have come to me first."

"Do you think she could have taken off with him?" I asked.

"Oh lordy, no! No way," she said, sounding horrified. "He'd be out of business in nothing flat if he did that. She's Pete Daniels' special girl."

"*What?*" I was stunned at this totally unexpected development.

"That's right," she said, nodding. "Amelia has to get

special permission from Pete Daniels to even see a client."

"Help me out here," I said. "Your Peter Daniels is one of Terry's clients?"

She started to chuckle but coughed and cleared her throat instead. It must have been the look on my face.

"He's a bit more than a client," she said.

She was silent for a moment, then realized she'd stepped over the line and she wasn't going to be able to pull back.

"Mr. Daniels... he's part of the operation."

"The escort service?" I asked.

Tiana shrugged. "All of it," she replied. "Everything."

I remembered Sandy alluding to the existence of a third tier, but she'd said she had no knowledge of its whereabouts or its workings.

I leaned back in my chair for a second, tapping my lips with the eraser on my pencil.

"Did she have a date with Daniels that Saturday evening?"

"I really don't know," she replied. "He usually comes to her place."

"And you've seen him there?" I asked.

"Sure. Plenty of times."

"Does he pay her?" Ramirez asked.

"Hah!" She laughed, just once. "I'm not privy to their financial arrangements, but I think Pete Daniels is her sugar daddy." She winked.

"An accountant for a car dealership has the kind of money to be somebody's sugar daddy?" I said, more to myself than to Tiana.

I need to tell Jack to dig deeper into Daniels' financials for potential off-shore accounts.

"He has a very hands-on approach to the operation," she said. "I'm sure he gets a cut of the profit."

"Does he keep the books, too?"

"Matthew does the books for the Green Lane operation, but the reports all go to Pete. He does the escort service's books, too, so I'm sure he probably does it all."

I looked at Ramirez. She raised her eyebrows, pursed her lips and shook her head but said nothing.

"Well," I said, glancing at the clock on the wall, "thank you. You've given us a lot to think about, and I'm sure there's more you can tell us; but for now, I think we can call it a day. If you'll give me your contact information, I'll be able to get hold of you if I need you."

"I was... I am concerned about Matthew and the two girls. As far as Terry's concerned, I just want my Tahoe back, hopefully in one piece. But Amelia, and the Daniels kids, too, it's just all too much to be a coincidence: the fire, the deaths, and Terry..."

"You may be right," I said.

She nodded. "Since you're in Homicide, I guess you're treating the two deaths as murder. The other stuff is Vice and Missing Persons, right? But in this case, I'm pretty sure it's all connected—"

"That reminds me," I said, interrupting her. "I was going to ask Sandy last night but didn't, so now I'll ask you. How come you're both so willing to talk to the police?"

She smiled slyly. "You think we can't afford a little house protection?"

"Protection? As in..." Ramirez said.

She sighed and looked at the ceiling. The expression on her face almost screamed what she must have been thinking: *Are you clueless?*

"As in asking Vice to look the other way," she said.

I knew it. Henry Finkle was the reason Knowles was never charged with anything.

"I get it, but that makes it even more gutsy; you walking in here," I said.

Her eyes narrowed. "I'm concerned about my friends," she snapped. "I'm not afraid of you. You don't know me. The way I'm dressed says something about me and my profession. It speaks of money and good taste. You could have taken Sandy in because she was soliciting. I could just be a gifted spinner of tall tales. But that's for you to find out."

Was she? I wondered. But when I looked at my notes and the incalculable value of the information she was giving us, I shut the hell up.

She paused to let me decide what to do. *She's smart*, I thought. *Beyond smart, and she's sharp*.

"May I continue?" she asked.

I gave her a short nod.

"The one I'm most concerned about is Charlotte."

"Charlotte? But you know that Emily's missing, too?" I asked.

"I know that. But Charlotte is my greatest concern."

"Why Charlotte?"

"I guess maybe it's my intuition. Her mother, Stacey, has no mothering abilities or mindset, and I only know that from what little bit Charlotte has told me about her. And...she's been abused."

I was about to speak, but Ramirez beat me to it. "Abused?" she asked.

"Probably physically. Definitely psychologically, but most assuredly, sexually."

I nodded. "Sandy told me Matthew was protecting the girls."

"Sandy was correct."

"Is it Matthew who's abusing her?" Ramirez asked.

"Obviously, you don't know Matthew."

"You're right," I said. "How could we? So who is it, Tiana? Who's abusing Charlotte?"

"Pete Daniels has been fu... screwing Charlotte since she was twelve."

I stared at her, stunned. "Good God," I said.

"I don't think God has anything to do with it," she said. "Pete Daniels deserves to rot in Hell."

She had slipped into street vocabulary, but I could tell she was genuinely disgusted and shaken by having to reveal it to us. The statement was so vehement that I was ready to add her to the suspect list. But now, I, too, wanted him to rot in Hell, and I found myself hoping that he was the one lying on the slab in Doc's little house of horrors, but maybe that was too good for him.

"Do you think he's abusing Emily, too?" I asked.

"No. That's what Matthew's protecting her from. He told me that she's daddy's 'pride and joy,' but who knows the extent of that? It might just mean he'd never touch her, or it might mean that he's simply biding his time. That's why Matt brings her with him every night, too, and keeps them both out late. It's the only way to keep them both safe."

I suddenly saw it in my mind's eye, Pete and Stacey in the downstairs bedroom and Charlotte tossing the match. But no, the latest fire report had set the characteristics of the fire as hasty, panicked.

"And you think Terry might be involved in... what?" I asked.

She took a deep breath, inflating her cheeks and blowing it back out.

"I don't really know, but I have my theories," she replied.

"Care to enlighten me?" I asked.

She sat and stared at me for a few seconds.

"Why not?" she said. "As far as I've gone now, I might as well step in it completely." She chuckled ruefully. "You see, Terry is one of those jealous, rebellious types. He constantly tests the boundaries. Pete Daniels was his boss, and he was really hard on him. Pete's just an all-around abusive guy. That's why Matthew is doing the books for the Green Lane operation. Matt loves the construction trade—" She paused, then continued, "You might not be able to tell from the outside, but the inside of the house on Green Lane is beautiful, even the garage. He turned it into a comfortable lounge for ladies and their dates. Matt would love to restore the entire property, which is why he talked his father into buying it in the first place.

"But Pete says do this, do that, forget the remodeling nonsense, manage the pros and keep my books."

"And what does this have to do with Terry?" Ramirez asked.

"Oh, sorry. I got a little off track there. I was simply offering an example of how Pete rules the roost. But, since Terry isn't his son, he has less control over him, but control nonetheless.

"So, Terry made overtures toward Charlotte... I can't tell you why. Maybe just because he thought he could, maybe just to be rebellious. Who knows, but somehow it got back to Pete, and he blew a gasket. And to show Pete he wouldn't be told what to do, Terry became even more aggressive with Charlotte. I thought it was just because he can't keep it in his pants, but now I have to wonder if he was *grooming* her. And I think Matt must have thought so, too, because they got into fistfights over it."

"Hoh-boy," I said, shaking my head. *And I was thinking I was going to be able to sort this out, but the thing with Terrance and Charlotte has given me more than a couple of new thoughts about the fire.*

I heaved a sigh. "One last thing, Tiana. Where does Stacey Daniels fit into it?"

Tiana shook her head. "I honestly don't know. Charlotte rarely mentions her."

"How d'you know so much about Charlotte's private life?" I asked.

"Originally, the escorts and the pros were together in the house on Green Lane. That's where Charlotte took a liking to me, and we started spending time together, then she started confiding in me. It was a gradual thing. I guess she needed to feel she could trust me. We're kindred spirits, in a way."

"How's that?" I asked.

Tiana shrugged, then said, "Probably because her story isn't too much different than my own. I'm lucky in that once I got away from home, I had therapy that helped straighten me out. Charlotte's still too afraid and enmeshed to get any distance from it, but she confides in me and I try to help her however I can."

"Let me show you something really quick," I said, turning my laptop toward her. "I don't think there's much doubt, but is this your Tahoe?" I pulled up the short video capture that Paul Burnett had provided.

"Yes, that's definitely my Tahoe, and that's the Knowles' house."

She stood then, looking at her slender, gold Gucci watch. "I have an appointment later this morning, and I need to get back to my apartment first. It was good to unburden myself and to be able to tell you about Amelia, and about Charlotte."

She handed me a dramatically designed rose linen and white card with a logo and raised gold lettering. "If you have any more questions or if you think I might be able to help in any way at all, please don't hesitate to call me."

"Likewise," I said, handing her my own card.

"Oh, wait!" I called as she was leaving the office. "I need a description of Amelia."

"She's a blonde, olive-skinned Italian. Her last name is Arvina. If I find a photo of her, I'll text you with it."

"Thank you," I said, adding Amelia Arvina to my list of persons of interest. "You be careful out there, Tiana. The world you live in is fraught with danger."

"Don't I know it," she said, and then turned and walked confidently across the situation room to the elevator, garnering many an appreciative look along the way.

24

Day 4, Noon

I HAD A LOT TO THINK ABOUT. IT WAS ALMOST midday. Tiana had been gone for just a few minutes and I felt... as if I hadn't slept for a week. So I went to the restroom, splashed some cold water on my face, and washed my hands. Then I leaned forward, put my hands on the rim of the sink, propped myself up, and stared at my face, not really seeing it, just thinking. I rearranged the strands of hair that had worked their way out of my ponytail, but then I looked again at my eyes.

They say the eyes are the window to the soul, and after twenty-two years on the force, I'd seen just about everything and would say my soul was pretty well seared; nothing fazed me anymore.

I've seen countless homicides: women, victims of sex-related crimes—rape victims, prostitutes—but somehow, when they're dead, I never made that much of a connection. You see them on the slab and they're not quite human anymore, just slabs of meat awaiting the butcher. I compartmentalize. But child abuse is one thing I never could accept. And Pete Daniels forced himself on his own daughter for more than six years... *Geez! What a sick son of a bitch.*

And now they're on the run. Running from the law? Running from Daddy, or what they did to him? Or is someone holding them against their will, using them as pawns in some power struggle? Where the hell are they?

Did Pete Daniels die as a result of an accident? Did Charlotte or her brother whack him and set the fire to cover up what they did? I can't see the twelve-year-old being involved... but stranger things, right?

I heard the door swing open, so I washed my hands again. It wasn't so much that I worried someone would wonder what I was doing. I think it was more of a metaphor for wanting to be done with the whole sordid business.

Usually, we were able to wrap up in four or five days —the first forty-eight, if all went smoothly—but this one? We were four days in and farther from a result than when we started.

"That was some interview," Tracy said as she stepped up to the sink next to me.

"Informative," I said. "Let's bring the others up to date. Ask them to come to my office in fifteen. I'll order in. What d'you want, Mexican or Chinese?"

"Mmmm, how about Japanese? There's a new sushi-to-go place."

"Whatever," I said, not really wanting to be bothered with it.

She smiled and nodded.

"How about Stacey Daniels?" I asked. "Anything?"

The smile disappeared. "Just bits and pieces really.

It's hard to track anything down. She has a sheet, but only for a DWI. She hadn't been drinking, but a blood test showed she was on prescription pills."

"Opioids?" I asked.

"Sedatives," she replied.

"Okay, we can talk about it in my office," I said, opening the bathroom door.

"Yep. I'll be right there," she said.

Hawk was the only one who balked at ordering Japanese, but he came around once he looked at the menu. And Tracy explained everything to him.

"Okay," I continued after twenty minutes or so of small talk. I was becoming antsier by the moment. "Time's a-wasting. Let's talk while we eat. You'll have heard by now that we interviewed Tina Stafford, aka Tiana, this morning."

I stopped to take a bite of my California roll, which of course necessitated consuming the whole thing in one bite. Needless to say, I won't be doing that again while I'm conducting a briefing. *They'll think I learned my table manners from Samson.*

"Let's break it down," I began. "Corbin, you do the boards."

I paused and consulted my notes. "Tiana stated she hadn't seen Terrance Knowles, the three Daniels children or her best friend and next-door neighbor Amelia Arvin since Friday. She also said that both Matthew and Knowles are involved in the running of the Green Lane operation, and Knowles has a second escort business operating out of an as-yet-unknown location. And then she dropped this bomb," I continued. "Apparently, Peter Daniels is Knowles' boss and is running the entire operation. Tiana also said that Amelia Arvin is an escort and

Peter Daniel's... girlfriend and that he's extremely jealous over her; keeps her on a tight rein."

I looked at Corbin. He nodded and drew lines out from our nucleus, Peter Daniels and his family, connecting them with Terrance Knowles; Knowles with Amelia Arvin. He drew another line from Matthew Daniels to Tiana and from Tiana to Sandy.

"Draw a line from Pete Daniels to Amelia," I instructed. "According to Tiana, Amelia was Pete's 'special girl,' his private stock. In fact, she referred to him as Amelia's sugar daddy."

"So Daniels," Hawk said, "who has a wife and three kids and is an accountant for a car dealership, is also a high-end escort's sugar daddy? Nice!"

"Yeah, that was my reaction, too," I replied.

"Could he have been laundering the money through the car dealership?" Anne asked.

I looked at Jack. "That's a good question. Jack, I need you to take a deep look at Peter Daniels' finances. See if he has any off-shore accounts, shell companies, and the like."

I continued, "Tiana mentioned that Daniels was abusive with his kids, especially Matthew and Charlotte... Charlotte in particular. He was sexually abusing her from the age of twelve on. He also abused Matthew physically, and all three children mentally, which accounts for how they were perceived by the neighbors and at school. And Charlotte..."

"She was being groomed for something else!" Ramirez said.

"Well, we're not really sure at this point," I said. "But it doesn't look good."

"But Terrance Knowles is the one who earned most

of Pete's scorn. In addition to riding herd on the hookers and escorts and having to reconcile the nightly take, Knowles had a thing for Charlotte. Tiana was sure it was a one-way street. That could be another reason why Matthew and the girls are in the wind.

"It could also be the reason Knowles has disappeared, considering his overtures toward Charlotte."

"So first, Pete Daniels' is screwing his own daughter," Anne said. "Then he's sugar daddy to the escort, not to mention being insanely jealous. So one has to wonder if he found his wife in bed with somebody else? What is he, half man, half rabbit?"

"Just lucky, I guess," Jack said sarcastically.

"Middle-aged crazy, more like," Cooper said.

I nodded. "And then there's Terrance Knowles, who, in my estimation, is just a Pete-Daniels-wannabe. Tiana said she wasn't sure if he just can't keep it in his pants or if his interest in Charlotte was an act of rebellion."

"Maybe he wanted to groom Charlotte for the biz," Hawk said. "Do you know whether he groomed the other two, Sandy and Tiana? Maybe he likes to break them in personally."

"The perks of the job," Cooper said. "Like auditions."

"Hmm, maybe I could see that with Sandy on Green Lane," I said. "But I'm thinking Tiana has been in the business for a while, maybe even before Terrance."

"How long do you think this business has been in operation?" Cooper asked.

"I've no idea," I said. "And, as far as we're concerned, that's not important. What is important is that she also said that somebody in Vice is being paid off to look the other way, which is why Knowles has a clean sheet. I need to talk to somebody in Vice."

Tracy shook her head, looked at me askance, then said, "You know you'll have to go through Tiny, right? Good luck with that."

They all knew that Henry "Tiny" Finkle had once been my nemesis. Back in the day, when I was still a lieutenant and he was a deputy chief, he'd harassed me for years. In the end, though, it caught up with him, and I got him bounced to Vice and they busted him down to captain. It couldn't have happened to a nicer guy. But now we were of equal rank, I was hoping we could talk on equal terms.

"Of course I do. But thanks, anyway," I said, flashing her an artificial smile.

I took a deep breath. "Okay, then. Give me our best suspects thus far in the investigation."

Corbin stood at the board with his marker poised.

"Everyone," Anne said. "Assuming it's Pete Daniels lying on the slab, it could be Matthew, Knowles, Charlotte, and person or persons unknown."

"Yeah, what she said," Hawk said. "But put Daniels up there as well. We still don't know if he's the male victim or not."

I nodded and said, "Let's consider both scenarios. But if it's not Pete Daniels on the slab, it could be either Knowles or Matthew. And if it's either of them, where the hell is Pete? Geez, what a tangled web we weave."

They all stared at me. I stared back at them and said, "Yeah, right. Tough questions, to which we have no answers. Jack, any word on the dental records?"

"Nope," he replied. "I'm told the Daniels' dentist is

on vacation somewhere in Florida. He's gone fishin' and won't be back in his office until next Monday."

"But surely there's someone there who can help us out," I said.

"Nope," Jack replied. "It's a one-man practice and the office is closed. All I got was his answering service."

"Geez!" I said and shook my head. "Okay. Let's move on. Corbin, you want to say something?"

"No matter if the male died as a result of an accident or a whack on the head, the fire was deliberately set and, if I understand it correctly, that's what killed the female victim. That makes it a homicide. So, your method, for any of the suspects, is both possible blunt force and arson."

"True," I said. "So, who's our prime suspect?"

"Assuming Pete is the male victim," Corbin said. "Terry Knowles, then Matthew."

"Everybody agree?" I asked. They all nodded assent.

Robar spoke up. "What about Charlotte?"

"List her, too," I said. "She certainly has motive."

"But don't you think..." Tracy started to ask.

"That she would have had to have had help?" I finished for her.

"I'd say yes," Corbin agreed, adding her name to the board. "If she didn't do it, she may certainly be an accessory."

"Who next?" I asked.

They were silent for a few seconds, then Cooper said, "What about the mom? We're assuming it's her on the slab, but we don't know, not for sure. It could be Charlotte, and if it is..."

"Maybe *she* came home and found Papa in bed with

somebody else, Amelia Arvin, for instance," Ramirez said.

"That's a definite possibility," I said. "But I'm putting my money on Charlotte. There's a long history of sexual and mental abuse, and if her father was turning his attention toward her little sister... That would've been enough to push her over the edge."

"That could be said of the wife too," Hawk said. "Her husband was screwing her daughter. How about this. She takes an overdose of sedatives, bangs him over the head before she passes out, hauls him up on the bed, sets the fire, then collapses on the bed next to him and passes out."

We all looked at him in astonishment, and then Cooper started to laugh.

"What?" Hawk asked.

"That kind of thing happens only in pulp fiction," Jack said.

"I wouldn't be too quick to think that Stacey Daniels didn't know," Anne said in defense of her partner. "Statistics show that often in those cases mothers do know. The reasons for them turning a blind eye are many, and sad, and complicated."

"If she was brutalized throughout the marriage and kept from butting in to protect her children, she might very well be motivated to kill him. That would be enough motive for me," Tracy said.

I sighed and said, "Okay, Stacey Daniels goes on the board."

"And Mom might have spirited the kids away, too," Tracy added. "So maybe they're all together somewhere."

I nodded but didn't comment. We were basically

throwing crap at the wall again, and all because we had no ID on the victims.

"We don't think that Pete Daniels is the top rung in the operation, either," I said, changing the subject. "And, if that's the case, well, the possibilities become endless. Especially if he is or was skimming the profits."

"Or sampling the product," Tracy added.

"Okay," I said. "That's enough. Let me think... Jack, see what more you can find out about Terry's father, Ambassador Knowles. Someone needs to inform him that his son is missing and ask him if he has any idea where he could be.

"Coop and Tracy, see what you can find out about Amelia Arvina and her current life, friends. Once you get some info, then get on the street and follow it up.

"Hawk and Robar. I want you to interview the women over on Green Lane. Maybe they have information to share."

"What about us, Cap?" Corbin wanted to know.

"I'm going to talk to Vice," I replied. "You're going to put out a BOLO on Tiana's Tahoe, Amelia, Knowles, and the Daniels kids.

"Jack, do some more digging. We need to know about the third tier. That's a complete black hole right now. Sandy and Tiana know about it but have no idea who's actually at the top. All they say they know is that it exists. It might or might not. Maybe it's just a ruse Daniels uses to keep the girls in line. Or maybe it's another hush-hush kind of service. Whatever it is, we need to know."

"Are we really sure that Daniels is not the head of the organization?" Corbin said.

"No, we're not, but we need to find out. Jack?"

Jack nodded, and I continued, "We need to work fast, people. We have missing kids. That's a game-changer. Okay. Get out of here and get on with it. Corbin, you stay."

They all left except for Corbin. I made two cups of single-serve coffee and handed one to him.

"Corbin," I said as he hovered over my desk. "It's time to issue the BOLOs to patrol. Talk to Chief Johnston and find out how much of an area we can encompass. We need it to be as wide as possible. It's been four days now. If they're not lying low in town, they could be running, and if they've crossed a state line..."

"I get the picture, Cap. I'll get right on it."

Corbin went out, and Jack stuck his head in. "Cap," he said. "I went down to Miss Pierce to have them make the call to the Ambassador."

"Good." I nodded.

"She told me Belgrade is six hours ahead of us. The person I spoke with said that he wasn't sure when the call would be made since it wasn't a death notification, but that someone would get back to us tomorrow."

"Tomorrow, and tomorrow, and tomorrow," I quoted in frustration.

"Isn't that how it always is, boss?" Jack said.

I sighed. "Yes, it is. Now kindly get the hell out of here and let me get on with some work."

25

Day 4, 2:30 p.m.

THE MOMENT OF TRUTH HAD ARRIVED. AS MUCH AS I dreaded even being in the same *building* as Henry Finkle, I needed information that only he could provide. It was an unpleasant task, but someone had to do it.

Besides, I figured I could always de-louse after I was finished.

The civilian receptionist at the front counter, Vice's gatekeeper, lowered her glasses and gave me an up-and-down once-over, then she nodded toward the corridor.

"He's expecting you, Captain Gazzara. Second door on the left."

Oh yes, I'd called ahead to make sure I didn't get the runaround. Hopefully, that little icebreaker would take some of the chill off our little tête-a-tête. I knocked on his door.

"Enter!" he called.

I pushed the door open, stepped inside, and there he

was in all his unprofessional glory: legs crossed, feet on his desk, arms folded across his chest.

"Well, well," he said, grinning. "Captain Kate Gazzara. Just like old times. Never late. What brings you slumming to my sordid little piece of real estate?"

"Henry," I said, closing the door behind me. That little show of respect was all the deference he was going to hear from me today. Uninvited, I moved toward the one chair facing his desk and, realizing that the chair's position would position the soles of his shoes uncomfortably close to my face, I pulled the chair to one side, to a more advantageous angle and sat down.

"You know, I work with every section in this department," he informed me without any prompting on my part. "We collaborate, you see. It's not, like, just one person showboating and taking all the credit when things fall into her lap. Which is why I think it's so rich that here you are, obviously needing something from me. You must really be desperate because, seriously, Kate, if there's anyone I have less respect for than you..."

"Whoa," I said, getting to my feet.

"It's those idiots who took your side and aided and abetted my demotion and banishment to Vice," he finished.

"You had your hearing, Henry. That was your chance to convince the board what a wonderful cop you *were,* and you couldn't. So here you are, years later, still blaming me for your ethical lapses. I would think you were sick of the taste of your own tears by now. It's time to man up, Henry."

His feet came off his desk so fast I thought he was going to leap at me. His face was red, and his eyes bulged like they were going to pop out of his skull. We glared at each other, fists clenched. I was determined that if he made even one wrong move, I'd take him down so fast it would make his head spin.

"What the f... What d'you want, Gazzara?" he snarled.

"Thanks for asking," I said with a smile as I sat down again and crossed my legs. "I'm working an arson case with two burnt bodies on the side. Peter Daniels, an accountant at the John Roberts Auto Circus, was one of the crispies. Apparently, he moonlighted as a bag man for an escort business and a well-stocked brothel on Green Lane. Sound familiar?"

Finkle's face had dimmed to a pinkish hue, but he didn't respond. He just sat staring at me as if I was speaking a language he didn't understand.

I continued. "Pete Daniels' three children are also missing. We don't know if it's an abduction or if they're dead, like their parents, but one of them is a minor, so that's a concern. Speaking of missing persons, an escort by the name of Amelia Arvina and a pimp named Terrance Knowles are also missing; both are connected to the Green Lane enterprise, and there's a good chance they're both dead."

Finkle seemed to be hearing me at last, but it took a few moments for him to return to my orbit. He blinked several times before he spoke, struggling to keep his voice calm.

"I am aware of Roberts Auto Circus. I bought my Ford SUV there. Years ago."

"Good," I said, gifting him with what I considered to be my sweetest smile. "Now we're getting somewhere. What about the other stuff?"

"Sorry. I can't talk about any of that. You know how it is. Ongoing investigation and all that crap."

"I understand," I replied. "I'm not asking you to cc me on every aspect of your operation. I just want any background you might have on the people I mentioned."

He looked out the window and pulled on his lip with his finger and thumb. He looked like he was calculating the bare minimum of info he could provide to avoid seeming uncooperative, should I make a complaint, while still satisfying me enough to leave.

"I don't know anything about the kids, of course," he said, steepling his fingers. "That whore, Amelia whatever? Yeah, we know her. We track the websites. She's expensive. We know some of her clients. We could go in anytime and make a bust, but maybe we have a reason for biding our time. Maximum impact. It ties into our investigation. That's all I can say about her.

"Terrance Knowles? He's just a punk, but we know him. If someone were to stab him or run him down with a truck, he'd be replaced within an hour. Maybe he and Amelia did one of those murder-suicide pacts. Hopefully, it was in some other county.

"And Pete Daniels?" he continued. "You think he's some kind of sex trafficking kingpin? That's rich. Who's your source on this stuff? Some disgruntled hooker?"

"Can't say," I said. "Ongoing investigation and all that crap." I gave him a quick, phony smile. "So that's it? That's all you've got?"

"What can I say, Captain Kate?" he leered, beginning to recover from his earlier state of shock. "I'm not some stooge you're sweating in a box. I'm running a high-level investigation involving various echelons of law enforcement, and you just aren't privy to our inner workings. I wish I could help you more, but frankly, I think you should just turn over all your files to Missing Persons. It doesn't sound to me like you have anything much going on. Speaking frankly, of course."

"Thank you for your cooperation, Henry," I said dryly and stood up and walked to the door and opened it. And then, in classic Columbo style, I swiveled, smiled and said, "Oh, by the way, Tiny. May I call you that? I always wondered where you picked up that nickname. It's none of my business, of course, as you so eloquently put it, but I heard from a very reliable source that the house on Green Lane is 'protected'"—I made air quotes to emphasize the point—"from law enforcement. Vice in particular. Now I took that to mean that someone in the department's being paid to look the other way. You wouldn't know anything about that, would you? Because I'd think Vice would be the logical department to bribe, wouldn't you?"

The color was returning to his face. "No, I don't know anything about that. And if you start stirring up shit for my department, you'd damn well better have some hard evidence to back it up. And let me say this," he snarled. "Come after me again and I *will* take you down, Gazzara!"

I still had the door ajar. I hoped everyone heard him squeal.

"As I said," I replied, "it's just something someone told me. I'll let you know if I find out anything more. Don't worry, though. I'll try not to crash your top-secret sex ring party."

I left his door open and headed back down the corridor to the elevator, half expecting a shoe to come flying after me. That didn't happen, but I exited quickly anyway.

Back in my own office, I flopped into my chair, prompting Samson to stir, looking at me expectantly.

"Well, what do you think?" I asked him. "You weren't there, but you can probably still answer the question. Did I learn anything from my encounter with our unfriendly neighborhood Captain Finkle?"

Samson cocked his head and stared at me.

"I agree with you," I said. "I learned nothing except for confirmation of our mutual dislike, which wasn't news to me. I don't know why I expected anything different. The next question is, did I accomplish anything? Well, at least he knows that Vice is on my radar, but I couldn't tell one way or the other whether anything he told me was relevant."

Samson laid back down, his head on the edge of his bed, staring up at me.

So what exactly did I learn? Finkle admitted to knowing Amelia and Knowles, but he dismissed the idea that Pete Daniels had anything to do with it.

No, that's not quite true. What he implied, I think, was that I was crazy to think that Pete was a criminal mastermind. So, was there one? And if so, who? Were there people involved that we still didn't know about?

I didn't have any of the answers, but I was determined to find them.

26

Day 4, 3:00 p.m.

I SAT FOR A MOMENT STARING AT SAMSON AS HE stared balefully back at me. "Fat lot of help you are," I muttered. He lifted his head for a moment then laid it down again and closed his eyes.

I shook my head and picked up Tiana's business card, then picked up the phone and called her.

"Tiana, It's captain Gazzara," I said when she answered.

"Hello, Captain. What can I do for you?"

"I was wondering; were you able to find a photo of Amelia?"

"No. Not yet," she replied. "But you might want to go to our escort website. There are plenty of photos of her there."

"Oh?" I said, wondering why she hadn't given me that information earlier. "Okay, what's the website address?"

I grabbed my phone between my ear and shoulder

and turned to my desktop. "This doesn't look like an escort service," I said. "It's a—"

"Yes, I know. You'll have to look at the drop-down menu. You'll find it there," she said.

"Okay... Got it," I said. "Many thanks. Sorry to bother you."

"No problem at all," she said. "Enjoy the rest of your day." And she disconnected.

Once I started examining the website, I realized why she hadn't given me the website from the get-go. There was a lot of information there we could use. I paused and stared at the screen. *I guess she must have decided she wanted to tell me more than she did,* I thought, *and that this was the quickest way to do it without having to come back to the police department. Smart girl.*

At first glance it could have been a jeweler's website. It was professionally photographed and styled. On the landing page were clusters of gems and single jewelry pieces, both vintage and modern. The text spoke of top-tier craftsmanship and innovative designs. But here's what made it unique. When I opened the drop-down menu at the top left of the page, I was provided with a list of gems. When I tried clicking on any of the categories, I brought up a paywall asking me to create an account. I clicked on that and was asked my birth year, then to create a username and password and then to enter my credit card information. I entered my department American Express. That done, I was asked to create an online name for myself.

Now I was having fun. I grinned and typed in Jasper and was immediately taken to another page, "Our Most Exotic and Sought-after Gems," with a large button that invited me to "Enter," which I did.

I shook my head. I couldn't help but wonder who their photographer and website designer had been. It was, at the same time, both glamorous yet tastefully ostentatious. I chuckled, wondering whether those two words together constituted an oxymoron.

The first page showed a luxurious room with glittering white columns, a marble floor, flokati rugs, and loungers, upon which were five lovely young women dressed in silk and gems. Their flawlessly coifed hair and perfectly blended makeup were designed to... They looked like Greek goddesses under a dome which was painted fresco-style, half with blue sky and sun, the other half with a lapis sky above the moon and stars.

I looked for another link to go deeper into the site but found none. I clicked on the menu again, but there was nowhere to go from there. I knew there had to be more to it than that, so I started clicking around the page—on the women themselves, the columns, the most prominent pieces of jewelry—all to no avail. I even clicked on the artwork pictured on the wall of the room. When the word "artwork" went through my mind, I looked toward the top of the screen and clicked on the dome. It was not until I clicked on the night sky half of the fresco that anything worked. When I clicked on the moon, however, the words "Cosmic gemology" appeared, and a banner appeared warning me that I was leaving the secure jewelry site and did I wish to continue or go back?

"Here we go," I said as I clicked and was taken to another website. The first page was titled "Exclusive Gems." Each frame showed a glowing gem beautifully presented in an exquisite setting. The frames were titled:

June's Emeralds, July's Ruby, September's Sapphire, Tiana's Topaz, and Amelia's Amethyst.

I clicked first on Amelia's Amethyst. I was taken into a dramatically appointed boudoir where Amelia stood at the end of a royal poster bed, wearing a translucent fabric gown adorned with what must have been paste amethyst and citrine. There was a poetic description and the mention that when heated, amethyst turned to citrine. The portrayal was followed by a link inviting me to click for "more information."

Before I clicked, I looked at the model again. She perfectly fit Tiana's description, and I hoped there were other photos. I was not disappointed.

I clicked on the info link and was taken to a page with a tastefully intimate portrait of Amelia along with a romantic description of her, her character, and tasteful client reviews, mostly about how Amelia had been the perfect companion for various events and the quintessential evening out. There was one more link to her "services," which, for the moment, I didn't go into. I got the idea. Everything seemed to be on the level, and I was sure even the description of services would be worded to appear legitimate while, at the same time, provocative.

I right-clicked on the photo, saving it to my hard drive. Then I backed out of Amelia's page and clicked into Tiana's Topaz page. There she was, sitting on a fur-covered throne, covered in many layers of topaz jewelry, both gold and blue. Her surroundings were predominantly royal blue and gold, set in what appeared to be an exotic kingdom. I clicked on her next page to see her photo. This time, I was too curious not to check out her "services" page because I wanted to know what kind of money we were talking about.

Whoa! I thought as I went through the list of various services. No wonder she can afford lavish digs and college tuition.

I went back to the menu. I searched through its entirety to see if there was anything I had missed. I had hoped Tiana was giving me a clue to the third tier.

I thought about what to do next, then picked up the office phone to call Jack.

"Cap," he said.

"Jack," I responded. "I need you to come to my office for a few minutes."

"Righty-ho," he said. "On the way."

Two minutes later he opened the door and stepped inside and, as usual, Samson raised his head, sniffed the air, then lay back down.

Jack plopped into the chair opposite mine. "How can I help?" he asked.

I turned my laptop around. I had returned to the "Our Most Exotic and Sought-After Gems" page.

"Cap! I didn't know you were into gemology."

I grinned. "Just these particular ones. I found some very interesting material, but I know there must be more. Could there be hidden pages on a site that only those in the know can access?"

"Sure, there could, but not for what you're looking for. The kind of stuff you're looking for, boss, is not available on the open internet."

"It's not?" I asked, already knowing the answer.

"You're looking for third-tier stuff, right?" he replied.

I nodded.

"That will be on the Dark Web," he said.

"I knew that," I said. "Can you show me how to access it?"

"It's better that you don't get into it, Cap. It's a huge security risk for our entire network if you do. I'll do it at home. I have a Black Hat source. Let me take care of it."

I sighed and said, "All right," and handed him a slip of paper with the URL written on it. "Thanks, Jack." I wasn't up on the terms and technology of cyber-crime, but I'd heard the term Black Hat, and it spoke for itself. "Just don't get yourself in trouble," I added.

He shook his head and raised his hands, palms out, to reassure me. "Not looking for trouble, Cap."

I nodded and he left. Me? I called the chief, and without downing Finkle, I brought him up to speed on our conversation. I also mentioned that we were hoping for the BOLOs we'd issued to produce some results and that we were pursuing connections between the Green Lane operation and the Daniels family.

"Yes, Captain Finkle brought that to my attention, Kate. You must've gotten the better of him. He was red-faced and angry when he came to see me."

I didn't say anything; I could tell that the chief's words were a prelude to something else.

"Seems you cast some aspersions on him, his character, and on the Vice department in general."

The little rat. He couldn't be man enough just to suck it up; no, he had to go tattling to the chief.

"I'll admit it got a bit heated," I said. "And, of course it was entirely my fault. I shouldn't have gone to him for help, not with our history."

He was silent for a moment, then said, "Knowing Captain Finkle as I do, I'm sure your assertions as to his character were accurate descriptions. The problem is you included the entire Vice department."

"Maybe I was a little out of line, Chief, but I know

for sure that someone in Vice is protecting the Green Lane operation. And if it's not Finkle himself, then it has to be someone in his department."

"What makes you so sure, Kate?"

"I have it from two insiders," I said. "I don't think there's anything... bent going on. I think the protection is part of a much larger, ongoing Vice investigation; he even mentioned there was such an ongoing investigation. But if that's the case, why is he so uptight about it?"

"I'll have a word with him," Johnston said.

"I don't mean to make trouble for Vice," I said. "All I wanted was a little help, some information. I got nothing other than threats. I tell you, Chief. I don't intend to revisit the past, but I don't intend to let him walk all over me, again. Your mandate to us is cooperation between departments. I'd like to see that happen."

There was a moment of silence, then he said, "As I said, Catherine, I'll have a word with him. In the meantime, I suggest you've probably gotten all you can from him, so I assume you have no plans to revisit him."

"Not at the moment, Chief," I said, to which I'm sure he raised his eyebrows. I grinned, hoping he would know I was half joking.

"Not funny, Kate," he said. "Keep me informed." And he hung up.

"*Finkle!*" I snarled through gritted teeth.

Samson lifted his head and snapped his jaws.

27

Day 4, 3:15 p.m.

I LEANED BACK IN MY CHAIR, LACED MY FINGERS together behind my neck, and stared up at the clock. I was bored, antsy, and itching for something positive to happen. Then I had an idea.

Thinking maybe I could get some answers right away, I picked up my office phone and speed-dialed Harry Starke.

Harry answered in his usual chipper demeanor, "What's up, Kate? Long time no hear from you."

"Yeah, sorry about that. How've you been? How are Amanda and Jade?"

After a couple of minutes of chitchat, I said, "Look, Harry, I need a little input. I'm working a case that's growing bigger and more confusing by the hour. We've put a lot of the pieces together, but, well, you know how it is. What I need is a new pair of eyes. You up for it?"

"This about the fire?" he asked.

"Yeah, how did you know?" I asked.

"I saw it on the news, of course, and when I heard it was Pete Daniels' house, I knew there would be something more to it."

"You know the name Pete Daniels, then?"

"I do. Pete Daniels, the Auto Circus—perfect name for that establishment—and Daniels', shall we say, indiscretions? Kate, I was just about to head out to run some errands. How about I come by and we go get some coffee?"

"Sure," I said. "How long will you be?"

"I have a couple of stops to make first, so thirty minutes?"

"That'll work," I said. "I'll be waiting."

"Hey," he said. "You have Samson with you? I'd love to see him. Last time I saw him, he wasn't in the best of shape."

"He will surprise you now," I said.

"Okay, then. I'll pick you two up in half an hour."

"Looking forward to it," I said, "as is Samson, I'm sure."

Just as I put the phone down, Anne and Hawk walked in, and I called out to Corbin.

"Hey, you two," I said, gesturing for them to sit down. "How did the Green Lane interviews go?"

"It turned into kind of a group interview," Anne said. "We didn't learn much we didn't already know, but after probing a little deeper, we found out something we weren't exactly expecting."

"Do tell," I said as Corbin sat down.

"The reason we've had trouble putting some elements together is because of where it's happening, who it's with and who's in charge," Hawk added.

"Ah-hah," I said.

"According to the ladies—"

"Ladies? How old are these ladies?" I asked, interrupting him.

"They all appeared to be over the age of eighteen," Anne said, "but sometimes it's hard to tell, you know?"

I nodded. "Go on."

"It appears," Hawk said, "that they're harboring groups of foreign girls—nobody referred to them as women—at Green Lane overnight. One of the Green Lane gals said that one of the visitors spoke broken English with a Russian or Eastern European accent."

Corbin raised his eyebrows and looked at me. I frowned and nodded slightly.

"The girl said they were there waiting for someone to pick them up and take them to Nashville."

"Nashville? Hmm, so this little local operation may just be part of a larger network," Corbin said. "We knew there was more to it, but it sounds to me like this is something the feds need to hear about."

I contemplated that for a moment. "You're probably right, but let's set that aside for a minute. Our goal is to find the Daniels' kids and find a killer. Nashville is way out of our bailiwick, but we'll keep it on tap." I looked at Anne and said, "That it?"

They both nodded and Anne said, "We'll keep digging to see what we can come up with." And she and Hawk left to go to their own desks.

I tapped my pencil on my desk pad, musing. "I feel like this whole thing is about to blow wide open. I don't know how much more we can handle without some extra manpower. This thing is escalating faster than a speeding bullet. It's now graduated to international sex trafficking," I said. "Definitely beyond our purview, but we need to let Vice in on everything we know at some point."

"Wasn't that the purpose of your visit to Finkle?" Corbin asked.

I shrugged. "That... didn't go well," I said. "We both triggered each other. It's funny, but after all this time, you'd think I was beyond that kind of thing. I do know this; you're coming with me next time."

"Of course," he said, nodding.

I looked at the clock and jumped up. "Samson and I are meeting with Harry Starke. He's picking us up. In fact, he's probably out there waiting."

"Okay, boss," Corbin said. "Is there anything you need me to follow up on right now?"

"You can go find Cooper and Ramirez and see if they've tracked down Amelia Arvina. And if Jack's around, see what he's up to. I'm not sure he'll tell you about his top-secret assignment, but you can probe. If not, I'll have him come talk to us when I get back."

"Sounds good. See you later, then. Are you going to see if Harry can add some new perspective?"

"That's the plan," I replied. "It sure would be nice if he could put a few bricks together for us. He already said he knows Pete Daniels."

Corbin nodded. "Give me a buzz when you get back, then." He left the office.

"C'mon, Sammy," I said, "Let's go see Uncle Harry."

Samson stretched his back legs, then the front, then looked up at me, his eyes bright, sparkling.

28

Day 4, 4 p.m.

I CLIPPED SAMMY'S LEASH ON HIM, ADJUSTED HIS VEST and badge and made ready to leave. I took one last look at the boards, shook my head and said, "Come on, boy," and together we walked across the situation room to the elevator.

I was right. Harry was already there, parked in front of the PD, waving to us from his Range Rover. As I walked up, he rolled down the passenger-side window, and the new-car smell rolled out on the breeze. I hesitated.

"C'mon," Harry said, "it's all right. I laid a car robe across the back seat for Samson."

He got out and came around, opened the rear door and squatted to Samson's eye level. Harry seemed to look down Samson's spine the way you'd look at the line of sight over a rifle barrel, then he stood, nodded his approval, and said, "Look at you! You're doing well, pal. I'm impressed." He ruffled Samson's ears and then stood aside. Samson took the open door as an invitation and jumped right in.

I took that as my cue to get in too. Wow! I'd had a used Range Rover in the past, but nothing like this. I'd always thought of them as a utility vehicle, but this was beyond the most luxurious vehicle I'd ever been in. It was made for elegance and ultra-comfort. No matter how short the ride, I was going to enjoy this.

"Nice wheels, Harry," I said.

"Ya think?" he chuckled.

"Whatcha gonna have, Kate?" he asked as he stopped at the Starbucks drive-through window.

"Coffee, black, no sugar," I said.

"Hmm, I think I'll have the same."

He ordered and then drove to the Greenway and parked.

"So, how've you been, Kate? Haven't seen or heard from you for weeks."

"Me?" I said. "Same old same old. Busy, busy, busy. You know how it is. The wheel never stops turning." I took a sip of my coffee and then continued, "By the way, I went to see Finkle today."

"Oh, and how did that go?"

"How d'you think? It was a total waste of breath and effort. He's about as helpful as a bag full of turnips, maybe less so. How's Amanda? Doing well, I hope."

"Oh yeah," he replied. "Jade, too. Keeping her and Maria on their toes. So, whatcha got, Kate?"

I took another sip, swallowed it, closed my eyes for a second, then looked at him and said, "Every day, I keep finding more layers of this pesky crime, but it's all stuff I need to be feeding Vice. There are links to my homicides, but my latest piece of information suggests the need for federal involvement."

"Trafficking, huh?" he said. "Which is it, sex or drugs?"

"Sex," I replied. "Linked to a syndicate in Nashville with connections in Chattanooga, and from what we've learned, Daniels is—make that was—up to his neck in it. I'm pretty sure he's my unidentified male victim."

I paused for a second and stared out through the windshield. "We talked to a couple of pros working the Green Lane operation. They told us someone is importing young women, possibly Russian or Eastern European, and using the house as a stopover before moving them on to Nashville. But that's all outside of my investigation. Though, as I said, I'm pretty sure it's all connected. My focus is on the homicides and finding the three Daniels kids."

"Suspects?" he asked.

"Hah!" I said, shaking my head. "That's where you come in. It all revolves around the identities of the two bodies. Until we know who they are, the possibilities are many. Peter and Matthew Daniels, Terry Knowles or perhaps even a person unknown. Same with the female: Stacey Daniels is who we think it is, but it could be Charlotte Daniels or a missing escort, Amelia Arvin. Any one of them could be a victim or a killer. All have motives of one sort or another."

"Have you interviewed anybody at all?" he asked. "Any of the suspects, I mean?"

"No! They're all either missing or victims."

"The Green Lane house and Terry Knowles ring a bell. He's Ambassador Knowles' son, right?"

"Yep."

He grinned at me. "That's what I thought. There's your East European trafficking connection."

"What? Say that again?" I asked.

"Well, it's just a thought," he said. "I mean, think about it. What's the son of a United States ambassador doing working as a pimp in a whore house? Maybe those girls are—"

"Coming from Serbia," I said, interrupting him.

I CLOSED my eyes and shook it off. "Okay, okay," I said. "This is just getting bigger and bigger, and it's all moving in the wrong direction."

"Except it's not—not entirely," Harry said. "Just to be clear, what, exactly, does sleazy Pete Daniels have to do with it? If he is your victim, I don't think he'll be missed."

"He's kind of the middleman, I think," I replied. "He's an accountant, and he keeps the books for the operation. And, I get the impression that he might be some kind of a big shot, but not *the* big shot. I think maybe he's a middleman in some kind of super hierarchy."

"And you have no names yet, for any of the higher-ups?" he said.

"Nope, not a one. "

"And that's why you went to see Finkle?" he asked.

"Yeah. Him."

"Bad idea," Harry said, then took a sip of his coffee.

"Yep! I thought we could both be adults about it after all these years. But within seconds, it turned into a bruhaha. Though he did give me a couple of nibbles, but only in retrospect."

"Well, Kate, my advice is if you've got evidence of something this big, especially if it involves a US ambassador, you'd better bring in the FBI."

"Thanks, but no thanks. Not until I've solved my homicides."

The words were barely out of my mouth when my phone rang. It was Corbin. I looked at Harry. He nodded. I took the call.

"What's up, Corbin?"

"Cap! Just got a call on the BOLO from Campbell County. They've spotted the Tahoe at a motel in LaFollette. They want to know what you want them to do."

"Geez," I said. "That's way out of our jurisdiction." I paused for a second, thinking. Then I remembered something. "Campbell County. I know the sheriff. We went through the academy together. I'll give him a call and get right back to you."

"You didn't take your car with you. Where are you? I'll bring it to you."

"No need," I said. "Harry will drop me off."

I looked at Harry and raised my eyebrows. He nodded and started the motor.

"A breakthrough?" Harry asked after I hung up.

"Yep. Looks like we have found the Daniels' kids. The car we're looking for's been spotted in LaFollette. I need to call the Campbell County sheriff."

"Go ahead. I'll take you back to the PD."

"Thanks, Harry, you're a peach," I said as I scanned through my contacts for Joel Taylor's number. I hadn't spoken to him in years. His was one of those numbers you keep just in case.

I found it and made the call as Harry swept out of the parking lot.

"Campbell County Sheriff's Office. How may I direct your call?"

"Hi. This is Captain Gazzara, Chattanooga PD. Is the sheriff in?"

"He is. He's expecting your call, Captain Gazzara."

That was the way Joel was, always a step ahead of the game.

"Kate!" Joel said as he picked up the phone. "It's been a coon's age. How the hell are you?"

"I'm doing great, and you?"

"Healthy but busy. I'm running again. You know how that is. Okay, knowing what I do, I assume you're wanting to enter the county in an official capacity."

"Yes, sir," I replied. "I'll be heading your way in about forty-five minutes. What's the status of the Tahoe and its occupants?"

"All's quiet," he replied. "They're in a Motel Six and seem to be in for the night. What do you want us to do in the meantime?"

"Just sit on them unless they look like they're leaving."

"Will do."

"Okay, then. It's now... four-forty. We should be with you—geez, how far is it, Joel?"

"From Chattanooga? About one-fifty, but it's interstate all the way."

I quickly did the math, then said, "We should be with you in Jacksboro... between seven-thirty and eight. How far is LaFolette from you, by the way?"

"About five minutes is all," he replied. "In the meantime I'll keep them under surveillance, and if anything changes, I'll let you know. If they try to leave, d'you want me to detain them?"

"Absolutely," I replied. "They're murder suspects, but tell your officers to go easy. One of them's just a kid. But if there's a Terrance Knowles with them—stocky build, sandy-haired—watch out. He could be trouble."

"Good to know. And the kid. How old?"

"There are two—well three. The brother Matthew's twenty-one. The eldest girl is eighteen, and the young-ster's twelve."

"Gotcha," he replied. "See you soon. Looking forward to it, by the way."

"Me, too," I said, "and thanks for your help." And I ended the call.

Ten minutes later, Harry dropped me off at the PD.

"Take care, Kate," he said as I let Samson out of the back seat. "Let me know how it goes."

29

Day 4, 5:25 p.m.

I MADE A QUICK STOP IN MY OFFICE, THEN STRAPPED
Samson into his harness and jumped in the passenger
seat of my unmarked cruiser; Corbin was driving. Then I
called Chief Johnston.

"Chief? Gazzara, here. The Tahoe's been spotted up
in Campbell County. I'm on my way up there. Sheriff
Joel Taylor's a friend; we were at the academy together.
He's keeping an eye on them until we get there. Corbin
and I are in the car, but I wanted to check in with you
first."

"You're going to bring them back to Chattanooga?"
he asked.

"That's the plan," I replied.

"You don't think Campbell County can handle that?"

"They could," I replied. "Of course they could. It's
not that. I need to question the occupants of the Tahoe
right away. I'll have them taken to the county jail in
Jacksboro, then we'll see how it goes from there."

"I think you should let Taylor handle it—"

"Chief, the suspects must be transported back to Chattanooga sooner rather than later, so the sooner we go, the sooner we'll have them back in the city. And, sir, maybe it does sound like a trust issue, but those two young men, Knowles and Matthew Daniels, are real wild cards. Both are young and hotheaded. I'd really hate for some equally hotheaded deputy to tangle with them and one or more of them get injured or dead."

"Very well, Kate," he said. "But know that I'm only permitting this on the condition you do it by the book. Understood?"

"Understood, Chief, and thank you."

I could have said more, but once the chief says yes, it's better to accept it and be grateful.

"I'll keep you apprised; well, either me or Corbin."

"You do that. And be sure to read them their rights. I don't want any surprises after the fact. Moment by moment if you can, please."

"You got it," I said and disconnected before he could change his mind.

I looked at Corbin and rolled my eyes. "He wants a blow-by-blow account as it's happening," I said.

"I understand," Corbin said. "He's anxious, too, and he doesn't want anything to go wrong."

"Which is why I'm glad we're going to be there. We can de-escalate if anything goes sideways. Unless we find ourselves dealing with Knowles. Then who knows."

Corbin didn't respond, so I looked at him. He half-grinned.

"You do know, don't you, that you don't know the Daniels kids any more or any less than you know Knowles?"

"Of course I do," I snapped. Irritated that he would even ask such a thing.

He didn't answer, kept his eyes on the road. By then we were passing through Ooltewah and heading up White Oak Mountain on I-75, and in heavy traffic. Mountain is a bit of a stretch, but White Oak Hill doesn't have quite the same ring to it.

I glanced at the time on the dashboard. It was almost five-thirty and we were about ninety minutes out of Knoxville. I flipped on the blue lights and siren, and Corbin eased onto the hard shoulder and drove on in silence.

My phone rang. It was Sheriff Taylor. "Joel?"

"Just a quick update. I have a deputy camped out at the motel in LaFollette. Your people are moving about. The tall guy went across the street; to get some food, I guess. Other than that, my deputy said they're just milling around and looking bored."

"They don't look like they're planning to bolt?" I asked.

"If they are, they'll probably wait for dark," Taylor replied.

"How many are there?" I asked.

"He thinks three: the tall guy and two females."

"Okay, thanks, Sheriff. We're about forty miles out of Knoxville, so we'll see you in another hour, with luck."

"I'll keep you apprised."

"Thanks," I said.

Corbin looked over in anticipation.

"So no sign of Knowles, then? Sounds like it's just Matthew and the girls. I suppose he could be sleeping."

"Who knows?" I said. "Maybe he's at home, laying low. We need to get a warrant tomorrow and find out."

"Could be. But why? Why not business as usual for him? There's something hinky going on with him. He abandoned the Green Lane girls. He could be the male victim."

I shook my head, frustrated to hell and back. We didn't speak again until we were about five miles out of Knoxville.

"Methinks there's a need for speed," I said. "I don't know if I'm just antsy or if I'm picking up on something."

Corbin looked at me. "Wouldn't be the first time, Cap."

I hated what I called my "free-floating anxiety," but sometimes it was more than that. More than once it had been a precursor to an incident while on a case.

I picked up the radio and called Knox County, letting them know we'd be passing through Knoxville shortly, lights-and-siren.

"We're aware of the situation, Captain," the dispatcher said. "You'll meet with a state trooper in Jacksboro who will accompany you to LaFollette in case the suspects try to get back on the highway. He's on his way now."

"Name?" I asked.

"Trooper John Wells," the dispatcher relayed.

"John Wells. Got it. Thank you."

"Let's go, then," I said to Corbin. "Light up the grille and hit the siren. Let 'em know we're coming."

We zipped through Knoxville and soon were on our way north to Jacksboro.

And then, and I mean literally, just as we pulled into the Campbell County Sheriff's Department parking lot, we intercepted a radio transmission saying that it looked like the Tahoe was getting ready to rabbit.

I got out of the car, looked around and saw the state trooper's cruiser just a couple of parking spaces away, obviously in receipt of the same transmission. He rolled his window down just as Joel ran out and waved to us.

"Let's go!" he shouted. "I'll lead the way." And he jumped in the front seat with the trooper.

I leapt back into the car, and Corbin reversed out of the parking spot before I could close the door. Then, with tires screeching, he shot out of the parking lot, lights on and siren howling.

"Looks like you were right," Corbin said. "It appears they got a jump on us and are now at the mercy of a single county deputy."

"Yeah, right," I grumbled. "What I'm afraid of is that he went to get coffee and they grabbed the opportunity and ran for it as he came out of the donut shop."

"Oooooh," Corbin said. "Not good."

By then we were out of Jacksboro, speeding toward LaFollette. Me? I hoped to hell the deputy at least knew which way they'd gone.

"They must have spotted the deputy," Corbin said.

"We don't know if that's the case," I said. "But it's a real possibility. I'm just praying they don't make it to the state line and cross over into Kentucky. That would create a huge problem."

"How far is it to the Kentucky state line?" Corbin asked.

"I-75 to Jellico is about thirty miles," I said. "The state line's right there, just a hair's breadth away," I answered him.

Samson sat straight up in the seat, animated by the

surge in speed, tongue lolling out as if to say, "Oh boy, oh boy, oh boy, oh boy!"

We kept driving, tailing the state vehicle directly in front of us.

Jacksboro Parkway—25W—is a four-lane highway and an easy drive. Even so, I began to worry we'd find the Tahoe upside-down in a ditch. It was almost eight o'clock, and the sun was low in the western sky.

We blew through Jellico and headed out the other side.

I've no idea where the deputy was. I don't remember passing him, but the trooper pulled into the left lane, leaving us the right, and I realized we were fast coming up behind the Tahoe.

Suddenly, the Tahoe slid sideways, swaying as it tipped from side to side for a second, and then came to a halt. We screeched to a stop behind it and jumped out of the car, weapons drawn.

Corbin shouted for them to get out of the car with their hands up. The driver's door opened first, and out stumbled a young man who, by the looks of him, was Matthew Daniels, tall, slim-hipped, with muscular arms.

"Get your hands up where we can see them," I told him. "Do it now!"

He stretched his arms high above his head, palms out, shaking his hands so we could see they were clear. His eyes were as big as saucers.

"Please! Please!" he begged. "I'm just trying to protect my sisters."

Both the front passenger-side door and the one behind it opened at the same time, and the two girls got out.

"C'mon," I said. "Hands above your heads."

They raised them tentatively, and the taller one, who I assumed was Charlotte, said, "It was an accident."

I wasn't sure what she was referring to, but this was not the place for a confession of any kind.

"Get down on your knees, both of you, and put your hands behind your head!" Corbin shouted.

I'm pretty sure he meant Matthew and Charlotte, but Emily took it to mean her, too.

Matthew immediately dropped to his knees and stared down at the pavement. Charlotte sank down more slowly, looking up at us defiantly. Emily got as close to Charlotte as she could before dropping to her knees. She, too, looked at us, but with shock and fear, like a deer in the headlights.

Corbin and I holstered our weapons and stepped forward toward the kids.

Corbin cuffed Matthew's wrists. I went a little easier on Charlotte, not cinching them as tight as I normally would, although, by the way she looked at me, in any other circumstance, I wouldn't have done so. Next, I went to Emily, but I couldn't do it. I gently helped her up and held her by the arm.

"It's okay, Emily," I said. "Nobody's going to hurt you. You're safe now."

She didn't answer. I looked at Matthew and said, "Where's Terry Knowles?"

Charlotte looked at me now in bewilderment, then turned toward Matthew, her eyes wide.

Matthew looked at her and shook his head almost imperceptibly, but I caught it.

"Fine," I said, "you don't want to talk to me now. That's okay. I'll give you time to think about it until we get you in the box."

I gestured to Joel and John. "Would you take Matthew to Jacksboro? Let's have someone bring the girls separately."

The Sheriff nodded. "I'll radio ahead."

"Where are your keys, son?" the trooper said to Matthew. Matthew gestured to his front pocket with his head, and Joel pulled out the Tahoe keys with a lavender rabbit's foot and a green translucent troll doll on the fob.

I smiled. They were a woman's keys, no doubt, and yet they didn't quite fit Tiana's profile.

The trooper tossed them to a deputy I didn't recognize and told him to take the Tahoe to the station.

Joel handed the girls off to a backup unit. One of the officers was a woman. I asked her to hold Emily by the arm and not to use the cuffs on her. She nodded. "Yes, ma'am."

I caught a glint just beyond the Tahoe in the fading light and saw the spikes which had been laid down by none other than the Jellico Fire Department. That had to be a first.

The traffic was piling up behind us as we began to clear the scene, and the Fire Department pulled in the spikes. The deputy checked the Tahoe all around, making sure none of the tires were damaged. Then he climbed in and maneuvered his way back onto the road, going south to Jacksboro.

30

Day 4, 8:30 p.m.

WHY *LaFollette?* I WONDERED AS I DROVE BACK TO Jacksboro. *Were they waiting for somebody? Knowles, maybe?* I had noticed Charlotte's confused expression when I had asked about him, as well as Matthew's warning not to say anything.

I decided to separate them into different interview rooms, but I had to call Rhonda Mackabee to come because we couldn't question Emily without an adult present. *Does she know her father and possibly her mother were dead?*

We arrived at the Jacksboro Sheriff's Department to find they, too, were having a busy evening and all but one of the interview rooms were busy.

Joel had put Matthew in the available room, but the girls were being held in the hallway by the female Sergeant Hudson.

I thought for a minute, then decided. "Just put the girls in with Matthew, for now, and take the cuffs off them; the boy, too," I told Sergeant Hudson and one of the deputies who had joined her. "Seat them behind him so they can't look at each other. No questions can be addressed to Emily, nor should she respond to any. And I want two deputies—one male, one female—present in the interview room at all times. And somebody please make sure they have something to eat, even if it's just a soda and chips." And then I headed back outside to call Rhonda Mackabee.

I stepped outside and stood on the steps and made the call. She answered almost immediately.

"Captain Gazzara! Do you have some news for me?"

"I do, Rhonda," I said. "Good news. We have all three of your sister's kids in custody."

"Oh, thank God," she said. "Are they all right?"

"Yes. They're tired but seem to be in good spirits. That being said, I need you to come and be with Emily and probably take her home with you. I also need to question her, and I can't do that without a parent or a responsible adult present. Right now, you're the only relation I can think of."

"Question her? And what about Matthew or Charlotte? Aren't they old enough?"

"Well, yes, but they're being questioned, too, so I can't use either of them."

"Are you talking about the police station down on Amnicola?"

"I'm afraid not. We're up in Jacksboro."

"Jacksboro? Oh, my Lord. Why Jacksboro?" she asked.

"We don't know yet. They were apprehended just as they were about to cross the state line into Kentucky."

"Well..." she said, hesitating. "I can't do it. I can't drive in the dark. My night vision is terrible."

"I understand. I apologize. I shouldn't have expected you to drive all the way up here. I can make different arrangements. I'll keep you in the loop."

"Do that, please, Captain. I'm so sorry I can't be there."

"That's okay, Rhonda. We'll work out an acceptable solution, then I'll let you know what we've decided."

"So, does this mean that Stacey's dead?"

"We don't know yet, I'm afraid," I said. "I hope we'll know more when we've interviewed the children."

"I understand, Captain Gazzara. So, I'll hear from you soon?"

"As soon as possible, Mrs. Mackabee. And thank you."

After disconnecting the call, I thought about transporting them all back to Chattanooga before starting any questioning. But before I could even settle my brain, my cell phone rang. I looked at it. It was Doc!

Yes! I thought as I swiped the screen. "Doc! My stars. Please tell me you have something for me."

"I sure do, Kate," he said. "I can tell you your two fire victims are *not* Peter and Stacey Daniels."

That knocked me back for a second. "You're sure, Doc?" I said without thinking. "Whoops! Sorry, Doc. Of course you are. I take it you have the DNA results?"

"No," he said, "but I do have dental records. Neither is a match for the Daniels couple."

"Who are they then?" I asked, irritated that I had been thrown yet another roadblock.

"I don't know, Kate. It doesn't work like NCIC. I can't just load the dental records into a database and see who they match. The records have to be requisitioned from the dentist, so we have to have a potential subject."

I was turning everything over in my mind. I thought of the gash on the back of the male victim's head, and Charlotte's words echoed in my mind, saying, "It was an accident."

"I don't know, Doc. I hate to just take a stab in the dark here, but you might check on Terrance Knowles and... Amelia Arvina. She's Pete Daniels' sugar-baby. I'm sure she's got a form, so it shouldn't be too difficult to track her information. You might even get lucky with a DNA sample."

"Sounds like a plan, Kate. Sorry I couldn't have made it easier on you. I'll get back to you when I have something."

"Thanks, Doc. By the way, we have the Daniels kids safe, so we're getting there."

"Good news indeed. Talk to you soon." And he hung up.

Wow, I thought. *The parents are still alive. Wait till I tell Corbin... But where the hell are they?*

31

Day 4, 9:30 p.m.

I CALLED CORBIN TO FIND OUT WHERE HE WAS.

"I'm outside the interview room, waiting for you," he said. "I have the two girls out here in the hallway. We didn't want to take them in until you got back."

"Okay, I want you with me," I said. "Listen, Doc just called. The victims are not Peter or Stacey Daniels. So, take a deep breath, and let's see what shakes out."

When everyone was settled in the interview room, I asked, "Is there anything you need before we start talking?"

Emily raised her hand. "I need to go to the bathroom."

"Okay, just a second," I said. I looked at Sergeant Hudson. "Can you take her?"

"Of course, Captain."

Emily and Sergeant Hudson left the room and closed the door behind them.

I took a moment to look at the two kids. They were

a good-looking pair. Matthew had wavy chestnut hair, blue eyes and was quite buff. Charlotte's hair was more honey blond and curly. Because of their complexions, I would normally have questioned whether or not they were brother and sister, except that they both shared a couple of almost identical features: the shape of their eyes and noses.

"Look—" Matthew said.

I held up my hand to stop him. "Be patient, Matthew. We're going to get to the bottom of this, hopefully tonight. But we have to do things by the book, okay?"

He nodded.

"First," I continued, "I need to read you your rights." I stood up. "Stand up, both of you."

"You have the right to remain silent. Anything you say can be used against you in a court of law. You have the right to an attorney. If you cannot afford an attorney, one will be appointed to you. Do you understand these rights as I have read them to you?"

Matthew nodded, and Charlotte said, "I get it."

It was at that moment that Sergeant Hudson and Emily returned. "Just a minute, Sergeant," I said and backed out of the room and closed the door behind me.

"How is your work schedule this evening, Sergeant?"

"Everything's good," she said. "The Sheriff has assigned me to you for the duration."

"Good," I said, smiling at them.

"Emily," I said, bending down a little. "Sergeant Hudson is going to take you somewhere to get you some dinner. Is that okay?"

She hesitated at first but then nodded.

"Take her somewhere nice," I said, "and don't come

back till I text you, okay? I don't want to keep her here in this environment any longer than I have to."

Hudson nodded.

"Text me and let me know where you are, and make sure you keep an eye on her. I don't want her to try to make a run for it. Not that I think she will, but you never know." I gave her my cell number.

"Will do, Captain," Sergeant Hudson said.

I returned to the interview room, we all sat down, and I immediately started the tape.

When the recording signal indicated to begin, I stated the time, date, and purpose of the interview, then said, "Present is Captain Catherine Gazzara." I nodded to Corbin and he said, "Sergeant Corbin Russell." I then said, "Also present are," I nodded at Matt.

"Matthew Daniels," he said.

I nodded at Charlotte.

"Charlotte Daniels," she said, her voice rising in the end almost as though it were a question.

I nodded, looked up at the two cameras to make sure they were on, then read them their rights again for the recording, then continued, "Sergeant Russell and I are from the Chattanooga Police Department," I said. "Do you know why you were stopped by the Campbell County Sheriff and the State Police tonight?"

"Maybe," Matthew said. "I'm not sure."

I looked past Matthew at Charlotte, who was looking frantically at Matthew.

She didn't acknowledge the question at all.

"Maybe?" I asked. "Why maybe?"

"For one thing," Charlotte finally blurted, "we had nothing to do with the fire. We didn't even know about it until the next morning, till we saw it on TV in the motel room."

Matthew frowned and glared at her. He obviously didn't want her to say anything.

"Motel room, where?" I asked.

"In LaFollette. We left the house and drove straight up here," Matthew said.

"That was four days ago," Corbin said. "Were you meeting someone?"

Matthew looked surprised and shook his head.

"Did Terry Knowles give you the keys to the Tahoe?"

"Sorta," Matthew said.

"Sorta?" I glanced at Charlotte, who was trying to be stoic but was not managing it very well. I didn't need a stethoscope to tell me her heart was racing.

"I took them from him," Matthew said.

"You took them from him?" I said. "What's that supposed to mean?"

He shrugged, looked down at the table, but didn't answer.

"What was the plan, then, Matthew?" I asked. "Were you and your sisters going on a little vacation? Is that it?"

"Sorta," he said.

"That's it, sorta?" I asked. He shrugged but didn't answer.

"What d'you mean, Matthew," I said.

Again, he shrugged but didn't answer.

I looked at Charlotte and said, "The first thing you said when you got out of the Tahoe was—"

"I know what I said," she snapped.

"And you," I said, turning back to Matthew, "you said you were—"

"Matthew and I were just trying to protect my sister," Charlotte said before he could speak.

"What were you protecting her from, Matthew?" I asked. "And what did you mean when you said it was an accident?"

They looked at each other, then Matthew said, "Do I need a lawyer?"

"You haven't been charged with anything," I told him.

"But how do I know it's all right to tell you anything?" he asked.

I did not want to go down that road.

"Look at it this way," Corbin said. "This is your chance to tell your story, to help yourself. If you've done nothing wrong, you've nothing to worry about. If you did do something wrong, yes, you need a lawyer."

Matthew stared at us. I could see sweat beads breaking out on his forehead, and his hands were glistening.

"Didn't you just say that we have the right to remain silent and to have an attorney present?"

"Do you have an attorney?" I asked.

"Pete does," he said.

"Who is it? I asked. "D'you want us to call him?"

No answer.

"Help yourselves here, Matthew," Corbin said. "Somebody burned that house down. Was it Knowles?"

Neither of them moved.

"Who wants to hurt your sisters, Matthew? Is it something to do with the accident?" I asked.

No response.

I sat back in my chair. "Okay, let's go back a bit. Sergeant Russell and I are homicide detectives. We have reason to believe the fire at your house was a deliberate act of arson resulting in the death of two persons. That—look at me, Charlotte—that is murder. Our job is to find out who killed them. Nothing more than that."

"Who are the victims?" Charlotte asked in an anxious tone.

"Well," I said, "we now know it's not you three, and we also know it's not your parents, so who do *you* think they might be?"

Charlotte leaned forward, with her elbows resting on the table and a weird-looking expression on her face; a look of relief, maybe? But she said nothing.

"Charlotte?" I said. She didn't respond.

"Wh-where did you find the victims?" Matthew asked, his irritation now visibly turning to fear.

I looked at Corbin, who shrugged slightly.

"They were in the master bedroom," I said. "On the bed, together."

"That it?" Matthew said.

"What do you mean?" Corbin asked.

"I mean, that's it, then," he said. "How do you know the fire was started on purpose?"

"That's something we're not at liberty to discuss," I said as I glanced down under the table and noticed something amiss. "What size of shoes do you wear, Matthew?"

"Uh, twelve. Why?"

Corbin and I glanced at each other again.

"What about your dad?" I asked.

"Ten and a half, I think," Matthew said. "Maybe eleven."

There was a moment of silence.

Charlotte sat up, seemingly interested in this new line of questioning.

"Matthew," I said, leaning forward, "what did you do with the size nine cowboy boots that your Aunt Rhonda bought you for Christmas last year?"

He flushed red. "I regifted them to Terry," he said. "I knew Aunt Rhonda would never know."

"Strange gift," I said.

"It's what he told me he wanted."

"Why didn't he buy them himself? He surely has more money than you."

Matthew shrugged. "Why does it matter?"

"It doesn't. I'm just trying to get something straight in my mind. The day of the fire, forensics found an imprint of size nine boots under one of the windows. Was Terry there that morning, before the fire?"

Charlotte was looking at Matthew. He kept staring straight ahead.

"I have to go to the bathroom," she said.

I sighed. "Interview suspended at nine-forty-four PM."

"Corbin, you stay with Matthew. Sergeant Hudson isn't back yet, so I'll take Charlotte to the bathroom."

He nodded.

I walked her out and down the hallway toward the restroom. As we got to the door, she turned to me. "Can I please talk to you alone?"

"Well, what do you mean by alone?"

"Without Matthew or the other man, Sergeant..."

"Sergeant Russell," I said.

"Russell," she repeated.

"Can Sergeant Hudson be there?" I asked.

"Is that the policewoman who went with Emily?"

I nodded.

"Yeah," she said. "That's okay."

"Let me see what I can work out. Do you still have to go to the bathroom?"

"Yeah," she said.

I looked along the corridor and turned toward the front desk, where I could see a female officer talking to the desk sergeant.

I waved my hand to get her attention. The desk sergeant spotted me, said something to the officer and nodded in my direction. She turned and looked at me. I gestured for her to come.

"Trying to stay out of the fray?" I asked, smiling at her.

She rolled her eyes. "Damn right, I am."

"I need a little help here," I said. "I need to make a phone call. Would you mind taking this young lady to the restroom, then return her to interview room three?"

"Sure, no problem...?" she said. I saw her looking for my badge.

"Gazzara," I said. "Chattanooga, Homicide."

"Captain Gazzara," she nodded. "I'm Officer Shirley, Sara Shirley, Knox County Sheriff's Department."

"Knox County?" I said. "What are you doing out here?"

"This mess," she said. "Campbell County put out a mutual call, and I got called in."

"Hey!" Charlotte said. "I wasn't kidding. I need to go."

"Sorry. Charlotte, this is Officer Shirley. She'll take care of you and return you to the interview room. I'll call Officer Hudson."

"Come on, girl," Shirley said. "This way."

As they walked away, I thought about poor Samson still in my cruiser. I needed to do something about that.

I was on my way to the front entrance and reached the door just as Sergeant Hudson pushed through with Emily. "Hey!" I said, "I was just about to call you. How was dinner?"

"Good," Emily said. "We had spaghetti with spumoni for dessert."

"Awesome!" I said, my own stomach rumbling as I realized I hadn't eaten all day.

"Emily," I said, "do you like dogs?"

"I love dogs," she said. "I've always wanted one, but Mom and Dad always said no."

"And you, Sergeant Hudson. Are you, by any chance, afraid of dogs?"

"Heck, no," she said. "In fact, I want to be part of a canine unit someday."

"Okay, good," I said, "then I've got someone I'd like you to meet. Is there a park nearby?"

"There's a dog park just down the street."

"Even better," I said. We walked to my car, and Samson heard me coming. He sat up, clamoring for me to open the door.

"This is Samson," I said.

"Ooh," Emily cooed. "That must mean he's strong."

"Strong and very smart," I said.

I clipped on his leash and released him from his harness.

He danced around in a circle.

"Oh, he's a police dog!" Sergeant Hudson said.

"A very special police dog," I said.

"Samson, this is Emily and..." I looked up at Hudson.

"Kelly," Hudson said before I could finish my sentence.

"Emily and Kelly. They're going to take very good care of you, Samson. They're going to take you for a walk, get you some water." I handed Emily a red, collapsible water bowl. "And then get you a bite to eat."

"There's a food bowl and some kibble in the back," I told them, handing Kelly my keys. "I really, really appreciate this, Sergeant Hudson."

"Thank you, Captain," she replied.

"Oh," I said, "and he's very strong, but he heels if you ask him to. He was injured a couple of months ago, so I haven't let him run too much yet."

"This will be fun," Kelly said, turning to Emily. "Do you want to walk him first?"

Emily lit up as she took the leash from Kelly. "C'mon, Samson. Show me how strong you are," she said.

I went back inside and went looking for Joel. I found him in his office, up to his armpits in paperwork.

"D'you have a minute, Sheriff," I asked.

"For you, Kate? Always. What can I do for you?"

"I'm wondering if there is any space available," I said. "I need to interview the elder sister separately."

He smiled wanly, looking tired and harassed. "I really don't, Kate. I'm sorry. This has been a real mess, and it's going to be a long night."

"I know, and I'm sorry all this had to happen on your turf... And... there's something else. I have my K-9 with me, so I can't transport them all back to Chattanooga together."

He nodded. "Sergeant Hudson is assigned to you for

the duration. She can take a patrol car and follow you to Chattanooga."

"Thanks so much, Joel. I hope I can make it up to you sometime."

"Maybe you can let me take you to dinner sometime," he said, grinning.

"How about I take *you* to dinner? Maybe we'll both have a little downtime once our crises are over."

"Over?" He chuckled. "When is it ever over?"

"Sometimes they let me eat between cases," I said. "I'll give you a call in a day or two."

"Think you're going to wrap this up that quickly?"

"I certainly hope so. Mine is just a small part. Vice will be handling the rest."

His eyebrows went up. "You'll have to tell me all about it, sometime."

"For sure," I said. "But right now, if I ever get any time off, this will be the last thing I want to talk about."

"Understood," he said, still smiling.

We nodded goodbye, and I was off to find all the necessary parties.

32

Day 4, 10:25 p.m.

BACK INSIDE, I GRABBED A YOUNG OFFICER FROM THE break room and sent him to catch up to Sergeant Hudson, Emily and Sampson.

Me? I returned to the interview room.

"Sergeant Russell," I said upon entering the room. "Take a quick break."

He nodded and approached the door.

"We're going to transport them back to Chattanooga," I said. "I was having a problem with logistics, but I've got it covered now. You and I will take Matthew with us, and Sergeant Hudson will follow us with the girls."

"That works," Corbin said and stuck his head inside the room. "I'm going to get something to drink. Do either of you want anything?"

They both shook their heads, and Corbin said to me, "I'll be back soon; how about you? D'you want anything?"

"No. Thank you," I replied. "I'll brief them while you're gone. Don't be too long, okay?"

He nodded, turned and walked away.

I stepped inside the interview room and said, "Okay. Change of plans. We're going to transport you back to Chattanooga. We'll finish the interview there."

Matthew nodded and pinched the bridge of his nose between his finger and thumb. Then he looked at me and said, "I still don't know what I'm being accused of. You tell me I haven't been charged, but here I am—"

I put up my hand to stop him. "Please don't say anything else until Sergeant Russell returns."

The door opened and he stepped inside.

"That was quick," I said.

"I just went to the machines in the breakroom," he said. "The coffee is... well, it's not good."

"Par for the course," I said and glanced up at the cameras to make sure they were still on.

I nodded to Matthew. "I think I explained earlier, but let me be explicit. Somebody burned down your house. That's arson. Two people are dead; one of them as a result of the fire. That makes it a homicide."

"So, you're holding me on suspicion of arson and murder?"

I nodded. "Until we can prove that you didn't start the fire, yes."

He looked dumbfounded.

Charlotte spoke up. "I told you we knew nothing about the fire until we saw it on TV."

"So you say. But at least one of the victims was dead before the fire started. How long before the fire has not yet been determined."

"Homicide, then, at the very least?" Matt asked. "Where did you find the victims?"

"Both were found in the downstairs bedroom, as I think I told you before," I said.

"And you don't know who they are?" Charlotte asked.

"No!" I replied. "We know they're not your mom and dad. So where are they?"

They looked at each other. Matthew shrugged. Then they both looked at me.

"We don't know," Charlotte said.

"Could they have gone on vacation or something?" Corbin asked.

"No, but..." Matthew said, then stopped. Something had dawned on him. I could see it on his face.

He looked at his sister. She slowly shook her head, obviously knowing what he was thinking. But whatever it was, I could also tell he wasn't going to say anything more about it. Not then, anyway.

"So, if it's not them," he said, "who else could it be?"

I stared at him for a moment. He seemed... a little more confident.

Hmm, I thought. *I wonder... It's worth a shot.*

"I talked to Sandy at the Green Lane—"

He literally froze. He bit his bottom lip. His eyes opened wide. *There we go,* I thought. *Got him.*

"She was concerned that no one had seen any of you, or Terry, since Saturday," I continued. "Oh, and Tina—Tiana—wants her Tahoe back."

He didn't answer. He continued to bite his bottom lip. I looked at Charlotte. Her face had lost its color.

Seeing him tense when I mentioned Tiana's name, I said, "She hasn't seen her friend, Amelia Arvina, either."

Charlotte wriggled in her seat, bent forward a little,

and turned her head to the wall, her lips clamped. I could tell she was bursting to say something.

A deputy knocked and came in. "Sergeant Hudson has returned with Emily and the dog."

"Good," I said. "Thank you, Deputy. Have Hudson bring them here, please."

He nodded and left. I turned to Corbin and said, "Get Matthew transferred to our car."

Corbin nodded, stood, walked around the table and said," Stand up, please, Matthew."

He stood. Corbin cuffed his hands behind his back, then said, "Let's go, son." And they left, leaving me alone with Charlotte.

"I can't have Emily here when I'm talking to you," Charlotte whispered.

"I understand," I said. "We'll have to deal with that when we get back to Chattanooga. I'll have your Aunt Rhonda come to pick her up."

"Before she gets here, though," Charlotte said. "I want to tell you this. I think Tiana's missing friend Amelia may be one of the fire victims."

"And if you knew nothing about the fire, why do you think that?"

Charlotte swallowed. "Because she was in bed with my dad when we left."

It was at that point Sergeant Hudson came in with Emily, so Charlotte stopped talking and looked at me.

"It's okay," I said. "We'll talk when we get to Chattanooga."

She nodded.

"You and Emily will ride with Sergeant Hudson. Sergeant Russell and Matthew with me."

"Awww," Emily said. "I don't get to sit next to Samson? Can he come with us?"

I smiled. "I wish he could, but his safety harness is in my car, so he has to stay with me. Sorry."

She nodded, looking disappointed.

"You'll have a chance to see him again when we get back to Chattanooga, okay?" I said. "Now, how about you and Charlotte go and sit on that little bench right there in front of this door for a moment, please. I need to talk with Sergeant Hudson."

Emily nodded.

I turned to Hudson while keeping an eye on the two girls.

"I'm sorry you have to make this trip," I said, "but I'm really glad it's you." I turned a little more inward to shield my mouth from the girls.

"How does Emily seem?"

Kelly narrowed her eyes and gave me an inquisitive look.

"Have you seen any signs that she may have been abused?" I asked.

Now her eyebrows went up. "None. She seems like a really smart and well-adjusted little girl."

I nodded slowly. "Seems like she's the only one in the Daniels family who hasn't, then. I don't think there's any need to cuff Charlotte, but that's up to you."

Sergeant Hudson nodded. "We'll be ready to leave whenever you are."

I nodded. "Thanks again."

A deep voice resonated through the hallway. "Hey, darlin'. What'd you do? Are they keepin' you overnight? You can share our cell. Hell, you can even sleep in my cot."

I looked out just in time to see a huge bald guy, half a foot taller than me, with a neck like a tree trunk, grab himself and thrust his hips at Charlotte.

Charlotte turned to me with a horrified look on her face.

"You sick son of a bitch. What's the matter with you?" I said. He turned toward me and made the same gesture.

There were three of them being escorted along the corridor, presumably to the cells, escorted by two smiling deputies.

"I'll get the girls out of here right now," Hudson said, pushing past me.

"I'm sorry, Charlotte," I said.

She shrugged. "I'm used to it."

There was nothing else I could say, so I nodded, turned to Hudson and said, "Come on. I'm ready to go." And I did.

Outside, the humidity hit me like a bucketful of warm water. I looked up at the sky. I couldn't see a single star. *There's a storm brewing, I bet.*

I walked over to where Sergeant Hudson was waiting in her patrol car with the girls. She had the windows open.

"You girls try to get some sleep," I said. "It's about two and a half hours back to Chattanooga, so that should give you some time to take the edge off."

Charlotte nodded. She looked exhausted.

Corbin had brought the car around to where I was, with Matthew and Samson both in the back seat. Matthew had his head back and his eyes closed.

"Forward ho," I said, climbing into the passenger seat.

"Are you sure you don't want to drive?" Corbin asked.

"Nope!" I said. "It's all yours. Feel that humidity? See that blank, black sky? I'll give you odds that we'll run into a storm before we get home."

"You might be right," he said.

I hated driving in the rain, especially at night.

"You okay back there, Matthew?" I asked. "Hope you don't mind the dog."

"Would it matter if I did?"

I looked back at him and saw his wrists had been cuffed and attached to a steel ring between his legs. It would be uncomfortable for him, no doubt, but as unlikely as it seemed, all we needed was one of us to get clunked in the head from behind. I smiled to myself. Of course *Samson would easily have taken care of that*.

WE WERE about a half hour out of Chattanooga when the storm broke loose. The rain lashed the windshield, and the wipers could barely keep up. Pockets of wind pushed the car toward the hard shoulder, and Corbin had to grip the wheel tightly to keep the car on the road.

I looked back at Samson. Storms always unnerved him, but not like they did some dogs. He just panted more and whined a bit, but he kept his eyes glued outside the window. Now and then he would quiver.

"Your dog's afraid of storms?" Matthew asked.

"Not afraid," I replied. "Just a little nervous." I turned in my seat and looked at him. "How about you?" I asked.

"Nah. Not so much."

I turned back to stare out through the rain-washed windshield.

A few miles further on, I turned to look at him again and smiled. Matthew was sound asleep. So was Samson, his head on Matthew's thigh. And I thought to myself, *If Samson knows who the bad guys are, then he must know who the good guys are, too.*

And I hoped, for Matt's sake, that was true.

33

Day 5, 1:30 a.m.

IT WAS JUST AFTER ONE-THIRTY AND THE RAIN HAD stopped when we arrived at the PD and parked at the rear of the building.

Corbin turned off the engine, laid his head back against the headrest, and heaved an audible sigh of relief.

"Made it," he said.

"Yes, thank you," I said. "Let's get them inside."

I got out of the car. I, too, was glad to be back in familiar surroundings. I opened the rear door, let Samson out and told him to stay, then I released Matthew and helped him out.

As always, the building was ablaze with light; the PD never sleeps. I key-carded the door and escorted Matthew inside, followed by Corbin, then Sergeant Hudson and the two girls.

I made them comfortable in two interview rooms then I went to freshen up. Fortunately, I always kept a spare set of clothing in my locker, so I let Samson into my office, then took a quick shower and headed out again to find Chief Johnston waiting for me outside the locker room.

"Kate," he said. "You're back."

"Chief?" I said. "What on earth are you doing here at this ungodly hour?"

"So, you brought them in," he said. "Everything went well, I presume?"

"Yes, sir. No problems at all."

"But no sign of Knowles?"

"No, sir. Not yet."

"Well, I'm glad you're back," he said, half turning to leave, then changed his mind and said, "Anything else? If not, I'll see you in my office in the morning. You can give me a full report then."

"I'm good, Chief," I replied. "See you in the morning... Around eleven?"

He nodded. "Eleven will be fine. Have a good rest of the night, Captain." And he turned again and left me standing there, still wondering what the hell he was doing there at almost two in the morning.

I shook my head, then went to find Kelly. She was waiting for me in the interview room with the girls. Corbin was in a second room with Matthew.

I told them I needed a minute, then went to my office.

As I walked through the situation room, I got another surprise. Tracy Ramirez was at her desk.

"Tracy," I said. "What are you doing here?"

"Corbin called me and said you were bringing the girls in and that you might need some help. So here I am."

"Well how cool is that?" I said. "Thanks, Tracy. That

means I can get Sergeant Hudson settled somewhere so she can get a few hours sleep before she heads back to Jacksboro. Have you met her?"

"Yep," Tracy said. "Already met her."

"Have you heard anything from Mrs. Mackabee?"

"Yep. She had a friend bring her in. She's waiting for you downstairs."

I stopped by the first interview room, where Corbin waited with Matthew, and poked my head in the door.

"This shouldn't take long," I said. "I don't want to keep you up all night, and the sooner you cooperate, Matthew, the sooner we can make other arrangements for you. Corbin, I'll join you in a minute."

Corbin nodded.

I was purposely vague on what those other arrangements might be. They depended on what we found out during the interviews.

Next, I went to the interview room where Sergeant Hudson was waiting with the girls.

"Emily, your Aunt Rhonda is waiting downstairs in the lobby to take you home with her."

"I don't want to go anywhere without Charlotte," Emily snapped.

"I understand," I said. "But we're going to talk about some serious stuff here, and it would just bore you."

"No, it wouldn't. I know the kinds of things you're going to talk about, and it involves me, too."

I'll bet you do, I thought.

"And you said I could see Sampson again tonight."

I smiled. Grown-up one minute and a child the next.

"I did," I said, "but I want you to go with your aunt and get some rest first. I'll have her bring you back in the morning. I need to talk to you, too. Samson will be here all day, and you can likely spend some time with him."

"Likely?"

"Okay, you can spend some time with him."

"All right," she said, obviously annoyed.

I smiled and held the door open for her, and just as she got to the door, she turned to Charlotte and wagged her finger at her, shaking her head. *What on earth was that about?* I wondered.

I looked at Charlotte and said, "Sergeant Hudson is coming with me. The door locks from both sides, inside and out, so you're safe in here, and I'll be right back."

Charlotte nodded, then looked down at the table.

"Oh, and Charlotte," I said. "Sergeant Ramirez will join you in a minute. She'll be with me when we talk together, okay?"

She nodded.

I hoped I was doing the right thing. After Emily's little scene, I wondered if the three kids were ticking time bombs.

Then I turned to Kelly Hudson and said, "You're not planning on driving back to Jacksboro tonight, are you?"

"Not hardly. I thought I'd find a nearby motel and get some shuteye before I started back."

"I don't blame you. Talk to the receptionist down-stairs. She'll give you a voucher for a hotel room."

"Thank you, Captain," she said. "I appreciate that."

"And I appreciate all you've done for us, and for Emily. Thank you."

"No problem. I feel like I'm somehow invested now. Hopefully, you'll let me know how it all turns out."

I nodded, smiled, then said, "I will, but keep an eye

on the media. They'll probably know before I do," I said dryly.

"Will do," she said, smiling at my attempt at humor.

"It goes without saying, Kelly," I said, "that if there is ever anything I can do for you, you only have to ask." I handed her my card.

"Thanks, Captain Gazzara. I really appreciate it."

As soon as she had departed, I called downstairs to tell them about the voucher and that the Chief had approved it. It was just a little white lie; I knew he would have if I'd had the opportunity to ask him.

34

I WALKED BACK INTO THE SECOND INTERVIEW ROOM. Tracy was already there, and Charlotte was sitting comfortably at the table.

I checked that the two cameras were on and went through the identification and time procedure.

"Charlotte, I need you not to be embarrassed to tell Sergeant Ramirez and me whatever you need to. We know a lot about Green Lane and about the escorts. None of that matters right now. What we are most concerned with, as I explained earlier, is the arson and the homicides. For now, unless someone gives me reason to believe otherwise, I believe that none of you knew about the fire until after the fact. But what about the victims?

"You mentioned before we concluded the interview in Jacksboro that you thought you knew who one of the victims was."

She nodded.

"Who d'you think it is?"

"Tiana's friend, Amelia, was sleeping with my dad in the downstairs bedroom when we left."

"Sleeping?"

She looked at me now through narrowed eyes. "No, probably not sleeping. We used the noise as a cover for our escape."

"And what were you escaping from?" I asked.

"That's not an easy question to answer," she said.

"Tell me this, then," I said. "If the male victim is not your father, who do you think it might be? Were they in the habit of sleeping with multiple partners?"

"Hell, no," she said vehemently, "especially if the woman was Amelia. Amelia was Dad's and nobody elses. He went into a rage if anyone else tried to touch her."

"Is it possible somehow that your dad went out, and when he returned, there was somebody else in bed with her, so he killed the man and set the house on fire in his rage?"

"No," she said vehemently.

"How do you know that if you weren't there?"

She sat silently for some thirty seconds or so. I didn't interrupt her thoughts, though Tracy looked sideways at me. Then Charlotte looked up at me and said, "Were you straight with us when you said you only found two victims in the fire?"

"I was," I replied. "But what d'you mean?"

Now she sat for a longer time. I could tell her mind was racing faster than her heart.

"I don't know why I'm telling you this," she said at last. "Somehow, I'm afraid that it will go hard on Matthew if I don't. I wasn't kidding when I said it was just an accident, and I'm as much to blame for it as he is."

"Go on," I said. She seemed much calmer now; cool, almost aloof. It was as if she was two completely different people.

"Terry," she said. "You keep asking about Terry Knowles. He had been quarreling, even duking it out with both Dad and Matthew, over me. Terry had a bad habit of zeroing in on a woman, treating them like his girlfriend, pimping them out, then dumping them and moving on to the next relationship, if you want to call it that, while keeping their share of what they produced for the house. Most recently, he had designs on me.

"There was no way Dad or Matthew, either one, was about to let that happen. I wasn't one of the girls. Well, it made Terry furious. They argued. They fought. Terry made threats—"

"What kind of threats?" Tracy said, interrupting her.

I cut Tracy a look; we needed to let the kid keep talking.

"All kinds," Charlotte replied. "He threatened to kill Dad, to kidnap me, to beat Matthew senseless, just about every rotten threat anyone could make. He even threatened to cut me up once."

And then she stopped talking and began twisting her fingers together so hard I thought she might break them.

"So, what happened?"

"So, on Saturday night, Dad and Amelia were downstairs, and we all went to our own rooms. It was hard to just carry on with what we were doing when they were going at it... Sometime after midnight, I was asleep... more like dozing in and out. And then I heard a loud noise. I like to sleep with my window open a crack on cool nights. Anyway. The window slid up with a bang, and Terry kind of fell in my bedroom window."

Ah! I thought. *Now I get it. The boot prints and the trellis leaning up to the window.*

"At first, I was so stunned, I could barely move, but then I remembered him threatening to cut me up. That was when I started sleeping with this big ol' trophy under my bed. I tried to grab it, but he jumped on me and I couldn't. He tore the bed covering off and all I had on was this little nighty thing. I thought he was going to rape me.

"But that's when it all went crazy. Matt must have heard the noise because he rushed into my room, grabbed Terry by the collar of his coat and threw him sideways off the bed. He stumbled backwards, tripped and fell and hit his big, old head on the corner of my desk. I mean, he hit it really hard."

"And?" I asked.

"And... he was dead. I guess."

"So, that's why you and Matt decided to burn the house down?" I asked.

"No. How could you even think that?" she snapped. "There were other people in the house—Dad, Amelia, and we weren't sure whether Mom was there or not. No. We didn't mean to kill Terry, and we weren't about to make it worse by killing anybody else. Matt got the keys to the Tahoe out of Terrance's pocket, we woke Emily up, and we just left. That's it. Period. We don't know who started the fire or why."

I sat there, thinking, slowly nodding. "So, if you left Terry's body upstairs in your bedroom, what happened to it?"

She shrugged.

"I mean, do you think he could still have been alive and gone downstairs where he encountered your dad?"

"That would have been stupid," Charlotte said.

"But not impossible, right?" Tracy asked.

Charlotte nodded, then slumped back into her chair and covered her face with her hands.

"All right," I said and looked at my watch. It was almost three in the morning and I could tell Charlotte was exhausted. I know I was. "That's enough for tonight. Tracy, would you please take Charlotte down to the cafeteria vending machines and get her a sandwich and something to drink. Then prepare the couch in the family lounge. She can sleep there until morning. And please, keep an eye on her. I want no screwups at this late stage."

"Of course," Tracy said.

"Is there anything else I can wear?" Charlotte asked. "I've been in these same clothes for the last four days."

I looked at her tall, willowy shape and thought maybe some of my things would fit her. "Tell you what," I said. "I can't do it right away, so you'll have to sleep in what you have for one more night, but I'll go home and get something for you to wear. Okay?"

She started to smile.

"Okay, you're tall enough," I said. "But I have some clothes I haven't worn for a while." *In years*, I thought.

"That would be nice," she said. "I don't suppose there's much left of my clothes."

35

Day 5, 2:45 a.m.

I WAS IN NEED OF SOMETHING; WHAT, I DIDN'T KNOW.
I was totally knackered, as the Brits would say. I sure as
hell needed to catch my breath and think things through
before I went into the interview room and started in on
Matthew.

Charlotte had both surprised and mystified me. I'd
expected a tearful diatribe about the abuse she had
suffered at the hands of her father. Instead, she'd at least
confirmed that Knowles was dead... or did she? He was
looking more and more like the second unidentified
victim, but the fact he was killed upstairs... *Geez. What
happened to his body? How did it get downstairs and on the
bed? Is it even him? The crack on the desk would suggest it is.
But maybe not. Who's the female victim? Who set the fire, and
where the hell are Charlotte's parents?*

It would be interesting to see how—make that if—
Charlotte's and Matthew's stories matched, and to see if
they'd formulated a plan during their time in hiding.

Charlotte was mature, articulate and self-assured, which made it hard to believe she'd been sexually abused by her father over the past six years.

Then there were the strange mood changes... well, I'm not sure one could call them mood changes, but she was animated one moment and wrung out the next. Bipolar, maybe?

And then there was the strange little scene when Emily wagged her finger and shook her head at Charlotte. What was that about? A warning, no doubt, but for what? It was obvious she was warning her sister not to reveal too much. But why?

Hmm, maybe Matthew can plug some of the gaps and round out the wheel. Maybe then the story will come together.

Corbin and Matthew were seated opposite each other on either side of the table, looking bored out of their minds. Matthew certainly didn't act or look as though he was worried that the law was about to come down on his head, and that made me wonder if he really did have no reason to be. And, if he'd accidentally killed Knowles while defending his sister from a life-threatening attack, he was right.

I sat down beside Corbin, who reminded him of his rights, and I began.

"Matthew," I said. "I've talked to Charlotte and she's told me her story of what happened that night; now I'd like to hear yours."

He stared blankly for a minute, no doubt thinking I'd given him the opportunity to either save or hang himself.

"If they're not my mother and father," he said, finally, "I guess the female's Amelia Arvina."

"Why would you say that?" I asked.

"Because she's the only woman he ever had the guts to kick Mom out of bed for."

"You mean, she was the only woman your dad was unfaithful with?"

He chuckled and shook his head, then looked up at me and said, "Hell, no. Dad will screw anything that walks."

"Does that include your sister?" I asked.

A flash of anger crossed his face but was gone in an instant. "What I meant was," he said, "Amelia's the only one Dad ever brings home with him."

"You didn't answer my question, Matt, so I'll ask you again. Is your father sexually abusing Charlotte?"

"Did she tell you that?" he asked.

"What do you think?" I asked.

He looked down at the table for a moment, then nodded.

"Was that a yes?" I asked.

He nodded, then looked at me and said, "Yes, he was abusing her. Look, all I've ever done is try to protect my sisters. But until a few months ago, I had no way to do that. That's why I agreed to manage the Green Lane accounts, so I could keep them with me as much as possible. Big mistake. Terry Knowles went after my sister."

"Was that really a surprise?" I asked. "Green Lane is hardly a healthy environment for two young girls."

He rolled his eyes. "You think? Believe it or not, it was a healthier environment than our home."

"So, what happened to Terry?" I asked, changing tack.

Hesitantly, he told much the same story as Charlotte had, and it didn't sound rehearsed.

"So how do you think Terrance's body got from Charlotte's bedroom down to the master bedroom and then onto the bed?" I asked.

He pulled a face, shook his head and said, "I dunno. I really don't."

"Are you sure he was dead?" I asked. "Could he have recovered enough to make his way downstairs, and your dad killed him? Or maybe even escaped altogether?"

"No," he said. "He was dead. I checked his pulse. There wasn't one."

"That means nothing," Corbin said. "It could have been faint. You could have checked the wrong place. Only a nurse or a doctor can tell for sure... Who set the fire, Matt?"

"He was dead, I tell you... Wait, how d'you know it was arson and not accidental? Amelia smokes; did you know that?"

"Because whoever set the fire used an accelerant," Corbin said.

Matt looked at us both, his eyes growing bigger and bigger.

"But couldn't it have been random?" he asked, almost desperately. He shook his head and then looked at me and said, "The only other explanation is... My dad must..."

He looked wildly back and forth between me and Corbin.

"Must have what, Matt?" I asked.

"He must have brought Terry's body downstairs, laid him on the bed with Amelia, and set the fire."

I looked at him and said, "Amelia, if that's who the female victim is, wasn't dead when the fire started."

"*What?*" he shouted. "You can't be serious. She burned to death? Oh my God. Poor Amelia."

"I don't think she felt anything," I said, trying to ease the situation. "She was heavily drugged. How did that happen, d'you think?"

"I don't know," he said, shaking his head as he looked down at the table. "I don't know... I don't know." That last was said almost in a whisper.

I stared at him for a moment, then said, "Why would your father set the fire knowing Amelia was there?"

"Who the hell knows why my father does anything? A whim? Insanity? Stupidity?"

I glanced sideways at Corbin's notes.

"When Emily left the room tonight," I said. "she turned around and wagged her finger and shook her head at Charlotte. What was that about, d'you think? Was she trying to protect you?"

Matthew looked down and shook his head, seeming bewildered. Then he looked up at us.

"You know?" he said. "It's really strange how she can be so incredibly smart and so utterly dumb at the same time. Emily is a daddy's girl. He dotes on her, more than's healthy. Charlotte tried to talk to her about it." He paused for a second as if thinking it out, then continued, "Charlotte knows Dad's going to start on Emily pretty soon. She was twelve when he started abusing her. He doesn't do it now. She's too old. He likes them young. But Emily thinks Charlotte's lying and trying to get Dad into trouble. So what you saw was Emily warning Charlotte not to say anything."

I nodded. "You think that's dumb?" Corbin asked. "I'd call it willful ignorance."

I looked at Corbin and frowned. *Where the hell did that come from, I wonder?*

"Ha!" Matt said. "That's what I thought Mom's problem was until I realized that she's just plain dumb, too. She knows what's going on. She just won't do anything about it. That's why I have to protect them."

I wasn't going to argue with him. He was obviously disgusted with both his parents. And rightly so, in my humble opinion.

"Last questions and then we'll wrap it up for the night," I said with a sigh. "Where are they? Your parents?"

"If she isn't with Dad, I have no idea where Mom is. She wasn't there the night we left. But Dad?"

He frowned and narrowed his eyes as if searching for an answer or... how to avoid telling us the answer.

Suddenly, he clapped his hand down on the table and looked up at us.

"If my dad was lucid enough to know what he was doing when he set the fire... His boss, John Roberts, has a cabin out in the woods above a lake. He's used it lots of times before. That's the only place I can think of."

"Where is this cabin?" Corbin asked.

"Harrison, sort of," he replied. "If I could see a map, I could show you."

A map? Are you kidding me? They don't make those anymore.

"Corbin," I said. "Go get my laptop, please."

While Corbin was gone, I quickly asked myself two questions—one, why were these kids so eager to give their dad up, and two, why did I so readily believe them?

As to the second question, I figured it was because they'd filled in all the gaps and it all made sense. Little had been said about the sex trade entanglements by either of them. That was another can of worms all together and none of my concern. As to the first question, I had no idea except maybe they'd been so badly abused for so long that any love for their parents had turned to hatred.

We're close, I thought, *to catching our murderer. But so far, what little evidence we have is all circumstantial, and barely that.*

The kids had led us in the right direction, I was sure of that. But they weren't witnesses to any crimes except their own, and that was enough to cast doubt on everything they'd told us.

Corbin returned with the laptop and I pulled up Google Maps.

It turned out the cabin was in a wooded area off Champion Road, still within the city limits, thank God.

36

Day 5, 4:00 a.m.

"WE SHOULD ALL GO HOME NOW AND GET SOME
sleep," I said, some fifteen minutes later when the three
of us, Corbin, Tracy and me, were gathered in my office.
It was almost four AM and I was beat, and we had to be
awake and alert early in the morning to go to the cabin
and see what we could flush out. "What d'you think?" I
asked. "Meet back here at... say, eight?"

Corbin looked at his watch. "I guess. Three hours
ought to do it. Sounds good to me."

IT WAS four-twenty-five when I pulled into my driveway
that Wednesday morning. That gave Samson and me
time to flop for a couple of hours' rest.

I let Samson out into the backyard, waited for him to
return, then closed up and hit the bed. I asked my clock

to wake me at seven, and that was my last conscious thought for the next two hours.

I woke to the exhilarating sound of a Celtic harp. *Geez,* I thought as I groped for the clock, *I need to change that.*

Ten minutes of yoga while Sammy was outside, five to shower, and five more to grab a good cup of coffee and a toaster pastry—old habits die hard—and we were on our way by seven-thirty. I radioed in that I would be there in twenty minutes.

By eight, Corbin, Jack, Hawk, Tracy, Cooper, and Samson and I were out the door, in our cars and on Amnicola Highway, heading north to Highway 58 and the Roberts' cabin. *And where does he fit into all this?* I couldn't help but wonder as Corbin turned onto 153. It would be some time before I got a definitive answer to that question.

WE PARKED some one hundred yards from the cabin. I grabbed Samson's leash, and we headed toward the structure on foot.

The cabin was a modest affair—log-built, three bedrooms, etc.—surrounded by dense woodland. While we were still in a thicket and hidden from the cabin, I signaled for Jack and Hawk to go around to the back.

The rest of us walked slowly up to the cabin—weapons drawn—and up the three steps onto the porch. Corbin knocked and we both stood to one side—Corbin to the left and me and Tracy to the right—and we waited.

There was no response, but we knew someone had to

be there because a sporty red Mercedes convertible was parked alongside the cabin to the left. It had a Robert's Auto Circus frame around the license plate.

Corbin pounded on the door again. "Open up, Mr. Daniels. It's the police. We know you're in there."

Two minutes later, the door flew open and we were face to face with a Sig Sauer pistol.

We raised our weapons. Samson growled.

Daniels took two steps back and aimed the pistol at Samson. How dare he! I hurled myself at the man's chest. Daniels went down like he'd been hit with a baseball bat. The gun flew out of his hand. Corbin jumped on him, too, and together we rolled him over and slapped the cuffs on him.

Somewhere toward the back of the house, I could hear Jack on his radio, calling for an ambulance. And I knew it wasn't for Daniels.

We hauled Daniels up into a sitting position and Samson stood over him, growling.

Corbin helped get Daniels to his feet while I went to see what was happening further on inside the cabin. I found Jack in the living room, kneeling beside a woman lying stretched out on the floor.

"She's alive," he said, "but her pulse is weak. An ambulance is on the way."

I knew from the photos in Rhonda Mackabee's house it was Stacey Daniels.

I turned to look at Pete Daniels. "Why'd you do it?" I asked. "Killing Amelia wasn't enough?" By then, both Tracy and Hawk had joined us. Cooper was still outside on the front porch.

He shrugged. "She's a total pain in the ass. She was

gloating because I killed Amelia. Silly bitch. Amelia meant everything to me."

"Then why did you kill Amelia?" I asked.

"She was going to leave me! Said she'd saved up money and was getting out of the business. That she'd met someone else who wanted to give her a better life." Pete's face had turned bright red with anger. "I wasn't about to let her leave. She was mine! And besides, she knew too much."

There were plenty of witnesses to his confession this time. Better yet, Tracy held up her cell phone and wagged it at me.

At first, I didn't know what she was doing, but then I realized she'd recorded the entire encounter from our approach right up until and after my exchange with Daniels. I could have kissed her.

I turned back to face him. "Peter Daniels, I am arresting you on suspicion of the murder of Amelia Arvina and the attempted murder of your wife, Anastasia Daniels." And then I read him his rights, after which Tracy and Coop walked him out.

I heard the ambulance coming up the road. I looked back at Jack, but he just pursed his lips and shook his head.

Make that two murders, you sick son of a bitch.

Me? I felt terrific until I realized it would fall to me to tell the kids.

I called Anne Robar. "Anne," I asked, "would you take a uniformed officer and go to Robert's Auto Circus and ask John Roberts if he knows Pete's whereabouts and wait for the answer? If he says he doesn't know, arrest him for aiding and abetting and obstruction of justice."

"Will do, Cap," she said. "We'll be on our way right now."

The ambulance arrived, followed by backup officers. They immediately began to cordon off the scene.

I put Sammy back in the car.

Stacy didn't make it. When the EMTs brought out Stacey's body, I stopped them, pulled back the sheet and looked at her face. She must have been quite pretty once, but the pills and alcohol and all she must have been through over the years had taken their toll. *Well, she's at peace now*, I thought as I covered her face again.

My team and I stood and talked for a few minutes while the uniforms finished securing the scene.

"I realize this has little to do with anything concerning us," Jack said. "But my deep dive into the dark web did reveal that there are many layers to the sex trafficking thing. Even the Nashville operation is small potatoes compared to some of it. I'll make a full report and turn it over to Vice."

"How about Roberts?" I asked.

Jack nodded. "As far as I can tell, he's the driving force behind the Green Lane operation and the escort service and—it gets murky here—there's some suggestion he and Daniels were into some kind of kiddy sex trafficking operation. I don't have all the details yet, but I will."

"Just give me a chance to go over your report before you turn it in, and make copies for the chief."

By the time we got back to the station, they were already processing Pete Daniels, but I asked them to put him in holding until I got Matthew out of the cell block. I didn't want them to see each other.

I was informed that Charlotte was up and had had

breakfast in the family lounge, and that Matthew, too, was up and restlessly pacing his cell.

I had him brought to the family room to join his sister, and I told them both what had happened. It wasn't pleasant.

"He killed my mother?" Charlotte wailed. And she crumpled into a heap on the couch, sobbing. Matthew simply stood there, his eyes closed, saying nothing. And I couldn't help but wonder what he must be thinking.

After all, when you think about it, who did Charlotte have to turn to? An aging aunt and a high-class escort? *Thank God she still has Matthew.*

I was determined to make sure he didn't serve a day.

And he didn't, though Larry Strange, the DA assigned to the case, and Terrance's father, the ambassador, took some convincing that Knowles' death was an accident.

Anyway, by the time I'd finished talking to Matthew and Charlotte, Rhonda Mackabee had arrived with Emily. I brought her up to speed, then asked her to let Matthew and Charlotte break the news to Emily.

37

December 20th, 10 a.m.

IT WAS DECEMBER 20, THE DAY MATTHEW WAS TO BE freed. Just in time for Christmas.

Larry Strange had offered him a plea deal: Involuntary manslaughter, time served and five years' probation. In return, he was to give evidence against his father and John Roberts. And so, after nearly four months in the county lock up, they turned him loose into the arms of his sisters and aunt.

Charlotte had gone to stay with her aunt while he was inside, but with money she'd saved, she was able to rent an apartment for herself and Matthew in a nice location close to Chattanooga State Community College.

I had no idea how things had gone with Emily. I'd seen her at her mother's funeral. She'd called Samson's name and waved at him but ignored me completely. I'm sure she blamed me for putting her father away where she couldn't visit him. They had sent him up to Knox

County to await his trial because we didn't want him anywhere near Matthew, who was in the Hamilton County jail.

As to the Green Lane and the other related operations, Henry and his vice squad had finally decided to clean it up.

Was there someone in the department looking after them? We'll probably never know. Ongoing investigations and all that baloney.

Further investigation had resulted not only in sex trafficking charges for Peter Daniels and John Roberts, but they were also linked to a club where children were used for sex.

I had no doubt that Pete Daniels was going away for the rest of his life, but I *did* doubt that it would be a very long life. Slimeballs like him have a way of dying unnatural deaths, especially when they're labeled "kiddie diddlers."

And so I closed the case. Chief Johnston called me into his office the next morning, congratulated me and gave me the rest of the week off—five days off. Wow.

I smiled at him as I said, "Thanks, Chief, but you and I both know the chances of that happening are nothing less than zero."

He smiled at me and told me to go home, which I did.

The vet had released Sammy two days later, saying he was now at full strength and had full range of motion in his shoulder. As for me, it was great to have my running companion back.

And talking about running, I'd tried to run with my nosy neighbor Brad a couple of times, but it was really difficult for me to have a conversation with a guy who wanted to talk about nothing but blighted trees or a new species of voles.

Now as far as that tall drink-of-water, Trooper John, was concerned, he was someone I could enjoy talking to. And the fact that we lived three hours apart was a big, fat bonus.

Author's Note:

I titled this story Charlotte, not because she was the central character in the story but because I think she would have been the one who suffered the most. It really is her story. She was abused sexually, mentally and physically.

Was Charlotte based on a true story? Yes, of course it was, and not just one true story, but thousands. Charlotte's story is played out by young women and children every day, all across the nation, and this book is dedicated to them. Bless you everyone.

Blair Howard.
June 2023.

KEEP READING FOR A LOOK INSIDE MY NEWEST SERIES!

THANK YOU FOR TAKING THE TIME TO READ CHARLOTTE. THE SEVENTEENTH BOOK IN THE SPIN-OFF SERIES OF NOVELS FEATURING LIEUTENANT KATE GAZZARA. THE NEXT BOOK IN THIS SERIES IS IN THE WORKS AND WILL BE AVAILABLE SOON.

WHILE YOU WAIT, CHECK OUT THE FIRST BOOK IN MY NEWEST SERIES, THE RANDALL AND CARVER MYSTERIES!

'So it seems that Blair Howard can just write anything and hook you.. Mallory is just as much as a spitfire as Kate is.. I think her and Tucker are going to give criminals a run for their money.. Kept me interested and guessing till the end.. Can't wait for the next one.' - C. Curry

Click the image to read a sample of Never Say Dead or flip the page

A LOOK INSIDE

Never Say Dead

A Randall And Carver Mystery

Book One

By

Blair Howard

1

Monday Evening

MALLORY CARVER LEANED BACK AGAINST THE BAR counter and stared up at the water stains on the ceiling.

She didn't know how long they'd been there. She'd worked at The Saloon since... she specifically remembered the help wanted sign had appeared in October after she graduated high school, but she didn't apply until after Thanksgiving. And only then because she needed to get out of the house for a few hours each day. But the part-time job turned full-time, and...

Thirteen years later and I'm wondering if I can sell pictures of the ceiling for Rorschach tests, she thought.

She imagined a decade of drunks staring up at them, some seeing their mothers, others seeing their dogs. Maybe some saw a traumatic childhood event; *those would be the drunks that cried into their beer,* she thought.

She'd seen every kind of drunk you could imagine during her thirteen years at The Saloon.

Back in the day, when she was first hired, it had been

the Old West Saloon and Cattle Grill. It was a nice place then—fun music, good, inexpensive beer, an attractive menu, and even some coin-op horses out front for the kids to ride. Then the owner died, and it became Mustang Sally's. Sally kept the entire staff, which had been a relief, and she'd been a good boss and had treated everyone well. But then she'd had an emergency and moved out of state. After that it became the Quick Draw, an apt name since people didn't stay long when they found out how much the drinks cost. And now it was The Saloon, where the drinks were cheap because they were cheap drinks. The speaker system was old, dating from Sally's time, but she and the live music were long gone. And Vinnie, who'd owned the place for the last six years, cared more about the pennies he pinched than he did complaining customers.

It's a hole. And I can't dig my way out, she thought gloomily.

She looked at the clock. It was a little before nine PM—what once was peak hour—but the only customers she had was a booth full of bikers drinking the most tasteless domestic beer they had on tap, and Art Peters ensconced at the end of the bar with his sleep apnea.

"If we don't have any business, I guess I might as well start cleaning up," she muttered, slipping an earbud under her long blond hair and starting her favorite podcast.

She felt that familiar thrill at the clanking sound of the clock tower and the bong of the hour as Devin Rudd began his podcast. "Not every terrible tale begins with a terrible event. Many times, the most mundane happenings can lead to the most horrific murders. This, then, is the story of a man who wished to be an art student, and what his desires wrought for those around him. This, then, is another... *Dark Tiding*."

As the music began, she wondered who it was going to be this time. As Devin Rudd began to describe the idyllic setting in which the killer grew up, she stepped around the end of the bar, collected the bus bin and hauled it off to the dishwasher.

Where could she be? she wondered as she filled the dishwasher and pulled down the hatch. *It was just a routine hike.* As the water began sloshing around inside the washer, she tried to concentrate on the podcast. She'd missed the name of the killer—something mundane, someone she'd never heard of, which was unusual. She thought she knew them all; all those of any note, anyway.

The door buzzer jangled. She hurried back out to see who it was, but it was only the bikers leaving, a half-pitcher of warm beer on the table along with a ten-dollar bill. *At least I don't have to deal with them at closing time.*

Why hasn't she called her mom? It's been six days. Maybe she's lying hurt in a gully somewhere. She pushed the thought away. She had to work.

She grabbed another bus bin and walked over to clear the table, wrinkling her nose at the lingering smell of strong tobacco. *I don't mind the smell of tobacco, but that stuff reeks.* She waved a hand at the invisible odors, but they persisted. She hurriedly scraped the last of the paper trash into the bin and turned to flee the stink, but found herself facing Deputy Kal Cundiff.

"Evening, Mallory," Kal said.

She stopped, startled, the bus bin on her hip. Outside, the sound of motorcycles revving broke the silence.

"Oh, hi, Kal," she said, frowning. "I didn't hear you come in."

"That's because you're filling your ears with garbage," he said and smirked. "Who are you listening to tonight? Ed Gein? Ted Bundy? Or is it a five-part series on Charlie Manson?"

"It's not like that," she lied as she marched past him. But when she dropped the bin out back, she paused the podcast, slipped the bud out of her ear and into her pocket, and returned to her place behind the bar.

"All right," she said. "What brings you in here tonight? And in uniform? Don't tell me your dad has decided to take us seriously."

"Nah," Kal said and pulled a face, unable to look her in the eye. "The Sheriff's office has decided it doesn't qualify as a missing person's case."

"How can that be?" she insisted. "A person just has to be missing for more than forty-eight hours. Julie's been missing for *six days*."

"Mal," he said plaintively, "this isn't one of those podcasts you listen to."

"Screw you, Kal," she snapped back. "Julie is a responsible young woman. She's an experienced hunting guide. She knows the trails like the back of her hand. Ever since Jared got hurt, she's been the dependable rock of the family. She wouldn't just... fly off and disappear without telling someone. It's not in her nature."

"Well, you know... sometimes the pressure builds up," Kal said in his best TV-cop voice. "All that responsibility, helping to run the business and all. And she decides to up and take a crazy vacation. It happens all the time. She'll be back. Mal, we never found her car, not at any of the trailheads. Not everything is some stupid criminal murder conspiracy."

"Is that what you think of me, Kal Cundiff? You think I'm bitching about my missing niece because I listened to a story?" She stepped around the end of the bar and stopped in front of him, using every inch of her five-foot-ten to loom over him. "My sister, Jennifer," she continued, "and my entire family is halfway to mourning because they think she might be lying dead up there in the forest somewhere, and all you can do is make sick remarks."

"Look, Mal, I'm sorry," Kal said, his face turning a rosy hue.

Mallory stepped back behind the bar and slammed down the hatch with a bang.

"Really?" she snapped. "You're sorry. Your dad is sorry. And my sister is at home crying over her missing daughter, and your department doesn't seem to care at all. Was there any other reason you stopped by to see me? If not, I have to close up, so you need to leave."

Kal reached around and pulled out a notebook from his hip pocket. "Okay. I was out of line, and I apologize. As it happens, I'm here to get a few details. Since you fancy yourself an amateur detective, you probably have them all memorized, right?"

She wanted to glare at him, slap the mocking smile off his face, but there was a sliver of hope: *Is he finally going to take it seriously?*

"Where do you want me to start?" she asked.

"You can gimme the basics first," he replied, his pen poised.

"Her name is Julie Romero. She's twenty-three, five-eight, slim, one-hundred-twenty-two pounds, with blonde, shoulder-length hair. She had her dog, Tobin, with her. Her parents have lived in Chattanooga for the last forty-four years. My sister, Jennifer, her mother, told me that she left last Tuesday morning for a hike on Red Grove Trail, off Highway 64; she didn't know which branch."

"Yeah, I heard," he said. "Red Grove. She oughta know better than to go into the forest up there by herself."

"And why not?" she asked, giving him an annoyed glare. "She's an experienced guide."

She knew that many of the locals had some wild ideas about the mountains and the Cherokee National Forest. And, while there were plenty of real-life dangers associated with walking through forests and mountains, centuries of Native American folklore and campfire stories had convinced half the population that the place was crawling with eldritch deities, dark forces commanded by witches, ghosts, territorial moonshiners, and cannabis and mandrake farmers. Most of it was bunk as far as she was concerned, but Kal didn't look too eager to check out the forbidding forest.

"Look, Julie isn't just some hiker," she said. "She's an experienced hunting guide. She works for her dad, Jared Romero, at his big hunting outlet off 64. She doesn't just get lost in her own backyard."

"Experienced hikers can and do get lost," Kal argued. "Happens all the time."

"Not Julie," she snapped. "If she was going to be late back, she'd have texted her father. What about her Bronco? That wouldn't just get lost, too, would it?"

"We've had an APB out for almost a week," Kal replied. "If nobody's found it, it means it's left the county. And with no evidence to the contrary, it looks like she drove it away."

Mallory opened her mouth to speak, but Kal beat her to it.

"Let me ask you something, Mal. Do you want to be here? In Chattanooga?"

Mallory paused.

"Because you just said she's lived here basically her whole life," he continued. "She's never been anywhere else. Never seen the big cities. Never tasted life outside of town or even outside her own family. How happy was she working for her dad?"

Mallory knew that Julie was frustrated with her dad at times. But she always smiled at everything... but was there pain behind that smile? Longing? Frustration?

How long had Mallory wanted to just pack up and leave? When exactly had *she* decided to stay? She had a sharp mind and a good education, with a 4.0 grade point average. Why did she stay? Why would Julie stay? *Because it's home. That's why.*

"See?" Kal said righteously when she didn't reply. "I knew you'd understand. Just give her another week and she'll come rolling back into town, apologize for being so thoughtless, and then brag about her big adventure in Nashville."

A part of Mallory wanted to believe him. It was an easy out, and it fulfilled all the criteria: Julie was safe. She was having a little reckless fun. Everything would be fine.

But it didn't answer the real questions, the ones her family kept asking. *Why* did she? *How* could she? *Where* is she? Why hasn't she called? And why is her phone off?

"We're not going to agree on this, Kal," Mallory said

sadly. "I guess we just don't understand each other. It isn't personal. No one will listen to us, so Jennifer is going to do something about it herself."

Kal looked alarmed. "You don't mean she's going to go trekking up there her own self? That's insane. She does that, we'll have a real missing person's case on our hands."

"No, she's not going to do that. She's not stupid, Kal. She said she's going into the city tomorrow. Though, I suppose she might have lied to us and planned to run away into the woods instead."

"What's she gonna do, then?" Kal demanded.

"She's going to hire Tucker Randall," Mallory said.

"*What?* That overpriced PI who takes on, what, three or four cases a year? Your family is seriously going to put trust in that hack?"

"We haven't been seeing any results from your department so far, have we?" Mallory said.

"Tucker Randall is a publicity hound," Kal replied. "He'll suck you dry and leave you looking stupid while he parades around on TV."

"Better stupid than useless." Mallory saw that her jibe had hit its mark.

"Well, I've got to get going," Kal said and stuffed the notepad back in his pocket.

"Get it all down, did you?" Mallory asked, smirking, knowing he hadn't written a word.

Kal rolled his shoulders, adjusted his belt, looked at her and said, "Good luck with Randall, but I ain't holding my breath." As he opened the door, he threw one last shot. "If he even takes the case, which I sincerely doubt he will."

Mallory resisted the urge to throw something at the

door. Instead, she stomped to the other end of the bar and gave Art a little shove. "Come on, Art. It's closing time. Do I need to call your brother?"

"What?" Art looked at her, then scrunched up his face as he tried to focus. "Nah-uh-uh. I'm good. I'll get home just fine."

I hope Julie gets home just fine, too.

2

Tuesday Morning 9am

IT WAS JUST BEFORE NINE AND A BEAUTIFUL MORNING, though Tucker Randall ignored the sunlight streaming in through slats in the window blinds as he studied the open manila folders spread across his desk. His eyes flickered over forensic photos and police reports, but the file he was most interested in was the Nebraska case, the one he was tapping with the fingertips of his left hand. He was pretty certain it would be the most interesting of the six cases, but he wanted to make his decision with more than just a hunch and a fee.

He turned his attention to the case in Jacksonville, Oklahoma. *If I take this one, Nate will start bugging me to visit his kids again...*

The door opened, and his assistant poked her head inside and said, "Mr. Randall?"

"What is it, Debbie?" he asked, hoping she wasn't feeling chatty.

"You have a call on line one. It's your brother."

"Speak his name, and he shall appear," he muttered as he picked up the phone. "Nate," he said. "How's my favorite brother?"

"Your only brother. At least that's what Mom says," Nate replied.

"You know," Tucker said. "Technically, I'm not open yet. So I'm going to add an inconvenience charge to your bill, and—"

"Haha. Very funny," Nate replied. "I figured you'd still be in bed. I figured you'd be jet-lagged?"

"Nate, it was LA, not India. I lose more sleep than that on an average night."

"See, Tucker, this is what I'm talking about. You just throw yourself into these things with no regard for your health. Take a week off. Come out here to Tulsa. It's Ella's birthday on Saturday, and Laura's making a strawberry cake. The kids would love to see you."

"While I do enjoy Laura's cooking," Tucker replied, "I don't think I'll have time." He picked up the Jacksonville file and set it aside. "Besides, you're the family man, not me."

"You can say that again. Mom's losing hope on that one." Nate sighed—and a crackle of static burst in Tucker's ear. "So you won't come to Ella's party?"

"I'll be in Nebraska," Tucker replied. "It has everything I like in a case, and they still have snow up there."

"Why do you do this to yourself?" Nate asked, exasperated.

"Obviously, because I like it. Otherwise, I wouldn't," Tucker replied. "What are you talking about, exactly?"

"Your MO. This thing you have about taking only one case at a time. I'm a cop, and you and I both know it can take months to close a case. You're limiting yourself,

Tucker, and you know you have more to offer, no matter whose hat you're wearing."

"I don't wear hats." Tucker paused. He could hear voices in the next room. Debbie was talking to someone. *A client? Arguing? No, two clients. Why are they raising their voices?*

"Tucker? You still there?" Nate asked.

"Yeah, I'm here. Just hold on a sec. Someone's in the outer office."

The arguing in the other room continued. *What the hell?*

His door opened, and two people burst in, a man and a woman.

"Tucker? Is this still about Marsha?"

"Sorry, Nate. I have to go. Clients. I'll call you later, okay?" And he hung up the phone before Nate could dredge up the past, again.

Whoever they are, they have a cosmic sense of timing.

"I'm sorry, Mr. Randall," Debbie said, flustered. "I tried to tell them you're not accepting new clients, but they wouldn't listen. They shoved past me. Do you want me to call the police?"

"No. Please don't call the police," the woman said, obviously distressed. "If you'll just hear us out. Give us five minutes, and then we'll leave. I promise."

He stood and looked at the couple. The first thing he realized was that the man was taller than he was. He had to be at least six-four. He towered over poor Debbie.

But that wasn't all. They both had that desperate look in their eyes, and there was also something about the woman. Something he couldn't quite place. She looked familiar. *I've seen her somewhere before, but where?*

"Please, have a seat," he said. "Thank you, Debbie. I don't think we'll need the police."

"I'm really sorry," the woman said as she sat down. "We're not normally this pushy. I mean, I've never—"

"There's no need to apologize," Tucker said. "Tell me about your problem, and I'll tell you if I can help."

She nodded, took a deep breath, and began, "I'm Jennifer Romero, and this is my husband, Jared. Our daughter, Julie, is missing. She went hiking, and she didn't return. We're hoping you can find her."

"Your daughter," Tucker said. "Is she an experienced hiker?"

"She's experienced," Jared said. "She works for me as a hunting and fishing guide. She knows the forest better than anyone I know. I own Romero's Outdoors out on 64, as you probably know. She's been hiking the trails since I carried her on my back when she was a kid."

By then, Tucker was only half listening to them. It was a missing person case, and he hated those. He'd spent more time during his years in the FBI chasing wayward kids than he cared to remember, and he was already regretting agreeing to listen to them.

In his mind, he was already setting up shop in a cabin in Northern Nebraska. He could smell the rich scent of crackling pine in the fireplace and taste the heat of strong black coffee on a cold morning.

He made a mental note to ask Debbie to check for the next available flight as he listened to Jared drone on about his daughter. Tucker told himself that as soon as they were done talking, he'd politely decline their business and refer them to another private investigator, but then he caught something Jennifer said that jerked him out of his reverie.

"...she went out to hike one of the trails, one that she's walked a hundred times, but she never came back. She didn't call. Her phone goes straight to voicemail. And her Bronco's disappeared. So has her dog, Tobin."

I could pitch this one to Billy, he thought. *He's nice, and he won't cheat them when the girl turns up in another day or two.*

"...and it's been a week now with no word."

"Wait," Tucker said. "A week? Why haven't you gone to the Sheriff's department? I'm just a private eye. They have far more resources than I do."

"We did," she said. "We filed a report, but they won't do anything. They won't even listen to us. They say there's no evidence and that she's probably just taken off for a few days."

He stared at her.

"They should be looking for her," Jennifer continued. "They really should, shouldn't they? But they aren't, and why would they? There are a lot of missing person cases in and around Chattanooga. It's a big city, and there are so many hiking trails around here, especially in the forests, and that just makes it worse. I guess they don't have time to investigate them all."

She was, he knew, referring to the Cherokee and Prentice Cooper forests, and many smaller ones besides. And he grimaced as he thought of the folklore and mystery that surrounded them, especially the Cherokee National Forest. It's vast, more than seven-hundred-thousand acres vast. Plenty of people had gone missing in the forest, never to be seen or heard from again.

"Exactly," Jared said. "I've talked to the county sheriff's office, several times, and the local police department. They won't even listen to us. They won't even acknowledge that she's missing."

Tucker raised an eyebrow and decided to play devil's advocate. "They could be right, you know."

Jennifer Romero stood up, slammed her hands down on the desk in front of him, leaned in and looked him in the eyes. And again, he was sure he'd seen her somewhere before.

"Julie would *never* leave," she said angrily. "Never! I know it. My husband knows it, and my sisters know it. All our friends know it. You have to believe us."

"We know something's wrong," Jared said quietly. "As Jen said, her phone goes straight to voicemail, and there's also been no activity on her bank account or her credit cards."

"You have access to her bank account?" Tucker asked.

"Yes. If she'd 'taken a vacation,' she'd need money, wouldn't she?"

"It was Mallory's idea," Jared said. "She's Jen's sister. She's a bit of a true-crime buff. She listens to podcasts about it all the time. Anyway, she insisted, so we keep all the important stuff, passwords, bank accounts and such in a folder."

A true crime nut. That's all I need, Tucker thought, resisting the urge to shake his head. It was a missing person case. He didn't do missing persons, and the mention of a possible amateur detective wanna-be drove the final nail into the proverbial coffin. So he dusted off the script he'd memorized for just such a situation.

"I'm really sorry," he began. "I understand how you feel, but I already have several commitments. And I just don't have the time to take on a new client. I can, however, refer you to my colleague, Will Preston. He is an excellent investigator, and he'll be happy to..."

He trailed off as Jennifer pushed a photo across the desk and said, "Look at her. It's my daughter, Julie. Look at her and tell me she's run away. Do it."

So he looked, and his breath caught in his throat. The photograph had been cropped, but the girl's face was a face from the past, a face that haunted his dreams. *Marsha! Marsha Cline?*

———

SIC DAVID LEWIS *was seated at his desk, leaning back in his chair, his fingers steepled in front of him.*

"Agent Randall... Tucker," he said, "I know this wasn't supposed to happen—"

"I did exactly what you told me to, David," Tucker said, interrupting him. "It was a done deal, you said. Marsha Cline's going to make it happen, you said. And all I had to do was to persuade her to make a statement. Which I did. She trusted *me, David. You were supposed to protect her."*

"There was an unforeseen—"

"Why, David?" Tucker shouted, leaning forward in his chair. "We're the Federal Bureau of Investigation, for God's sake."

"For what it's worth, Tucker, I really am sorry." He slid a glass across the desk. "Here. Have something."

Tucker took the glass, raised it to his lips, and felt the sting on his split lip where Lisa Cline had punched him in the mouth for breaking his promise to protect her daughter.

"You son of a bitch," he said, staring David in the eye and slowly shaking his head. "You had no intention—"

"It's not your fault, Tucker," David said easily. "It's not anybody's fault."

Tucker stood up, took a step forward and slammed the glass down on the desktop. It shattered with a sound like a gunshot.

THE GUNSHOT that had ended Marsha Cline's life.

He looked down at the scar in the palm of his hand. *If Marsha Cline had never met me, she'd still be alive,* he thought, then looked at the photo again. The resemblance was startling.

Julie Romero. Her eyes had that same overflowing joy for life as Marsha's once did. Her hair was a shade or two darker; her eyes were brown, while Marsha's were green. She was tanned, and there was a constellation of freckles spread across her smiling face.

Tucker could also see the resemblance in Jennifer Romero, and it pained him to look at her. If Marsha had been granted the chance to grow older, have a family, and live life to the full, Tucker was sure she'd look a lot like Jennifer.

He looked at her, nodded, sighed and said, "All right, I'll do it. I'll take your case."

"Oh, God. Thank you! Thank you."

And, as he looked into her eyes, glistening with tears, he wondered what the hell kind of a mess he'd just stepped into.

———

Order your copy at Blair Howard Books and continue reading now!

Genesis - "As always with Blair Howard's books, there are lots of dead ends and twists and turns . . . Great read!" *Alice - Online Reviewer*

Would you like to get a free copy of the first book in my best-selling Harry Starke Genesis series?
Visit www.blairhowardbooks.com

THANK YOU

Once again, I'd like to thank you for reading **Charlotte.** If you liked it, perhaps you would consider posting a short review (just a sentence will do). Word of mouth is an author's best friend and much appreciated.

To those many of my readers who have already posted reviews to this and my other novels, thank you for your past and continued support.

VISIT MY WEBSITE AT
WWW.BLAIRHOWARDBOOKS.COM.

From Blair Howard

The Harry Starke Genesis Series

The Harry Starke Series

The Lt. Kate Gazzara Murder Files

Randall And Carver Mysteries

The Peacemaker Series

The O'Sullivan Chronicles: Civil War Series

From Blair C. Howard

The Science Fiction Sovereign Star Series

ABOUT THE AUTHOR

Blair Howard is a retired journalist turned novelist. He's the author of more than 40 novels including the international best-selling Harry Starke series of crime stories, the Lt. Kate Gazzara series, and the Harry Starke Genesis series. He's also the author of the Peace-maker series of international thrillers and five Civil War/Western novels.

If you enjoy reading Science Fiction thrillers, Mr. Howard has made his debut into the genre with, The Sovereign Stars Series under the name, Blair C. Howard.

Visit www.blairhowardbooks.com.